IVYLAND

MILES KLEE

IVYLAND

MILES KLEE

OR BOOKS
New York • London

© 2011 Miles Klee

Published by OR Books, New York and London
Visit our website at www.orbooks.com

First printing 2011.

Cataloging-in-Publication data is available from the Library of Congress
A catalog record for this book is available from the British Library

ISBN 978-1-935928-61-4 paperback
ISBN 978-1-935928-62-1 e-book

Typeset by Wordstop Technologies, Chennai, India

Printed by BookMobile in the United States and CPI Books Ltd in the
United Kingdom
The U.S. printed edition of this book comes on Forest Stewardship
Council-certified, 30% recycled paper. The printer, BookMobile, is 100%
wind-powered.

For Mom & Dad

"... and yet it does not matter that he's all in bits ...
in a certain sense disintegration may have its advantages.
But of course it's dangerous, horribly dangerous. Suppose
you couldn't get back, out of the chaos ..."
—Aldous Huxley, *The Doors of Perception*

HECUBA /// IVYLAND, NEW JERSEY

forget all the progress we've made. The Van Vetchen procedure, a minimally invasive surgery that has saved untold millions of American lives, is now available through mobile immunization centers crisscrossing the country. You can't miss 'em! Flag one down and put your mind at . . .

She'd meant to see the miracle tree. Lenny passed it on a morning run to the nameless liquor place just beyond Ivyland's border and had nothing to report save the drive-by profanity he'd loosed on the jobless and devout gathered there. Hecuba laughed at that tossed-off barb, but more at his faked ignorance of the situation. If he hadn't known, why call them *that*? It wasn't the lucky marriage of enemy and epithet Lenny described, because he wasn't deaf to people's fascinations, no matter how little he listened.

With Hallorax gas, a cutting edge anesthetic, it's the quickest errand you'll run all week: you're awake the whole time and back to normal in minutes. A small incision is made here, at the base of the neck, where Endless's patented bodyguard solution is injected. Should you be exposed to H12, molecules from this reservoir will bond to the foreign particles, making them too large to cross the barrier from bloodstream to brain. Without Van Vetchen surgery, H12 can eat away at a brain's frontal and temporal lobes, disrupting speech, reasoning, memory, sleep cycles and cognitive stability over the course of a day, a month, or possibly years before a fatal brain...

The radio would've been preferable. "Recharging America"

was on Storm 89.9 right now, in-depth stuff on the Zeller Bridge collapse or, even better, maybe the moon mission. The run-up to launch had lent her a risky hope not known since DH found his way home. He was asleep face-down on the pullout when she left that morning, and she wondered how he'd cracked his insomnia. Cocooned in a blanket, her son still looked cold. She rolled him onto his back, finding the puzzled face of chemical naps.

New strains could be engineered to make mental decay long-term and less traceable, meaning prevention is no luxury; it's essential. That's why Congress and President Fullner have renewed the Healthy Bodies Act, keeping the Van Vetchen procedure mandatory for citizens age five and . . .

The bus she drove wasn't subtle. ENDLESS ENDLESS ENDLESS, it said on each side. END, read a pair of seats along the aisle. LESS, read the trio opposite. END LESS. Lest we forget whose money kept Ivyland afloat. It's not enough to clamp down on the booze, Lenny would say. Gotta shove their crap in my face and lecture me on the crap besides. He'd done a few months in Whitman max instead of a full year in Essex min—crowding or some quota shuffle—but missed the transition anyway, hearing only distorted prison rumors. Hecuba had quickly accepted the shift along with a job from Second Chance, shocked that they'd let her near a bus again, and carried on much as before. With Lenny back, though . . .

I think it's nice what they're doing for the town, she told him a week after he got sprung and found corporate Ivyland creepier than convict gossip supposed.

"Only here cause Jersey's made for tax dodges," he'd said, scratching a scar that ran with his jawline and hadn't been there when he began his sentence. "Don't give a shit about your second chance. You and this town are just cheaper, more desperate. You trust easy. I mean fuck: you trust *me*."

He went for a kiss after that.

Not all. We've turned the tide in the War on Drugs, our isotope signature research allowing authorities to stamp out origin and distribution points for many illegal intoxicants. Our innovative development team has produced Belltruvin, the most successful over-the-counter anti-anxiety medication in history, and Adderade, a groundbreaking beverage that spells the end of unfocused energy. We have entered sure-footedly that transhuman era when at last we can break free of DNA, change our bodies at will, revolt in earnest against aging and decay, ugliness and mental anguish. But we've done so with a noble, feeling soul. Here we stand, engineers of a sustainable global village, awaiting a brighter . . .

She made a third left in a row, noticing Fong Friday's new graffiti: someone had turned squat Chinese characters into a pudgy gang, adding heads and guns and those angled snap-up sneakers, complete with subtle E.Clipse logos. Not bad, she decided, checking the dash clock. Nine minutes till she was due at the day's first stop—yes, the miracle tree had to wait. It would give her time to think of a prayer. There was a static click, and the not-long-enough silence.

Welcome aboard and enjoy your ride, courtesy of Endless Nutraceuticals. As you can see, we've made a few changes around here. . .

Wouldn't kill them to update the video loop. Everyone knew this one by heart. Hecuba killed time by reacting with mock surprise to the mezzo soprano's recycled urgings. Ask my *doctor*? Still, when she turned the ignition, she was happy to hear a confident woman start speaking mid-sentence, exactly where she'd left off the night before. Hecuba liked to say, "Hold that thought, honey," as she put the bus in park and the screens powered down.

Fourth left in a row, a wide turn onto Mytrex Street. Still seven minutes. Idling at the Pureol Ave stop made sense. But certain parts of Hecuba weren't ready to face the route. She'd circle the block one more time.

. . . *know that life can be hard. We're here to help. Slowly but surely, things will get better. In the meantime, don't forget all the progress we've made. The Van Vetchen procedure, a minimally invasive surgery that has saved untold millions of American lives, is now. . .*

CAL /// IVYLAND, NEW JERSEY /// TWENTY YEARS AGO

Thanksgiving.

Sitting on the front lawn, the grassy precipice of a grassier hillock. Formal. Distracted. Fingering the waxed, prickling leaves of a manicured bush. Some older cousins wrestle and throw each other down the steep, tiny incline, staining khakis green. Across the street, the emptying of a peeled house by people in white biohazard suits and gas masks. Two of them try to force a pink couch through the door, slapping it when they pause to regroup. A third is on a ladder, boarding up windows with a nail gun.

Seven or eight: the age at which curiosity fades. Taking this bush apart, twig by twig—something Mom and Dad tell me not to do, like bite my nails or leave lights on when I leave a room. Conserve. I try.

The pink couch finally pops out, scudding onto the porch. One mover turns and slips back into the house. The other stalls, sits on an armrest, bent forward with elbows on knees. There's nothing about him except exhaustion. No face. His mask a staring question mark. Some weaker cousin is crying now.

Mom told me I couldn't eat the berries off of this bush, they're poison on purpose. To keep deer from eating them. I'd thought only things packaged in bottles and boxes could be poison. How had the toxic element escaped? When I get hold of a berry, I crush it between my thumb and index finger, wipe the goo on my blazer. I prick my palm (long overdue) and suck off a metallic bead of blood. I look up again. The man on the couch is waving at me.

My brother Aidan is beside me, wearing my old church clothes, waving back.

"Don't wave at him," I say.

"Why not?" he asks.

"You don't know him."

Aidan turns to me, still waving. I seize the hand and bunch its bones. He shows baby teeth and starts to whine. But the small hurt sound, bucking history, eases into a smile instead of a yell. I consider what he deserves for that.

There's something foreign at my back. It wraps my torso, fills the slender ribcage grooves, a finger settling in each one. A realization, quick crystal. That's why Aidan smiled. I let go.

Dad's huge hands toss me up, and when I come down we're face to face. He laughs; I laugh and panic. He spins, needing no reason. I'm his helpless satellite. We're weightless. Everything is spun and the light. I piss myself.

Aidan stands close by. I see him vanish and appear again over Dad's shoulder, watching. A blur that knows, and this heart rolls an inch. My water cooling as it travels. Pure release, and Dad shines on. I love him. He loves me.

He's making me fly.

*

Mom has the next day off; she takes me to the doctor for VV.

"We're giving you the gas now," the doctor says, "so breathe deep."

"You'll feel sleepy, but you won't be asleep."

AIDAN /// SANDPIPER, NEW JERSEY /// SEVENTEEN YEARS AGO

Henri and I met as kids one summer. Nothing's changed.

I'm re-peeling salty swim trunks off a scorching vinyl bus seat, stewing over something unfair, when the boy with a scarily huge birthmark on his neck sits next to me.

"My VV incision got infected, want to see?" he asks breathlessly, jabbing a thumb at it. Guess it's not a birthmark. Cal is silently laughing up front that this freak has joined me, turning back to whisper with Phoebe.

"H'lo I'm Henry, nice to meet you," is the rehearsed intro he blurts when I say nothing. *Fuck you, kid. That's right: I say the F word.* I face the window in my best antisocial hunch, which poses the difficulty of being heavily interested in a beach slum whizzing by and later, the faceless Jersey Dunes.

"It's garbage."

"What?"

"The dunes," he says. "One big landfill under the sand."

"I know."

"When did you get VV?" he goes.

"I never did."

"They make you. Maybe when you were born. What's your name?"

"Aidan."

Henry, chubby-palmed, sweating excessively, taps his fingers on hard plastic, hands laid atop a personal lunchbox cooler screaming HENRI ACTON (not 'Henry,' I note disgustedly) in blue marker. Like what my Uncle Karl uses down on the shore for beer. He pushes the white peak of the cooler back until it clicks, revealing fat translucent blobs sloshing in an inch of seawater. Suddenly I'm struck by a summer memory of standing in the shallow bay at Cape May and noticing slimy pink alien tendrils plastered to an ankle. Then shimmering, electric pain.

He must see my apprehension, because he's quick to assure me that these are the White Ones: harmless. White Ones don't even have tentacles, they're just sort of crazy big cells. Henri touches to demonstrate, even picks one up. I can't tell if they're alive or dead or how one could be expected to tell the difference. Their middles have small concentric circles, more clouded but still see-through. Get close enough, you see they're made of lines all shooting out from the circle's center. I'm finding it pretty damn impressive, really, that Henri's gone about collecting these nasty creatures with no concern for the trifling matter of What Will Mom Say When She Finds These In My Lunchbox?

"Here. Feel how slippery?" I'd rather not but try to be macho, half gripping, half poking one with three fingers and a thumb.

"Know'd be funny? Throw it out the window." I release a high-pitched yelp/laugh. "Do it," he prods.

"I don't think—"

"Watch."

We do an intimate dance to switch seats, trying to avoid skin contact in the rank humidity, or pouring jellyfish brine into our laps, and Henri has window adjacency. He gives me a second of eye contact, a covert *here goes nothing*, but he's visibly happy with what he's attempting, confident that only good will result. My brain sort of unhinges calculating the audacity, one eye beginning to warble back-and-forth superfast, knuckles gripping seat flesh with rapturous dread, every uncertainty attached to this thick slab of clear gelatin Henri is now hefting in his hand, having determined it to be the biggest. He fondles it a bit more to get his grip right and, not even checking for counselors, flips the jellyfish into an arc over his own buzzed head and out through the upper rectangle of window.

Flight barely registers before it's out of immediate view, but we stand and whip our heads, hearing a meaty *thwap*, as though a superhero had decked a crappy henchman, that announces contact between the creature and the windshield of a black convertible in the left lane, followed by the fatal high-pitched *skreeee* of this car's total swerving, a maneuver that makes the jellyfish do lazy migrations across the glass, trailing slime behind it and obscuring the bewildered driver's all-important view even further. At last the sparkled behemoth slides free and is airborne for one ludicrous ripple before the sizzling asphalt claims it.

It's a question of when, rather than if, someone tells; and dumb ponytailed Phoebe, wearing adult perfume that precedes her physical presence by quite a bit, the long-ago rat who snitched to our first grade teacher when I showed the class my new Spider-Man underwear, is instantly at the front of the bus with an eyewitness account. Next, the swarm of gray-shirted counselors, monochrome YMCA rainbows stamped on teenage chests, encircling Henri off the shoulder outside to get visual confirmation on the tossing of his gelatinous family into a sandy ditch as Ms. Hecuba, the same spacey woman who drives the regular schoolbus, buries her face in the steering wheel, trying to muffle her gaspy laugh.

"Don't worry," Henri says before he's yanked into the aisle, "I'll tell them it was just me."

It should seem hollow. I've done nothing. But there's fun in the conspiracy. He's playing with me; I know how to play back. Barely have to.

When Henri re-boards, he's beaming. He flops down next to me, shiny and wild-eyed, snorts as he tries to keep from cracking up. Laughter punctures him anyway.

"Good news," he hisses through giggles. As he slowly opens

his cooler I recognize the contour of one last jellyfish, salvaged and smuggled.

Henri's shaking with anticipation. He's fluttery as a ghost.

"THUNDERDAN & THE LIGHTNING ROD" /// EPISODE 904A /// NEW YORK, NEW YORK /// ONE YEAR AGO

FEMALE VOICE

You're listening to ThunderDan and the Lightning Rod on Storm 89.9. They're with you alllll the way home.

THUNDERDAN

ThunnnderDan and Lightning Rod-er-*ick* now bring you—

Opening bars of "Dies irae" *from Mozart's* Requiem Mass in D minor *play.*

LIGHTNING ROD

(*Vincent Price voice*) The news! (*Back to radio host voice*) Now hold on a sec, you geek over here, with your event ticker, Mr. Amateur Journalism, what makes your reportage good enough for people sitting out in traffic this very minute, trying to, y'know, keep their road rage in check?

THUNDERDAN

Don't shoot the messenger, but if you're not home by now, there's something wrong with your car.

Clunking, sputtering car noises.

LIGHTNING ROD

Woah, that's tough love.

THUNDERDAN

Just foolin'—we're with you all the way home. And seriously, if you have car trouble, it's probably cause a bunch of those gross caterpillars ate your transmission. Ugh! Things creep me out.

LIGHTNING ROD

North Jersey is in for a lot of butterflies, huh? I visited my parents in Ivyland this weekend and the house is *covered* in caterpillars. Like a bad horror movie. Weirdest thing I ever seen!

THUNDERDAN

Gotta disagree with you, given the big news today, Rod. We got Storm's own Frank Vader riding above the city in the— get this—the Endless blimp—

LIGHTNING ROD

No way.

THUNDERDAN

Endless blimp, no fooling, and Frank is going to tell us a little something about the Statue of Liberty situation as it stands. Is that right Frankie?

FRANK VADER

(*Light distortion*) That's right, Dan. It appears preliminary reports on the Statue of Liberty's vandalized exterior were largely correct—infamous French-American agitator and Ivyland College professor Azura Carcassone, known for her radical anti-EU stunts, was captured by authorities in a campus building there about an hour ago. She's since confessed to directing a home-grown terrorist cell responsible for dumping a chemical compound on Our Fair Lady's sculpted copper sheeting from the reopened crown observation deck, partially dissolving her signature green coating. From the blimp I can get a pretty good view of the corrosion, a big white-ish stain trickling down the front of Lady Liberty's toga. Now, Carcassone has previously claimed the U.S. doesn't appreciate or deserve what she calls "transcendent French art," a sentiment officials are saying motivated this terror plot. What they're at a loss to figure out, meanwhile, is how Carcassone and her conspirators were able to denature the statue's interior iron framework, damage they have continued to deny responsibility for, despite an admission to the superficial damage. The result of the warped frame is remarkable: our statue's proud posture has been traded for an uneven slouch.

THUNDERDAN

Getting your footage online here, Frank—it's like a giant bird went to the bathroom on her. Think she'd be used to that.

Laughter.

LIGHTNING ROD

You know how every so often, a news story brings this, like, new word into the conversation? Who ever heard of the word "denature"?

THUNDERDAN

But you say—if I'm hearing you right—say she's not owning up to that part.

FRANK VADER

Not at the moment. But if she's half as smart as they say, she will.

LIGHTNING ROD

Uh, she kind of has to.

THUNDERDAN

Thanks, Frank. Keep surfing the airwaves out there, and we'll check back with you later. Now's your guyses' chance out there to weigh in on the Statue Fiasco. Caller, you're on the air. What's your name?

ANTHONY

Anthony. I think I might know why that terrorist lady says she didn't do the framework.

LIGHTNING ROD

(*Impossible to tell if ironic*) We'd love to know. We're stumped.

THUNDERDAN

How do you know, Anthony? Are you with the ... shhh ... (*whispered*) government?

"Hail to the Chief" plays. Laughter.

ANTHONY

I know because my wife left me today.

LIGHTNING ROD

Hold that thought for one sec, Romeo—we got ads coming at ya!

FEMALE VOICE

(*With plaintive piano underneath*) The Van Vetchen procedure has saved millions of American lives, and yet many would not be protected in the unthinkable event of a wide-scale H12 outbreak. That's why Congress and President Fullner have passed the National Healthy Bodies Act, making VV compulsory for all citizens over the age of five. Your body is a temple—let's keep it that way. A friendly reminder brought to you by Endless Nutraceuticals, architects of a sustainable global village.

MALE VOICE

(*With bouncy electronic music underneath*) Hey, commuters. Do yourself and your community a favor when you finally get home: leave the lights off. In fact, always limit use of electric appliances—that way we can reduce stress on the Northeast power grid during its continued reconstruction. Fight for Light: Do It in the Dark.

THUNDERDAN

Folks, if you're just joining us, our caller says his wife leaving him today gave him the insight to understand why French terrorist Azura Carcassone won't reveal how she denatured the Statue of Liberty's iron framework. I have that straight? Anthony?

ANTHONY

I'm sorry. Little shaken up, blurted it out. But it's true.

LIGHTNING ROD

S'alright, buddy, your fellow men feel for ya. Now, why is it your wife walked out?

ANTHONY

She was calling every day to ask when I'd be home, since the commute takes so long, and I'd always say, I'm in traffic, I'm in traffic, and she got so fed up today she goes, "You don't get home by eight and help me with dinner and the kids *tonight*, that's the straw that breaks my back." She says, "I know you stay out late to screw your receptionist." I don't even *have* a receptionist.

THUNDERDAN

You should, they're hot.

Wolf whistle cue. Laughter.

ANTHONY

I go, "Baby, it's the commute. You don't know how bad it's gotten! Everyone is this late getting home, every day." Takes three hours to get to Ivyland, and that's right outside the city! And since those couple suffocations on the trains, sure not riding *those* again.

LIGHTNING ROD

Amen. Ain't that why our show goes till 10? Some guys have it even worse than you, you know.

ANTHONY

Only today I was even later than usual, so I didn't have a prayer. Had to walk home partway cause of these psychos. Shot one of the guys I was riding with.

Four seconds dead air.

ANTHONY

These psycho gas-heads saw the ice cream truck and I guess thought it would be an easy score, only they didn't stop us first, they just shot, and the guy who was sitting next to me, Sal, or Sam, I'd only just met him—he's dead now. Shot through the windshield. Cop too, both dead. Guys jacked the truck. I just got out and walked the rest.

LIGHTNING ROD

Hallorax junkies shot at you in—in an ice cream truck.

ANTHONY

Oh yeah, I didn't say? Cops drove some of us home in ice cream trucks. Was a fleet of them practically. Commandeered cause of the black-and-white shortage in the department, they said. Plus they could fit more people.

LIGHTNING ROD

So now our *finest* are riding around in ice cream trucks. Huh!

THUNDERDAN

Certainly not an ideal situation, Anthony … they were driving you back to Ivyland, is that right?

ANTHONY

Yeah. That's the least they coulda done.

LIGHTNING ROD

Settle down, chief, sounds like they were doing you a favor.

ANTHONY

Nope. They were driving a bunch of us who got stuck on the Munchausen Bridge escape.

THUNDERDAN

Anthony, now you really lost me. I thought this was—well, rubbing salt in your wounds—this was about your wife?

ANTHONY

Yeah. Well it was the escape, cause it was never finished, I guess. Me and these other guys were out following the signs on the escape walkway, headed toward the Jersey side. I mean obviously. But it was a dead end. They never finished the … never even finished the emergency walkway part. So we walked back to the New York side and then the ice cream trucks were there to take us through the tunnel instead. The ones who survived.

LIGHTNING ROD

Survived? (*Laughter*) Traffic *that* bad, Anthony?

THUNDERDAN

(*Laughter*) Who is the "we" we keep hearing about?

ANTHONY

The survivors. Of the Munchausen bridge collapse.

LIGHTNING ROD

Tony, the Munchausen bridge *didn't* collapse.

ANTHONY

Sure it did.

THUNDERDAN

We would've reported …

ANTHONY

You mean you haven't?

LIGHTNING ROD

Tony, I love a good crank call as much as … but our affiliates and spon—

High-pitched bleep.

THUNDERDAN & LIGHTNING ROD

FCC.

LIGHTNING ROD

We're with you, guy, but you gotta watch the language. Now, this is a pretty tasteless joke, you can admit.

ANTHONY

Rod. I saw the Munchausen upper level cave in. I saw it.

THUNDERDAN

(*Sotto voce*) Caller …

ANTHONY

People got crushed.

LIGHTNING ROD

Jesus.

Whispering, something about "the screener."

ANTHONY

Crushed when the Munchausen "denatured." It went all bendy. That's why that French lady won't fess up. Because something else is doing it, did it to the Munchausen and the statue. Maybe they built it wrong in the first place, or it just got old. Maybe something got in the air—I saw this white smoke all around, only it didn't move like smoke. Maybe it'll happen to a lot of other buildings and bridges—what was the story with that big bridge in Michigan a couple years back? And some of us'll walk to the dead ends of escapes and get picked up by cops in ice cream trucks trying to evacuate the place, and on the way home gas-heads'll kill two guys in our truck and hijack it, and by the time we walk up the front steps our wife'll be gone already and the kids'll want to know if we could have macaroni and cheese for dinner and we'll look in the pantry and see our wife, God, this woman I love, she even took the last box of mac and cheese.

A click. Six seconds dead air.

THUNDERDAN

That's what we in the business call "dead air."

Five seconds dead air.

LIGHTNING ROD

You know who makes a great mac and cheese.

THUNDERDAN

Your wife!

LIGHTNING ROD

Yeah, you knew.

DH /// KELVIN, NORTH CAROLINA ///
LAST SUMMER

For whatever reason, chest-deep in a bathwater ocean, "Dr." Leviticus Van Vetchen is screaming with joy.

"It's alive!" he screams, and I'm ringing hard enough to be equally revved minus the exact circumstances of why.

"It's alive!" I scream.

He pulls what's alive from the water, cupping it like communion. I stumble closer through the surf and freak when a fish grazes my leg.

"A sea dollar," I sing admiringly when I finally see.

"A sand dollar," Lev corrects, turning it over. "An *alive* sand dollar."

To my revulsion, the sand dollar has actual moving parts on the underside, wiggling hairs arranged in a star. The amount of Belltruvin in my system plus plain old revulsion makes me barf hard.

"Can I keep it?" I hear as a wave tosses my barf right back. One and only time he's asked *my* permission. I spit and look again. The sand dollar's hairs are churning frantically. "I'll keep it alive."

"This, what you're doing right now," I murmur, spitting, "is I think killing it."

"Nonsense," says Lev, who stabs a hole in it with his lucky scalpel. He threads a bit of seaweed through for a leash, ties it off and drags the little guy up the beach like some reluctant toy dog as wave after wave chops me down.

*

Hold on. Giving you the wrong impression. Lev's dad, Brutus Van Vetchen, is a respected medical mind, inventor of the operation that bears his name. Leviticus inherited a fairly great brain from the man and zilch from his mom, who died of ignored appendicitis in some Hare Krishna offshoot commune whose pamphlets regular Krishnas wouldn't wipe their asses with.

"Here," Lev was telling me a few months ago, poking a dirty mechanic laid out on the silver table in the back of our truck. The business of stripping cars continues undisturbed in the garage outside, screams of metal cutting metal. "Just got to cut in and do the injection. Easy."

"O. So what's this guy actually want?" I pat the dude's ample belly and something inside adjusts with a groan.

"Doesn't matter what this guy *wanted*; I'm training you to assist me in something a little more complicated and lucrative than cut-rate coz surgery. If an Adderade drip would help you pay attention, say so."

"VV."

"VV."

"You can do that?"

"If ably assisted. Like I said, surprisingly easy."

"Why so expensive, then?"

"That's the thing. When my daddy was first working things out, he lost all these volunteers. Tried different anesthetics, but these guys weren't waking up. The surgery worked, aside from the fact that no one lived through it."

As the machinery outside fades down, you can hear our guy snoring lightly.

"And out of nowhere one day, Daddy says, these three guys walk into his office, real genteel assholes in matching suits, even, say they're with Endless, and they give him a tank with their weirdo insignia on it. Hooked up to a mask. All they say is he should call when he's ready for more."

"Hallaxor?"

"Gas of the gods. Keeps operating prices high. Plus it scrambles your brain's limbic system for life if you're among the allergic 2% of males, not that they admit it. Read a case where the kid lost. The ability. To laugh."

"How'd they make it?"

"Think he asked? This was a miracle dropped in his lap. Ordered a million cases and kept his mouth shut."

"Wish we had a tank. Mystical."

"Lucky for you, we'll need it for our new operation. A lot."

"Don't have that kind of money. Or a hookup."

"Won't need money."

"D'you say only *guys* can be allergic?"

There's a grunt. We watch the fat mechanic wake up and absently grope his legs.

"Where the fuck are my calf implants?" he goes.

*

"Funny," I tell Lev the day before. It's spring in Ivyland, and Lev's living room is puddles of water and sun, and a bunch of those furry caterpillars are hauling themselves from surface to surface. "I remember this dumbshit Henri Jackson I think?"

"Henri," Lev repeats, glassed over and ready to ramble.

"From high school. Said so many poor people died cause they couldn't get VV."

"Shit's unethical, scare you into getting something can backfire that bad. Hundred times more people growing up half brain-dead and hormonally insane cause of the gas than dying cause of H12. God. Or you never got VV, and someone offers you gas at a party: shit, son, you can turn into the walking dead overnight. Speech fucked, and forget higher language processing. Circulatory system a shambles. Emotionally unbalanced."

When the lights go out, we each ask if the other paid utilities. Lev tries his pirate juice-sucker in the basement, flipping the switch peevishly a dozen times. No dice: not a rolling blackout. Blotted sirens in the distance confirm—it's citywide. We swallow some pills and head out to the corner, where we find Jack gnawing on Motherclucker Wings in his squad car, which is covered in caterpillar silk, meaning he'd sat there all day. Looting reports seep out of his transmitter.

"Jackalope," Lev says, knocking on the roof. "What's all this then?"

"Look up," Jack says, snapping the transmitter off with a sauced finger.

If the bright new street sign isn't a prank, Clark Ave. has been renamed "Bladderade Boulevard." As in, the Adderade flavor that helps old folks with urine flow and control.

"Someone's taking a territorial piss," Lev says.

"And the locals would rather starve, given their history with that someone," Jack says, opening a wet nap and wiping his chin. "Add the caterpillar invasion and fuck. Don't know why we even try this law-and-order thing anymore. Let a dump be a dump."

The distant sounds of shouting and breaking glass are like a TV heard through cheap walls. As we walk around to see which other streets have been changed, I wonder: when was the last time someone told me anything? Estronale Avenue. Belltruvin Lane is getting tear-gassed by a phalanx of beefy contract riot cops, who cheer and chest-bump each other when a can actually hits a civilian. Sure beats a Middle East war zone, boy. Hallaxor Heath is already empty, its trees stripped by caterpillars. Shreds of protest signs wheeling in the breeze past compliant brick row houses, building blocks that a kid outgrew, organized for neglect.

"I'm not sure they know what a heath is," Lev remarks. "I'm not sure *I* know." He concentrates. We float on. Things that happen here don't matter.

We stop in Sipwell's. I finish my Belltruvin and get really ringing, rejoice at the return of color. My line of piss glows in the destroyed bathroom stall, flecked with these piercing neon sparks. It's heavenly. Sighing never felt so good. A crack cuts across the wall above the toilet, a small Φ engraved farther up. Maybe supposed to be an ass, because nearby someone's written "Greeks ♥ Sodomy," and below that, "The South done fell again," and below that, "to get sodomized by Greeks."

What strikes me as so funny is that nothing's funny at all, and I take a moment to collapse with painful gasps of laughter that are themselves the funniest things and over too soon.

Back at the darkened bar, ThunderDan and Lightning Rod are on the air, roasting a stuttery caller alive, and Lev bobs sharply, swatting away candles as Patrick the bartender attempts to set them up. I nod a what's-up to Leo Clafter, the only other guy around. He's drinking Puff Adderade and grimaces at the bottle after each sip, flicking caterpillars that show up on the bar. Speaking of people messed up by gas. Even having Lenny around half your life is better than being that guy.

In walks the bald bouncer-looking Belltruvin Fairy, picking me out right away.

"Slow day," I say, taking out my expired driver's license so he can stick it in the slot of his chunky black handheld for a photo record. Lev says they use the info to spike your health insurance premiums with "suicidal tendencies," but I don't have insurance, so win-win.

"We got you on file," the Belltruvin Fairy smiles, "forget it." He tosses me a sample bottle. "You're lucky," he says. "Here last night, some joker tried to steal the whole bag." Patting a duffle, the rest of his supply rattling inside. "Had to break the kid's nose." He heads for the bathroom, punching his open palm nostalgically.

"Sorry, Lev, don't like it any more than you," Patrick is saying.

"You love it," says Lev. "Gives you a boner."

"Wiseass, I talked to the Ivyland Mayoral Council fucking *today*, soon as I found out. They're wiped. Broke as a joke."

"Just *try* to sell out harder than this."

"I'm supposed to feel sorry for you? Can't make a living selling this Adderade shit, 'cept maybe to crazy DH right here.

Endless's got no alcoholic stuff at all. Thank God Lenny isn't here to see this is all."

Damn but Lenny is mean—probably worse when he gets paroled. I forgive him. Hell, I forgive everybody. And Ivyland, I love you too: a castle of cards that against sick odds just doesn't fall over. Schools keep slashing budgets, stolen car parts spend a day under your hood before the next guy takes them, and craziest of all, people can still be polite. The pharma giants that built us up got crushed by Endless a decade ago, and now Endless is here to claim the spoils. Easier to change a place's street names than bulldoze and redraw the map.

"Shot of tequila, please," I say.

"Fuck's the matter with you," Lev goes.

"Hey. Rememberator 5000. Just got through saying there's no alcohol," Patrick reminds me.

"No tequila?"

"No *nothing*, DH, except this swill!" Lev yells, winging Leo's bottle of Puff Adderade at a rickety stool, breaking off a leg. Leo seems vaguely satisfied.

"My mom's sure not going to be happy," I realize.

"I'm dreading this, yes," Patrick sighs.

"Patrick," Lev says, "during Prohibition they had these things called 'speakeasies.' "

"You can stop right there," says Patrick. "Might just sell."

Lev's face goes loose.

"To . . . Endless?"

"Or any lunatic who wants to run a bar stocked with their garbage. Or shit yes, Endless, if they want. They're taking the whole rest of the block."

"This kind of horseshit makes you go deaf," sneers Lev. "Let's go."

"You gonna pay for Leo's drink?" Patrick calls after us. "Wanna fix that stool?"

Finding the afternoon of hot early spring, I suddenly have the thought: why not be optimistic again? Ivyland smells uncommonly clean, or has simply lost its scent of smoldering garbage.

"Lev," I say, "Sipwell's is behind us. Wish I'd gotten some ice, now that I think about it. But see how peaceful." I breathe in the peace around us, an insane peace. Every cell in my body abuzz. I mean really—do you know how nice things get? Because when it's going good I can't even take it, I'm feathers inside.

The bus whips past a corner where it's supposed to stop. We drift toward the duck pond and Christ, this time of year, with the baby ducks … I'm pretty sure I'll weep with joy if I see a duckling dip its top half into tea-brown water and shiver off a spray of drops when it comes back up for air. And I do. A team of caterpillars hover just in front of my face, rappelling on invisible threads.

"I know," says Lev. "This place."

"I need to sit down," I say.

"I know."

"We could try The Grate?"

"Jesus, DH, every bar is gonna be the same."

"Wish we had some gas."

"I know."

Three Collars materialize with their popped pastel polos and cold silver neck chains and E.Clipse sneakers and bright hair frosted and dangerous in the sun.

" 'Sup, Leviticus," says their leader. "Know where a friend can get a T?"

"Bound to be more now that Endless is here, they make the shit," says Lev.

"Yeah. Fucking named our street after their tampons."

"Pussified our territory," says the one in lavender.

"But yo," says the leader, "I want the hookup with some cheekbones."

"What're you, fifteen? I shouldn't do anything till after puberty."

The other Collars laugh cruelly with sharpened teeth. Their

leader pulls out his well-concealed piece and strokes my throat with the barrel, but the metal chills pleasantly at least.

"Or you'll do it now," he says.

*

Back home, we've got him on the kitchen Ping-Pong table with the other two off in the living room, going to town on my free Belltruvin. Only because Lev said to let them.

"Sure you want?" Lev asks.

"I'm pasty-white and zitty as shit. Don't make me say I need it."

So Lev puts him under with a handful of tranqs and makes a diagonal slice in each cheek with his lucky scalpel. Then he starts looking around the room for something to slip into the bloody slits. He finds an old square coaster and breaks it into two jagged halves that really don't fit.

"Lev?"

"I know. Time to leave."

"Okay."

"You understand what I mean by 'leave'?"

"Go away."

"Go away from *here*. Ivyland."

Ivyland. Clark Ave., or Bladderade Boulevard. New Jersey and its backward natural law. This wet, eroding house. Its mold. Suddenly I couldn't be angrier at the places that made me, and a bubbling starts in my lungs from badly wanting gas, shrapnel that cuts up the bloodstream. This little pain is Lenny. This one is gridlock on Route 22. This is me fucking up with Mom. This is me, me, me.

"Let's," I say.

We leave the leader unconscious on the table and move into the living room, where his cronies are rung out and drooling—light poppers. We roll them over and take their guns and money and any Belltruvin they couldn't cram in. Before I can stop myself

I punch the lavender one in the face, to see how it feels, and he smiles back with a wet split lip.

Lev's car won't start.

"I feel tight," I say, muscles locking.

We walk towards the Parkway to hitchhike, back past the duck pond, eventually passing the pink slab of a middle school.

An ice cream truck appears on the road. After feeling for the Collars' money in my pocket I try to flag it down as Lev kicks at the curb, only when it won't slow up a change crashes over him like a wave: he spins into the road, pulls his gun and starts firing wildly as the truck skids, chuckling that we're going to get some ice cream satisfaction dammit, specifically a chocolate éclair bar he's craved since the end of last summer when the trucks stopped running, and he's so committed that *I* start shooting, which I maybe hoped would validate his gut reaction. Which I hoped said, "Hey, your emotions can't be wrong, and I'm also feeling that heady mix of frustration and adrenaline that makes shooting guns an attractive option." But only Lev hits the thing, a big white snaking crack on glass that goes red. Jesus do I swear that.

The truck finishes its swerve to miss us, coasting to a crunching stop in thick hedges alongside the school, and when we get to it we see it's crowded full of scared-looking people (for some reason most with briefcases), and the driver is hit—well, is probably dead.

"You killed him!" this woman with a goiter screams. "You gas-heads killed him!"

"What are you doing back here?" Lev asks, rubbing his temple with the grip of the gun, "This isn't a bus, people." Turning to me: "Don't think they're selling ice cream."

"The song wasn't on," I say.

"Okay, out out out," Lev says, and everyone bolts except the driver and one other dead person. As we reverse and get back on the road I turn the song on. It makes me ache just right. I drag the pair of bodies towards the back and go through every pocket. Lev finds an empty parking lot, grabs a wrench from the glovebox, jumps out, comes back in a minute with the truck's license plate in hand. He starts the truck again.

"Lev," I say, "it was a cop driving."

Lev takes us to the soccer fields at the foot of Floods Hill, where they're having a huge tournament. He pulls right in front of this other ice cream truck playing the same song as us, sweaty uniformed kids with fistfuls of money lined up. I remember the song out of nowhere, this ragtime number now weirdly overlapping itself, repeating on different cycles from two sets of speakers. The Johnstons' real kid practiced it all the time that year.

The other truck driver is leaning out of his window to yell, but we can't hear him over the songs grinding against each other in bad harmonies, and besides, he has a confusing accent. Lev tells me to sell ice cream while he handles things, so I shout to the kids that I'm giving away my stuff for free. They ditch the original line and mob my truck, shrieking, and as I go back and forth between the freezer and window I keep tripping over the bodies.

All this hoopla about the giveaway operation is pissing off the real ice cream guy even more; he jacks up the volume of his song, so I crank mine, and the kids in their muddy jerseys are so disbelieving it hurts. I shower them with popsicles and chocolate tacos and ice cream sandwiches. I need to be rid of it all.

Finally the real ice cream vendor steps out to get physical, but Lev appears between the two trucks, cocks his gun and puts a bullet through the guy's windshield, making a giant twisted snowflake. Now it kind of looks like ours. The kids scream and run in no particular direction. Parents and players turn around and look from sidelines. The driver shrieks in a language; he's lying in the grass, hands on head. Lev chucks the gun at him, jumps into our truck and drives drives drives.

"Won't fool the dumbest cop in this town, even if that guy is an illegal."

"Slapped our license plate on his truck to be safe," Lev says. "We'll get this to my cousin's chop shop in Newark, make some adjustments. Take our cosmetic on the road."

I get one look at the unrolling fields behind us, at Ivyland, at the children who fell over each other in the scatter, now staring down at their ruined ice cream like if they focus hard enough it'll jump back into their hands, clean of dirt and grass. A last look at the kid whose birthday it might be, because he's got this red balloon that he lets float away in the chaos, float up till it's the head of a pin, till it's nothing.

I got out of the hospital a while back. I'd never seen my mom cry like she did when I told them I didn't need to be wheeled to the exit. Her shoulders jumped horribly with each sob. Her body wanted to be rid of a presence—me, I figured. I knew enough to let her keep going. Finally, on the ride home, somewhere in the smear of pocked concrete and For Sale signs I was slow to recognize as home, condemned houses standing merely because demolition teams were booked solid the next two years, she stopped long enough to say one thing: Thanks for sticking around this time.

I consider the bodies resting up against the freezers, their surprised faces, the ragtime still on maximum, a lone caterpillar crawling up the window's rim, and I lose it. I don't know. I guess Lev and I ruin people on the operating table, but they know the risks. And Lev says to shut up, cause all my shots flew off harmlessly into the trees, he killed them and he's the one with peace to make. Now we'll fix things, he says, help people from here on out, these two won't die in vain. I say it's not that, it's that they didn't expect it, they didn't see it coming, and that's not even what I mean.

AIDAN /// IVYLAND, NEW JERSEY

If you ever have the misfortune of meeting Henri Acton, please note three things:

(1) Avoid the French reading of his name. He giggles unforgivably at this. It's really "Henry," like, as American as possible. His parents belonged to an endangered species of WASP that valued "exotic" spelling in names while clinging to the blandest pronunciations.

(2) Be prepared to endure one of the most repellent faces ever conceived. The features are far-flung, pieces of a Pangaea disassembled by continental drift. Piggish nose, epic forehead, lips crusty and peeling. Also high on the try-to-ignore-it list is this nauseating green rim of spongy fungus that's developed on the ridge where his left front tooth meets excessive gums. Even if the tooth isn't rotting out of his head (it protrudes a little where its partner recedes, flattened), it can't be considered a dental success. At this point I'd prefer a gaping hole.

(3) If you play an instrument, don't mention it. You'll be forced to jam with him pounding away on his broke-down keyboard before you can say "next year's battle of the bands."

When Henri starts talking to me, the first couple sentences don't register at all, dull sonorities thumping through tiny bone but not translated. Like meeting someone whose name you won't remember: acknowledgement of vibrations, inconvenient to actually sort them out. You hear *my name is blah*, blah being a variant, white noise, antiformants. Nothing.

Henri looks at me now, gearing up to ask a question, forehead pre-furrowed. He doesn't have a unibrow so much as a diehard colony of hairs that populate the upper bridge of his nose. He's releasing air through a puckered mouth in the controlled *whhhhh* that accompanies his thinking—but this is just further introduction, a way of signaling the extent of his confusion. A "pre-apology," as Professor Fleer would have said of some timid philosopher with rotten ideas in his back pocket.

Finally he releases and launches in. Again, we're not sifting through phonemes of speech; we're assigning Henri as their source, same as if he'd burped or farted.

I say: "O."

I realize too late that this is rookie. "O" will suggest that I'm to some degree surprised and therefore invested. After the next patch of talk, I correct with an "uh-huh." Bored, prepping for the brush-off.

Following the next bit, he chuckles to himself in this way where I know he's laughing at my expense. It's the way one eye collapses in accidental winks, the crooked smile, the quiet snorts. I mutter the punch line of a long joke, Henri's absolute favorite, and the fact that it's his favorite is about all you need to know. It goes, in full, like this:

Henri's Favorite Joke

Okay once there was this little kid, right? Normal, suburban little boy, nuclear family plus like the perfectly trained collie, the works. So his dad comes home one day and says, Son, Daughter (the boy's got a sister, see), Wife, guess what I bought on the way home today. So the kids and mom are guessing and guessing, but Dad's stumped them. The dad is all, I got us tickets to the circus this Saturday! The family is psyched and everything, but the little boy is Eck. Stat. Ick. It is un-*friggin*-believable how berserk this kid is about going to the circus—he's never been. He's just bonkers all week, off the wall in school because of the circus, won't shut up at dinner about the circus. Can't sleep at night, what with his circus-soaked delirium.

Finally, yes, it's the night before, and the kid can't sleep, can't even close his eyes. He's drawing ever closer to the circus. In the morning, he puts on his favorite of many dinosaur T-shirts (it features a grinning velociraptor), rushes the family through breakfast, demands to know why they aren't on the road already. Mom suggests he go run around the house a few times. Eventually, they get out the door, take a short car ride, and there they are— *unbelievable,* the boy whispers to himself—at the circus.

Now he's finally stepping inside. He's actually in*side* the tent: this, *this* is where it's going to happen. They move through the tent to amazing seats in the front row; he could cry he's so happy about the gloriously unobstructed view they'll have.

The show begins, and instantly the boy is blown away. Elephants, acrobats, tightrope walkers, balancing acts, trained lions, fire-breathers, please—the goddamn *ringmaster.* Everything is pitch-perfect, lives up to this boy's self-made hype, improbably enough, and tends the seed of his very young soul.

Between acts, a clown comes out and starts doing bits. Hey, thinks the boy, this clown is pretty funny! He puts kernels of popcorn on bald people's heads! His pants keep falling down! Soon enough the clown makes his way over to our boy's section, breezes past, then seems to remember a crucial fact. He slowly backtracks until profiled directly in front of the boy. Carefully he rotates his head as a barn owl turns its gaze on a field mouse.

"Excuse me, sir!"

The boy is thunderstruck. Surely the clown couldn't be talking to him?

"Excuse me?"

He is! Our boy hesitates.

Then: "Yyyes?"

"Are you the horse's head?" asks the clown.

Here was a problem. What did the clown mean? How could he possibly be the horse's head? Which horse was *the* horse? The boy has a million questions about the question, but a tentful of eyes are fixed on him, so he shudders and wagers a reluctant guess:

"No?"

"Well then," says the clown, "you must be the horse's ass!" He whirls about and bows deeply to the crowd, with not a little showman's flair, to thundering laughter and applause.

And the boy: my God, you can only imagine. Humiliated, his stomach flops inside out, his heart pounding so hard and nastily that it may as well be a ball of worms, squirmy and terrified. The hot tears come, of course, the source and result of shame, as the boy sees his family laughing along, assuming he's keen on the joke. Clearly, okay, he's not.

So he runs. He just gets up and runs.

He runs past the box office, out through the park, sprints across town and all the way home, body burning, face wet and crunched in pain. He heaves himself onto his bed and weeps. His family gets home soon after, and they want to comfort him, naturally, feeling awful about laughing at him back there, not realizing, but he locks them out, continues to sob for hours over the sound of his parents' embarrassment and apologies and loving words.

Around midnight, long after he's passed on dinner, it hits him. Why sit here and pity himself when he can *get even*? That's it! This clown is going to taste some bitterly cold revenge and wish to God he'd never made our boy the butt of his gag. He will hang his novelty shoes and seltzer spritzer up in shame when our boy is through with him.

He begins at the library, borrowing every book ever written on clowning, comedic acting, mime; he studies everything imaginable and/or academic on the art of theater, from Stanislavsky to the commedia dell'arte, all the method and the madness, and finally, when he's old enough, enrolls in a prestigious clown college.

He's mastered theory on the page but finds himself hopelessly lacking onstage—there's this one total bastard instructor who picks on him incessantly, says he's got no talent, no inner clown to speak of, is going nowhere in the cutthroat world of professional clowning. But our boy is not so easily dissuaded. He grits his teeth and endures all this bastard's snide insults and shitty sneering, works his ass off really, stitching each convoluted clown gesture into the fabric he used to call himself, and finally it becomes clear to the boy that this prof is trying to motivate him, trying to unlock some latent glimpsed potential, which he finally *does*, if you can believe it, achieving a naturalism awesome for this day and age, and the boy goes on to graduate top of his class, for whatever that's worth in clown college.

At last he is unquestionably prepared to confront the old clown. He has spite in his sweat and cunning to match. He is ready. Now it's merely a matter of tracking down, footprint by absurdly huge footprint, his only, ever and unwitting foe.

The circus could be anywhere by now, years after the fact, but the young man's desire to punish the clown seems to overcome all logistical snags, and after driving around the country for two months and countless interrogations of squinty locals, he finds the circus setting up just outside a Northwestern hamlet, among towering pines. He smells victory. Our boy buys every ticket to the show that night, using virtually his whole life savings.

As he sits, immaculately dressed in his only suit, alone in a tent smaller and more squalid than he remembers, he reflects on the simple brilliance of his plan. With no one else at the show, the clown will be forced use him for the horse's ass bit—a delicious setup for humiliating ruin. Okay, so the show begins, business as usual, all the other animals and performers showcasing their respective talents, slightly confused by the empty house but professional about it, the young man watching in a distant fog, biding his time, tensing and un-tensing muscles, starting to fidget in psychotic excitement.

Finally, the aging, near-retirement clown, sad face locked in rictus, makes his fateful entrance, does some half-hearted solo shtick, meanders over to the young man, not recognizing his victim, and sets the trap in motion.

"Excuse me, sir!"

No response.

"Excuse me, sir?"

The young man can barely keep a straight face.

"Yes," he answers, too coolly for his own good.

"Are you the horse's head?"

Déjà vu. The young man is smiling too hard.

Through a sadistic smirk: "No. I'm not."

"Well then," says the clown (who would like to get this over with; doing private shows isn't really what he got into the business for, and he's about ready to have a drink with the lion tamer out back) as he whirls about to an imaginary audience, maybe even winking at an imaginary pigtailed girl in the front row, "you *must* be the horse's ass!"

There is a fleeting breath of uncertainty with that diseased logic frozen between them. The young man draws himself up to stand at an intimidating height, but if you were there, you wouldn't have noticed. The clown turns back, finds himself looking quizzically up at the tall young man, unable to see the angle, the trajectory, of what's next.

Suddenly our boy snaps his arm upward as if unholstering a gun. The clown is staring down the barrel of a knobby index finger that trembles a millimeter away from his red foam nose.

Moment of truth. Heart beginning to wormify, stomach contracting before the backsprings. Licking cracked lips, the grown and tortured boy speaks with undying hate and frothy venom, unbridled disgust and final superiority.

"Fuck you, Clown!"

End of Henri's Favorite Joke

Right—what I say to Henri is: "Fuck you, Clown." Can't tell if he loves the joke because he thinks the boy chokes on his moment of triumph or because he believes the revenge is somehow perfectly executed. He'd probably say for both reasons, if only to confuse the issue.

Henri continues, unfazed by the comment, which has lost its impact since we started using it to mean anything at all.

"I can't find paper towels," he finally interrupts himself to say.

"Behind you," I mutter.

He rips off a few squares and asks do I remember Larry M. from high school.

"He dated that girl with the hot star tattoo but hairy arms for like a day maybe?"

"Sure, Laura-who-came-out-afterwards. Plus wasn't he legally blind, I mean as far as getting to drive."

"No."

"Whatever, okay." His sentence cracks: o-*gnay*.

"And Laura was friends with the pregnant twins."

"Weren't both pregnant. One was pregnant twice."

"This is about Larry, anyway."

"Yeah. What'd you need paper towels for?" He's just holding a wad of them.

"Nothing. Listen. Remember when Larry was out for like a week of school and never said why?" Not really. "He was having surgery on his dick."

I want to find out who told him this and violently mute that mouth forever.

"Like enlargement," is all I can think to say.

"That's the thing: emergency room. He had to get stitches cause he cut it in an accident or some shit."

"Shut the fuck up."

"Seriously!" I can't believe he's bought this story, and probably off some deep-in-shit acquaintance from high school. "I ran into DH at Sipwell's a while back"—yep—"and he swears it's true, he's seen the scar."

"You in Sipwell's? I didn't think you'd been there since your open mic."

"So you have to at least acknowledge the scar."

"Must I."

"He gets the stitches. And afterward, guess what the doctor says."

"Never reproduce."

"He says, 'As long as you have these stitches in, you can't get an erection.' "

In the ensuing weird silence, I can divine the steady murmurs of a few collected voices outside.

"Can't as in … physically unable to get aroused."

"Aidan, brace yourself: Can't as in the imperative. I am ordering you to not get turned on."

"Lunacy. Never happened." Henri nods with sympathetically arched eyebrows and a sad-but-true face that nearly conceals his perverse amusement.

"He couldn't, or the stitches would pop."

"Have you called that tree guy yet?"

"For real." This clearly applies to his anecdote, not my question.

"Doctor can't expect that."

"I dunno, but it's not like they can just prescribe you pills, okay, there's not a huge market for chemicals that make your dick flaccid."

"Are you going to clean up whatever you spilled in there?"

"Dog could get it."

"We don't have a dog."

"I'm saying we should. You're not letting me finish."

After lengthy and falsely superior sighing meant to indicate I'm ready to hear the big finish, I prop my head up on my elbow, bored, and take a sip of orange juice, failing to recall I'd just brushed my teeth.

"So the reason he was out of school is *pffffhaha*, O, God, this is too good, okay, so he, he, the first day after the emergency room he's in math with Ms. Delacroix, right?"

I wish I weren't laughing at this, but now I can't stop. Henri nods, already falling apart.

"That tight blue sweater we loved …"

"No," I groan.

"He popped every stitch!" Henri exclaims. "Only Larry, man." Nostalgic head-shaking. "Heh, Larry."

"And the moral is … ?"

Henri disappears into the living room with his balled-up paper towels as I put dishes away.

"Sure are a lotta people staring at it," I hear.

The maple in our front yard got struck by lightning last night. I didn't see the bolt itself, but I can picture it carving the storm-tossed treetop and stabbing at what's now a charred and leafless ten-foot trunk. I did hear the crack of doom that accompanies a lightning strike too close to home, the kind of thunder that rattles bones in their sockets and would've had our theoretical dog cowering under the dining room table. Just grateful it didn't kick off more blackouts.

"They're taking pictures."

"Of a dead tree?"

"Check it out."

I walk in to see, and he's right. Several flashes go off in less than a minute.

"Doesn't it remind you of—"

I'm out the door in ratty sandals before Henri can make the trademark non sequitur. I let the screen door slam behind me, cursing when I hear one of the hinges break off and clatter on the porch.

"Don't any of you come suing me when that falls on you," I yell.

Only puzzled looks. Yeah, we all have total faith in this dead maple's structural integrity. A couple is poring over the blown-off twigs and boughs lying around. Across the street, open-mouthed and wary of the other onlookers, stands Grady, a mangled blue kite in hand. His dirty ferret is on the loose, exploring the drawers of a bureau left on the curb when our neighbors moved to Philly.

I smile at him but stop short of anything more. The smile he sends back is cautious, meant for a stranger. He's trying to look past me.

"This your tree?" a pale woman asks.

"Until they tear it down later today," I snap.

This fortysomething man, one of the Guatemalans who plays soccer down at Floods Hill on the weekends, takes a step forward and soberly corrects me.

"We cannot let you destroy this miracle."

"Excuse me?"

A stringy-haired character who must've been home-schooled in the worst way, wearing a seasonal sweater knitted by herself or an equally creepy sibling, moves one deliberate step closer to Soccer Guy.

"God has spoken through your tree."

Soccer Guy explains, in no inelegant fashion:

"Your tree, it embraces the Virgin." He ushers me into the street, indicating a side of the maple's black skeleton I haven't seen.

"Uh."

"You see?"

"Am I missing something? You did say virgin."

"Look." He steps forward and traces the outline of an overcooked vertical rift in the bark. "See?" I touch the ridges of the gash, darkening my fingers, soft black crumbs trickling off. Then I notice the split isn't just bark-deep—it cuts into the trunk itself.

"She is inside."

The rest of the peanut gallery, up till now content to let this guy do the talking, produces a knowing chuckle. Really knew how to blow a first impression.

"She is in there," the man says, as though he'd just made up his mind. I peer inside at the mangled tree guts, then step back off the curb.

"When you say …"

"The Virgin Mary is born of your tree."

The whole picture, top-down now. I move forward again, staring through the crack, know what to look for and finally see it. The narrow chin with rough-hewn mouth. Shoulders smoothly sloping back. Supple arms meeting around a perfect oval abdomen with fingers meshed ... like, linking, and she's pulling on that link—if it unclasped, the arms would snap gently off her pregnant belly. The trunk, blasted open at the top, allows the sun's designs to trickle down inside: dappled shadows thrown by the leaves of other trees, shapes that jump in slow electric flashes. The convincing effect of hair ruffled by wind. I blink with dust in my eye and whisper something into to my chest. Their spokesman introduces himself.

"I am Anastasio," he says.

I mumble, unsure, that my name is Aidan. Anastasio sticks out his hand.

"I will not let you tear down this tree," he says.

A glance at the rest of the crowd leads me to believe they pretty much agree.

OFFICER R. DANKE ///
IVYLAND, NEW JERSEY /// LAST WINTER

Let's be assholes, says Jack. So we are professional assholes. We prowl down the block collecting Christmas trees from the gutter and pile them in front of Tara Cable's front door because she refused to give Ed a freezejob. He cited hygienic advantages. She said it was perverted. Now Jack won't stop calling her "Ice Queen."

She and her housemates are the only ones with decorations still up, some with last month's eggs still crusted on. I spit into the circuitry of the Holiday FX module that makes it so it's always snowing lightly in a soft gaslight kind of glow, snowing only on their house. Melts fast in 72° January, but even so. When spit fails, I stomp the box till it sparks and smokes, then run. Jack says to hold up. He zips back and kicks over a plastic reindeer. Okay, he says.

We pull out of the dead-end, I ask where to go, and he says: Straight, who cares, be a man here. I hear him but ask again out of habit. Just straight on Estronale Ave, he yells, straight as a clitoris, if you've seen one.

It's like that.

*

Most of what comes out of Ed's mouth, you can tell he's whacked and body-ringing on Belltruvin anti-anxies. (Best line yet: Watch out for that lake—oh! it's just water.) When we pick him up, his opening gem is, really, "Do you think volcanoes are the places where Hell is spilling over?" He leaves his car out on the turnpike shoulder, traffic patrol dummy propped up in the passenger seat. Why not behind the wheel, I wonder aloud. Don't trust him, Ed says.

We detail the action at Tara Cable's place—he's pissed we didn't wait. I swerve to miss a cat, and Jack slaps me harder than he has to. I don't do that, I say. No, retard, he goes, that was Coach Syd you just passed.

In the side mirror Coach is taking the scenic route to nowhere, drunker than when he crashed our Fourth of July party last year, before Jack pulled up all the No Parking signs for a bonfire but after Bert tore his leg open on the Slip-n-Slide. I don't go in for those blowouts anymore.

I back up and roll down the window. Coach ambles over, smoothing his, like, eight hairs back.

"What's up, psychos?" He grins good-naturedly, recognizing no one.

Jack leans over me and pegs him in the moustache with an egg, point-blank.

"Fagmaster," yells Coach Syd, spitting shell, "I'll shove a whole carton up your dick." But we're gone, and odds are this little memory won't quite stick. Here's a guy who'd guess that AC/DC invented batteries and Braveheart wrote the Bill of Rights, who never reassembles the previous night. Even if tomorrow we were back in his joke of a health class, he wouldn't add things up. He'd just pause for a sec, studying us with a hint of attempted thought, before repeating that you can't always see visible blood with the naked eye.

We find Bertrand at the outdoor shooting range, and he hands me his target: planet-sized tits Photoshopped onto my sister, bullet-hole beauty mark and all. Starts laughing. I crumple it up and shove the sooty ball in his gaping mouth.

Guy thinks he's going to be a comedian. His "impression" of Teddy Roosevelt, he explains, he beats a teddy bear with a dildo.

How long does this go on, Ed asks. Till they laugh, Bertrand tells him. Your life is laughable enough, Jack says, polishing his nametag with a sleeve. We pass the sign with our town motto. *Ivyland: The Gateway to New York.* Abandon All Hope, Ye Who Gatekeep.

We stop for Atomic Motherclucker Wings from MexiLickin'SurfHog, but it's only 0130h and Sipwell's—I mean, the speakeasy that replaced it—is still going with some gay open mic thing, so we troop in and sit in the dark and drink the beer they serve in Adderade bottles as a joke. Ed, rung out, asks the bartender for a piece of ice and sits down with it. Jack says: Not here, freak. And in your pants? is what Bertrand asks, disappointed. So Ed gets up, testily rattling his Belltruvin bottle, and heads to the can, where he can get off by icing the back of his neck in peace, but on the way he spills his beer all over this twat in the next booth who is unwisely impolite in lecturing us on breaches of the social contract until Jack grabs him by the chin and makes a threat I truly can't hear on account of the noisy drunks and music.

Then out of nowhere it's last call. Blink later, lights out. At the door, we're getting shoved and jostled by these cologned-up frat boys from Iv College, real Grove Avenue jizzrags, some in the Collars, no doubt—matching chains, pastel polos, a snuffbox of rufies each. Mad rude.

Bertrand says, "Drunk and disorderly?"

Jack says, "Let's play this one by the book."

So we let them start walking up the street toward campus. We get the car and circle around the block three times, egging them worse and worse each pass till they're red and screaming that we're pussy Endless rent-a-goons and one chucks a bottle that shatters on the windshield.

"Is there a code for egging?" Ed asks as we screech off, and I say, "The hell do I know, look it up." He bends forward to scroll though the console for a while before announcing the closest he can find is malicious mischief. "Good ol' 594," Jack says, knowing the book down to the comma. How *was* that solo freezejob in a public bathroom, Ed? "Can't believe everyone doesn't masturbate that way," Ed says. "It doesn't work for *ev*eryone," I remind him. *Pos*sible side effect. Of Belltruvin ab*use*. "It's so much better when you don't have to touch it," Ed goes, "even if you gotta ice yourself."

"There's nothing to do," Bertrand whines, and I could just punch him in the throat, because aren't we doing things at this very moment? You miss high school, Bert? Miss ripping on me for being a crap-out, pass-out rich kid? Or the summer when you, you total waste, were with that busted skank from industry row in South Woodbane, and Jack, DH and I were driving around in Ed's mom's minivan with an Aqua Artillery 3000 and happened to pull up next to her as she was idling at a red light with the window open? Because I fondly recall the automatic van door sliding silently at the push of a button and the gun slung in a belt looped over the dry cleaning hook, a Blackhawk's deathbringer. I remember thinking Loki, god of mischief, had graced us, and purposely keeping that thought to myself. Two fingers curling around the giant trigger.

"Anybody been to visit Leo?" Bertrand then has the nerve to ask.

"Bertrand," I say, "you owe me five bucks."

"Burned," says Ed.

"It's a Small World" was played at top volume on repeat in the station's holding cell, and Bertrand failed to successfully masturbate—classic style—in said cell without lubricant or visual stimuli within seven minutes. Easy money. Bert claimed he was just rusty that way. "He'll buy you a slice," Jack says. "Not hungry," I say. "Fine," says Jack, "he'll cover you at the diner." There is something Jack is not, and that is a listener. He wants to go up to the Reservation and bust some homos, some gas-heads. Ed says leave the gas-heads be, only hurting themselves, poor fucks. Homos too. They drive like that, I say, the gas-heads, and all raged up when they can't get it. You're too drunk to have this argument, says Jack, and we end up hitting the Res at primetime.

There's a ton of people parked, too many to walk through and terrorize, so we flip on the high beams and slow to a crawl. Most of the cars back out and peel away, but at the end of the lot a black kid bails from a station wagon and bolts for the woods.

"Good thing he's fat," says Jack, and sprints after.

"I want to sit up front," Ed says after we've waited a while. "Hate that I can't open my own door."

Jack and his runner come panting back into the headlights, the kid understandably crying as he gets stuffed in the back with Ed and Bert.

"My mom's going to find out," he wails. "They'll take my scholarship. Please."

"Even worse," says Jack. "You'll be the freshest virgin asshole New Jersey's correctional system ever dismantled."

This gets a big wail.

"Unless you can spare pills," says Bertrand.

"Take it all," weeps the kid.

And Jesus was he holding.

"Liked him," Ed says when we're back on the streets. "Reminds me of me at that age. But blacker. Fatter." "Hardly fatter," says Bertrand. Jack tells me to pull over when he sees a bike propped on a yield sign by the train station. Fetching a chain from the trunk, he locks it to the signpost. Then he tears the basket from the handlebars and hops back in with it under his arm. Reminds me of junior year, Ed says. Remember all those bomb threats? So easy to ditch during evac and take your pick of the bikes. Well, says Jack, everything reminds you of everything. What's your beat, Memory Lane? Just trying to help a guy out. Someone'll cut it tomorrow, I say. Money says it'll be there for months, Bertrand goes. We'll forget.

Smooth Larry comes on the radio and we tell him to die. "Have some more gingersnaps," Bertrand says to the radio. "Eat them till you puke," adds Ed, because Smooth Larry did do that at a department Christmas thing.

Vince gets on, saying he has multiple 594s, asking do we realize we're the only units on tonight and are supposed to be in separate cars?

"We are?" I ask.

"Don't worry about those 594s," a pissed Jack radios while trying to pinch my nipple, "we took good care of them."

"I wouldn't worry if you weren't shitting on my face, Officer Duffy."

"By the way, how's that open homicide going, sir?" Jack radios. "The Volvo crash and shooting—two bodies, wasn't it? Any leads in that clusterfuck?"

"I will beat you with the biggest blunt object in evidence," Vince declares, and his voice pops off.

Ed has the bright idea to put yellow tape around Vince's house so he thinks his wife got murdered. If he's even married. "But," says Bertrand, "we'd have to call it in, otherwise he'd know for sure that nothing happened. Screw it, then." We swing by Fong Friday's Chinese takeout, which bribes us, too dumb to know we're not health inspectors.

Afterward it's back on the highway, past the next-door black-on-black that used to be Viking Putt, whose plastic dragon had its eye clubbed to shit by yours truly the night before the whole place got torched. An arson Ed actually tried to take credit for—until the real story came out. We stop to skeleton-key into the abandoned Luckbolster Vid and have a fluorescent light swordfight that ends when they're in a million pieces, some bloody.

"Bored, bored, super-bored," sings Bertrand, gauzing a wrist in the backseat. "Helpful," says Jack. We cruise around without the lights going, because what's the rush? We drink in the squad car and finish Ed's Belltruvin and the fat kid's painkillers, crisscrossing town. "When is daylight saving time?" asks Ed.

"Nobody cares," I say. Jack is carefully unweaving the stolen bike basket, slipping strips out his cracked-open window one by one.

"Really should visit Leo," Bertrand says.

"Novel idea," Jack finally says, watching me.

I mumble something and turn around, pointing us at Saint Barnabas. It gets quiet.

"Visiting hours are over," Ed says.

"Be less stupid," Jack says.

"We didn't even visit DH when he was in there," says Bertrand.

"He wasn't even in our class, really," Ed says.

"Prolly the tard who gave Leo the gas," I say.

"Actually," Jack goes, "DH skipped town." Better find someone else to blame.

"Leo should have known," Ed says. "Happened to his older brother, didn't it? That's why he never had VV in the first place, figured he had the allergy too. Dumbass never thinks shit through."

This is why I swore off those nights-of-mayhem: it becomes hard to notice when a dumbass acquaintance of yours is heaving and frothing and dying in the bushes.

"Cause I was thinking," says Ed, "that when you spring ahead, there's an hour you skip, so couldn't you commit a crime in that theoretical hour and then create an alibi for that same hour and never get caught?" "No," Bertrand says, "you'd need to do it when you fall back, so that the same hour would repeat twice and then you'd have, say, two different 3:30s. Man," he goes, "that would seriously . . . ! It'd be a crime *not* to kill someone."

"That can't work," says Jack, which I suppose is fortunate, because even I'd started to believe it made sense. Better than heckling guys through broken doors at porn café booths so they can't rub it out, or toying with a straight-edge like Smooth Larry. There's something creepy about a town that won't fight back. Impulse discovers you in places you refused to imagine.

First it was popping pills and dumpster diving, a donut or two in parking lots. But you adapt to your prey, and secretly.

"Ivyland: there's never anything to do," sighs Bertrand.

Which I guess is how all this nonsense gets started.

*

At the hospital, not even a badge-tap is necessary to get into the ICU and Leo's room, where he's hidden by a white plastic curtain.

"Y'all are his first visitors," the nurse says.

"Fucker's been here a week," Jack whispers.

We stay huddled until the nurse leaves. Then Bertrand opens the curtain.

It's a mistake.

Leo is as comatose as when the EMS dykes took him away from our New Year's party, shaking their heads at me, at us all, like we'd never get the call one day and find our noses in *their* shit. His face is swollen and monster-big, fattened veins like rubber hoses glued onto his arm. Breathing tube and a goatee of drool on the chin. Worst of all, eyes stuck blindly open, a leggy device overhead letting drops of moisture fall in every few seconds.

So this is what the gas allergy looks like. Bad to know.

"Nope, no God," says Jack.

"Sick," says Bertrand. "Why would any guy do it, knowing the risks?"

"Does it matter?" I ask.

"Would've been a lot worse if he'd got the gas as a kid," Bertrand says, "for VV. Imagine that."

"Being poor is a blessing, sometimes," Ed says, rubbing the back of his neck.

"Rather die of H12 than go through what his poor ass is," Jack says.

"Mind shutting up if this is all a joke to you?" I yell, suddenly furious, and it feels like a knife fight in my lungs. So none of us say anything for a bit, and we listen to the heart monitor beeping.

"Can't be like this," Jack says, yanking out Leo's IV.

"The fuck are you doing?" Bertrand says.

Jack doesn't answer, just drops to the ground, trying to get at the plugs of all the computers flashing Leo's vitals.

"Stop!" Bertrand screams.

Ed stares.

"Jack," I say with all my calm. "Don't."

He snorts, writhing on his belly, still pulling at cords under the bed. I kick him in the ribs so he rolls over and then place my shoe squarely on his chest, applying more and more weight, and I can see his teeth grinding.

"Don't."

*

At home I sit out in the thawed yard, listening to the night, wishing all Leo'd done was ignore me. Wishing I hadn't run blubbering to Jack after they took him, me so sloppy drunk. Wishing hardest that I didn't need his help.

But he'd listened and nodded and said, unbelievably: "It's not your fault."

"He wanted to try," I'd cried. "I said to be careful."

"How did he know you had any?"

"I don't know, I didn't tell him."

"Did you?"

"I've never done it either, I just took it from the evidence locker."

"So how did he know?"

"I don't know. I didn't say anything."

"Maybe you said something."

Fireflies have come out, a lazy yellow fog. Must've got their signals crossed in the warm snap. I see a bunch dead on the ground already. They have an agenda, but you wouldn't know it. They'd always been too trusting, too easy to catch, not like normal bugs that swoop and roll when you go to swat them— what is it their sensors don't say when the hand is coming?

I get up and find the twig I used as a marker when Jack wasn't looking. It sticks out of brown grass that rustles like paper. I get the shovel from under the porch stairs and cut into dirt that should be January-hard, dig till I hit the metal gas container that we put underground on New Year's after everyone left. I pull the Hallorax tank out, brush dirt off the Endless Φ. Back-to-back Ds? A circle cut in half? I try eating up time with all the wrong answers, but there are only so many. Lips already dry. I scrub the mouthpiece with my shirt, turn the valve up higher than normal, bring the mask to my face, and take the first deep breath of relief in a week.

CAL /// LUNAR ORBIT

Truth is, Emma Reyes and I are NASA's first to die in space. More arbitrary a milestone I can't imagine. Worse than burning alive on a botched dry run? Breaking up on launch, re-entry? It's something.

And we'll know in advance how this thing runs its course—"mild case of celebrity amplified by death," as my brother Aidan once said of a starlet who came to a lurid, newsworthy end. An actress with Emma's sort of look, in fact. Could be that everyone doomed shares a face.

"I'm scared, Cal," she says.

Whether Emma's accepted our lot remains a mystery from where I'm floating. She spends these hours staring out windows, cycling through all three. Terror and boredom are totals.

We don't know what happened; I assure myself that no one does. Malfunction. Nonfunction. It began with the lights dozing, dimming away. Preoccupied, we blamed our minds. Lines of communication scraped away to useless hums, hums then exchanged for thicker silence. We had acclimated to a thin, numbing drone, and the final switch shook us out of fake sleep. Without the melancholy note of white noise sustained, our voices clanged, blunt in stale air.

*

I screwed Emma once, long before all this, in a sleazy motel outside Cape Canaveral. The beaten town of Andronicus, Florida. A dip in the swamp where lizards that walk upright should evolve. Reminded me of home.

Neon VACANCY staining the room an arrhythmic lime. Passing traffic washed over her back. Headlights warped shadows into monstrous rhomboids, flying tombstones.

Strictly forbidden. Professional courtesies, teamwork concerns. Of course, we never quite expected a mission to materialize—evidently there's a space nut writing congressional budgets, and no one has seen fit to stop them. Nor had we begun to fret we'd be bumped up. But the first two teams fell to old-fashioned flu, and the public abhors unnecessary delay. We launched, our secret a stowaway.

The limits mattered. We did it because it wasn't an option. Tell me that doesn't make someone irresistible. Unfairly so. I didn't even have to lie. My inner asshole flexed its sphincter. There are women who want that callous truth. Even as we neared the end, I was thinking of someone, anyone else. A honeycombed pattern of female parts, motions and sounds that fit the contours of my broke-down brain. She caught a glimmer of the impotent rages I've collected.

Couldn't sleep next to her. I went to get some ice from the machine to chew on. Padded through the oppressively humid hallway toward the machine, bucket in hand. A small blond child with a mushroom cut and soft features rounded a corner and collided with my knee. It stared up at me through a shiny film of tears. It wore a knee-length red T-shirt and that may have been all.

"I can't find my mom."

"You checked the lost and found?"

"She left the room. When I woke up, she …"

"C'mon sport," I said, and offered my hand, which felt parental enough. We walked in a direction. It had a way of holding in its many sneezes, making a private huh-tunch *sound each time. Couldn't say if it was a boy or girl.*

"Does your mom love you?" I asked.

"Yes. She gave me a dumb haircut today, but she loves me. Does yours?"

"Yes."

"That's good."

"The best."

At the front desk I asked whether any moms had been seen about recently, explaining the situation to a twentyish acne-scarred girl who stopped whispering into her headset to listen. She smiled cravenly. The kid slunk off to push buttons on a Belltruvin vending machine.

"Prolly turning tricks, mister. Let the kid stay in the lobby if he wants."

"I think it might be a she," I said.

On the walk back to my room, we encountered the anachronism of an ice machine I'd been looking for, a huge silver chest of cubes that automatically refilled. You had to lift a heavy flap and dig it out. I put down the bucket and picked up the kid.

"Want to see something?"

I held it at an arm's distance and flew it into the open chest, skimming it across the ice and going woosh. *I expected it to be distressed or disturbed, but it stared dully up at me, bored. With all the bizarre things adults had done to it, I realized, this was hardly worth noting. Pulling it out of the low arc and setting it on the carpet again, I said:*

"Now everyone who has a drink at this hotel will get a little taste of you."

Back in the one-room suite, Emma did her thing.

"Either he leaves or I do," she said.

"I was hoping it would come to that," I said.

"I'm a girl," said the kid.

We watched a late night kung fu movie till she fell asleep on the sex-stained king-size, lips popping open soundlessly when unconsciousness came. She'd grow to be an object of obsession for sure, some fool's ridiculous symbol, a beauty who convinced you her beauty meant more.

I moved to the puke-colored floor. Sometime later the power went out. I noticed only because the surviving letters of VACANCY died and the muted TV infomercial for a revolutionary egg-cooker cut to black. Emma's absence made me feel better. I watched one corner of the blank hotel door and the light that bled through underneath before falling asleep. I knew she'd be gone when I woke. I tried not to think about it.

*

If you're already concluding that these are the toxic words of a man at stage three in some emotional trauma flowchart, stop it. I'm the disease that has got to be lived with. I can't be cured, but I'm quarantined.

These are not the thoughts of a man deranged with the idea of his fate as some unaccountable bounce of the dice, but one who half-expected a coda like this. And you, if you're even there, will just have to buck up and listen or not. These transmissions have no audience. Remember: I can't hear your helpless replies.

I can't hear you at all.

*

The ship is dying, dead. Glossing empty waves of space, we rotate to raw physics' tune. Sun: a maw of chilly blue light splitting starred fabric. Everywhere a tincture of this indifferent blue, of slipping glaciers. When the moon comes between us and the sun, there falls darkness so complete that escape is fantasy. A doomsayer would invoke the shadow of God. It's a solar eclipse without the halo, a circle of nothing cresting larger each time.

When we stray out of the ink, shadowlines pull blue over us again. The blue neither retreats nor returns. It's there the whole time, waiting to be drawn out and peeled away from impermeable sheets of dark. All that's left will be this blue. Dying bathed in its ancient tone. A parting trick of the eye.

I'm hunched in gut-blazing agony, sick, before a glass triangle that holds the Earth. An emptying like no other. I want to be dragged to a nameless field and shot in the head with no explanations. Nothing but a bare-bones execution. I'd lie in the field of swaying grasses, pink ruptured lobes lying close by, watch a stream of souls swim the width of the sky.

"I'm cold," says Emma, improvised Russian dolls bouncing

nervously in lap: her left hand wraps her right fist, which clenches an awful something tight.

"Put it away," I advise.

"It is away."

Daydreams like that, the thing in the field, I keep my mouth shut about. Years ago, after we successfully traded virginities (she convinced me to do it in Aidan's room after school, wanting neutral territory), I'd told Phoebe that I liked the idea of being hit by a car, that on my bike I was reckless to better those odds. She announced my death wish to the world. Wrong: I had to survive. That was crucial. I didn't imagine a well-attended funeral, or parades of pity along the hospital bedside. I got those when my appendix burst, along with garish flowers that made my roommate sneeze and sneeze, coating himself with bodily mists.

"Are you allergic?" I asked.

"Worse," he went, between fits. He looked allergic to everything, really. A red grid on his face, the history of how they'd stitched it together. I learned through plastic privacy curtains that he came to the hospital every third week.

No. What I wanted was something else entirely. A moment beyond what we have to describe it, reverse-engineered from its own aftermath.

I was hoping to be changed.

Early the next evening, Henri isn't bouncing about the kitchen, making the usual messes. I'm ready for work in record time.

Outside, Anastasio is showing the tree to an aged reverend who has to peer over his half-moon glasses to make out the Virgin, and I throw them a curt nod. Happily, there aren't as many spectators as yesterday. Whole miracle thing had run dry fast.

Doesn't bolster my optimism that the train sits in the station for a solid fifteen minutes, engineers flummoxed by standing water from last night's storm. Early in the rush hour, but it hardly seems to matter in terms of crowding—guy standing behind me has no choice but to sneeze directly on my shoulder.

This woman across the aisle gets hassled by a conductor because her ticket isn't a peak-hour, which costs a buck fifty more. The conductor faces three obstacles in trying to extract an additional one hundred fifty cents from this woman: she speaks no English, he speaks no Spanish, and she doesn't want to pay it.

"Why? No. No. Why?" she keeps going.

The conductor slows down his argument.

"This … [hands flapping to signify the train we're on] … is … [still flapping] … a … *peak* … train … rush hour. [pantomiming exchange of money] one … fifty … more."

The woman shakes her head.

Outside, on the far end of the platform, a homeless man whose face can't be made out in the glare is brandishing a sign that says

HeLLO, NeeD to GET SOMTHING OF UR CHeST??
4 ONe DOLLAR I WILL LeT U TeLL Me OF Say ANY
    THiNG U
WANT U KeN CURSe. YeL AND SHOUT AT ME,
    PriTeND IM UR
BOSS. I PROMISS I WONT GeT MAD !?!

He's wearing draw-stringed plaid pajama pants that leave pale flaky shins exposed. I brush some hair from my eyes and tuck it behind my ear—what I do when I don't know what to do.

A nearby passenger who can at least fake some Spanish keeps saying "mas personas" in a feeble attempt to mediate between the woman and conductor. When his two-word vocab is exhausted, the conductor squeezes through clustered bodies to find a better translator.

Should've called the tree people myself. Christians make me nervous. Wonder if I can get out on the platform, tell the homeless man I don't belong here, and be back aboard the train before it leaves. A sticky-faced kid exits the car's bathroom; shortly after, a finger of piss seeps out from under the door. I start on my bowtie. As I fiddle for that elusive ratio in the knot, the wrinkled guy in camo and dreadlocks sitting next to me develops an expression I can't account for.

"What," I say, starting fresh when my first bow comes out droopy.

"I knew it," he smiles. "You're not going into space. Nobody is. Could never afford it. Some hoax."

"Yep," I tell him. Most crazies just want agreement. "You figured it out."

The conductor returns to our car with a colleague and directs him toward the Spanish-speaking fare-beater.

"Un dollar y cincuenta," the new conductor tells her.

*

When I get to Fieldcrest Manor, sprinting a few uphill blocks from the train station and sweating fiercely in my polyester tux, the bridal party has already arrived. Standard doomed couple, bit more attractive than the usual gargoyles. I make a couple of passes at the sign-in sheet, waiting for authority figures to disperse. When they finally wander off, I erase the name of a doofus busboy and scrawl mine next to his punch-in time, then badly forge his signature at the bottom of the list.

"Aidan, where the shit have you been, we're partners," a voice chides. I turn around to receive a swift punch to the gut that doesn't hurt much. Still, wouldn't have volunteered. "For making me do the water glasses myself."

"You hate everything."

"Especially this." She indicates all of me.

Kidding. I think. Being partners with Phoebe, object of a cyclical schoolboy crush, will at least afford me someone to talk to. It also means I'll be punched more.

It falls to me to distribute the party favors, mix CDs of the couple's favorite songs, and lacy bags of candy. I pocket four bags and open a fifth, strewing the rest haphazardly over a table, knocking over the floral centerpiece and soaking some dinner rolls with vase water.

"Is 'Celebration!' the band tonight?" I ask.

"I've had a shattering premonition they are."

"You know, Phoebe, some people see the glass as half-full. Ours, however, are half empty, being that you suck at your job." I pop a candy and spit it out instantly.

"Was gonna warn you how bad those candies were."

"Thanks," I mutter, kicking the nasty menthol thing under a chair. "Virgin sex on the beach?"

"Always," Phoebe beams, and we race over to the bar.

*

A meaningful stride should make you untouchable. This is how I typically walk around Donald, a ranking ass who made me a pet project after I spilled goat-cheese salad on three extremely bearded Macedonians at a raucous wedding some weeks past. Tonight the stride backfires: Don clotheslines me in the chest.

"Stop. You're doing buffet plates."

It would be fair to call this a thinly veiled punishment. Fieldcrest has this practice of putting its china plates in a huge metal box that heats them to scalding temperatures, and you don't want to be the flammable chump who takes them out.

Donald is a balding control freak, obsessed with everything I find unimportant, shorter than me by a head and a half. I strive to make him painfully aware of this last fact, eliminating my slouch in his presence—puts him all the more on edge. So he enjoys his brief vertical advantage here, hovering over me as I struggle to remove dishes from the heater, fanning his face with a hairy hand, listing everything that hasn't been done.

"More champagne out, four more place settings at table twelve, [sound of several dishes breaking] be *care*ful, will you? O. *My.* God. This father of the bride is an awful one, he's already complaining that the band isn't set up, not that we have any real authority over them, of course, but they don't know that. People are coming down late to the reception anyhow, probably watching the shuttle launch in their rooms right now. Would be nice to see that, though. Don't carry so many plates at once, for God's sake! And where's your nametag?"

"Still haven't given me one."

"We'll get you one tomorrow," Donald promises, as he has every day since I got here. "Did you spill alfredo sauce on your tux already?"

"Must be from last week."

"Niiice. Taking a little pride in your appearance?"

"Can't be proud to be a slob?"

"Real cute. I'll tell you who won't think it's so cute is Sam: you'd better not jerk him around, boyo." I slam some more plates on the counter and open the next enormous sliding door. The head boss is Donald's empty threat of choice—the man wouldn't bother to acknowledge me if I got caught whacking off on a cake.

"Also, Aidan, Sam was telling me that you need to lose the facial hair, that's the policy, you know that. You're scruffy." The heavy metal door breaks off its hinges and lands on my foot.

"Fucking *cunt*!" I spit.

"Hey!" Donald barks, "I'm serious, he's spoken to me on several occasions about how scruffy you're looking." I drop another plate.

"Would you stop!"

"Sorry."

Donald mops his brow with a pilfered dinner napkin. His head looks waxed. I put another searing hot tower of plates on the counter and bend to retie a shoelace. It snaps off in my hand.

*

After work I'm the kind of tired where you can't make a convincing fist. Exhaustion is a tipping factor in my decision to let Henri pick a 24-hour place to eat. I regret it: he drives us to the closest MexiLickin'SurfHog.

"Here?" I ask. A wide customer is exiting the place with some difficulty.

"What?" says Henri. "Should be empty this late."

"You never go to these places."

"Not the ones with kiddie ball pits."

I mope up to the counter after him. A pale girl about our age waits patiently for orders, leaning on her register with one hand and examining the sparkly nails of the other.

"Man," Henri exhales, "decisions." He makes a satisfied grunt and strides dramatically up to the counter.

"I'll have the Hogwash breakfast sandwich," he announces with gusto. "And a Forest Steppe Adderade."

"No breakfast served after 11 AM." The girl doesn't have to look at the backlit menu to quote it verbatim.

"The small-mindedness," Henri says, sincerely. "Why are you serving Hang Ten Donuts, then?" He points at this scary woman hunched over a table, coughing food back into the colorful box she ate it out of.

"Because they're already made?"

"Don't they count as breakfast?"

"Could eat a donut for lunch."

"And yet I can't have a bagel for dinner? This policy seems to paper over relevant semantic issues."

"What?" She abandons her nails, squinting.

"Here," I'm compelled to interrupt. "I'll pay you an extra five to make him that sandwich." The girl palms the crumpled bill and shuffles into the back.

"I could have handled that," Henri starts in.

"That what you were doing?"

"Hold up. I *know* her." At first I assume he means the cashier. But he's staring at the woman with the box of donuts. She's paused, gaze lost in a faraway corner of the fluorescent room. Trying to remember the original restaurants that combined to make this Frankenstein chain, I imagine. Then the pose breaks and she pulls at her nose, apparently irritated by an itch within.

"Let me guess—she's the next Grady? Gonna turn her life around, too?" I should've known why we wound up here. More free-floating guilt to latch on to. More steamrolling tragedy to challenge and be flattened by. He's sitting at her table before I say, "Wait."

"Ms. Hecuba?" he asks. She goes in for another donut. "Ms. Hec? It's Henri. Grown up, now."

"Henri …" she says, spewing powder. Henri nods.

"Come on, man," I tell him.

"You used to drive the bus to school. And for camp! Remember Aidan?"

"She doesn't. Leave her alone."

"I drive the city bus," she says, and wipes a dirty finger on her teeth. "Endless one. Not a school bus."

"You used to … so you switched jobs, then. Congrats! Did you go through Second Chance, then?"

"Henri, it's not her, cut it out."

"What is this?" the woman wants to know. She sways and grinds her teeth like an angry sleep will come any second. "I don't know you."

"You sure do. How's DH?"

Wrong question. The woman snaps to, shoving the donut box across the table and into Henri's lap, and stands, knocking her chair over. She squeezes Henri's face between two trembling hands and speaks into his eye.

"Not well. You can just stay the fuck away from him."

"Miss," I say.

"No people like you. Nothing like that."

"He didn't mean anything," I say.

She faces me and stares.

"Aren't you supposed to be in space?" she asks.

*

"It *was* her, though," Henri says as he swings his weight through the open car door and bounces into the driver's seat.

"So what. She was insane. Could've admitted it and snapped your neck right after."

"Just being friendly." The ignition harrumphs a few times before turning over. Henri tears open his bag of food and downs half the sandwich in one bite before backing out of the parking space. I fog the window with my breath.

"Not everyone wants you to save them. Or be in your hypothetical band."

"I dunno. I see so much tunnel vision around here. Specially after the takeover. Carrying on with life as usual."

"They should. That's the only thing you can do. That's what the last person alive would do."

"Not me. I'd teach myself to swim or something."

"In the newly radioactive oceans?" I ask. He laughs and polishes off the sandwich. We speed through one of those stretches where most of the buildings are already gone, grass reclaiming the earth square by square.

"Okay, then, learn another instrument. To improve my solo act."

"Did you call the tree guys?" I ask.

"I think so."

Henri takes both hands off the wheel for a second to simultaneously scratch his balls and turn on the radio. A Beach Boys song seeps from speakers, and I up the volume. Commercial, it turns out. Henri slows for a red light, and we idle at a deserted corner where the church I grew up with sits in that curmudgeonly pose. "Here you are," it chants, "here you are." Ivyland. Stirring only when somebody tries to pry you loose. Maybe not even then. The light goes green, then flickers and dies completely. Henri pretends not to notice, massages his forehead with a knuckle as he hits the gas.

"Why wouldn't you drop it with Ms. Hec? Can't believe you were so set on something. Can't believe she thought I was *Cal*. Had to happen two times today before I got it."

"You don't look that different."

"Didn't think he'd ever go up. Never much wanted to."

"When'd you talk to him last?"

"He came for graduation last year when mom and dad couldn't make it out from Phoenix. All he said was I sure took my time. Shook my hand."

"You still holding onto that grudge? Because it's rightfully mine, I've just been letting you borrow it for years."

"He always seems worse than before."

"I imagine he thinks the same way," Henri says, brown eyes swerving with a current of blue before he goes stiff and his head hooks left. The steering wheel, in a mirrored gesture, gets spun so we cut across the wrong lane and lose the driver's-side mirror to an abandoned junk car in a burst of sparks that jolts Henri back to attention. He pulls hard right and overcorrects into a 180° spin, squealing to a stop against the opposite curb. We sit in electric silence until Henri mentions he might cry. I tell him he has a bloody nose.

GRADY /// IVYLAND, NEW JERSEY

I have ID from Harvey House, but police laugh and says the shit that comes out my mouth is classic. "Grady," says a policeman name of Ed, "the shit that comes out your mouth is classic." I ax him what's making drool and spit and upchuck classic. "See what I mean." He laughs suchlike I see all tooths and a broken. He goes, "Take it easy, Grady," and I says I don't take nothing but mine things. "You're all right," he says, and walking to the MexiLickin'SurfHog. I knowed he likes the donuts there, so I says one day to get strawberry glaze, cause that's a best flavor, of donuts anyway. "Don't get donuts, I get those fancy Adderade drinks." I say like a magic potion like some wizards? "Sort of." I says I knowed they had some drinks like them and sometime I went inside but a man with a green smock like Harvey House arts and crafts stood near and looked bad till I leave and whatever cause I'm not loving this place. The real Harvey House art class guy brung paints and crayons and everything else. I painted two pictures and make a little clay pot suchlike my thumbs pushed out the bowl and plus to that a clay space shuttle like for the moon visit. Ed looks mad at me. "Bunch of bastards in there. You get your french fries somewhere else." I says I don't like faster foods. He says: "Whudju want from MexiLickin'SurfHog then?" I says I was curious. The policeman laugh like his way. I ax always again if he knowed what scoundrel locked up my bicycle for when I'm leaving it by the train on accident. Police don't hear me sometimes or get busy so they forget what I axed

and I have to ax them tomorrow, and months of tomorrow.
Okie-doke. They got it hard enough without me being super
curious. One police name of Vince never forgets. He believes the
scoundrels locked up my bike. "Grady," he says, "looks like they
locked your bike up good, I admit." Some police don't believe.
They says, "I got to see ID," so I show my ID from Harvey
House. They laughs and forget and go to MexiLickin'SurfHog.
Okie-doke. Job is no picnic. For one thing, no blanket. For
another: no basket.

*

I had a basket for my bicycle, but from the look the scoundrels
had removen it. I carry Dr. Hal Rockefeller in the basket. He
loves to play and squirm when I ride. Sometime I ride to the park
and we seen some kids play baseball. Don't care who win or lose,
I have some fun, I don't mind to tell. Dr. Hal don't know butt
'bout baseball, but never sad to lie in some sun. When games go
empty we leave to Freddy's Baseball Memorabilia. I'm gonna sell
Freddy my Mickey Mantle rookie card for bazillions of riches.
Always say I can't wait to've brung my Mickey Mantle rookie card
to sell. Freddy goes: "Well why dontcha then?" He likes to think I
don't have a Mickey Mantle rookie. I do. Just gotta find it. When
I do, boy—watch out! I'll buy a boss car with the riches. I brung
Dr. Hal Rockefeller in there hundreds of times, but Freddy is
always forgetting his face. "Can't have no weasel in here," Freddy
says. Okie-doke. Freddy goes, "Well get him out!" I says you says
no *weasels* and he's a *ferret* but Freddy's too mad at me so always
I try to go out on the sidewalk and put Dr. Hal Rockefeller in
my jacket and come back in. Mostly Freddy can't see, but once
when Dr. Hal was fooling Freddy says, "Something moving in
your jacket?" I says it's prolly some Mexican jumping beans and
you bet I runned my butt off to get out. Freddy says I'm Some
'Spicious Character. What, I says, little old me? "Yeah-You," says
Freddy, "scaring kids away." I says I hasn't seen kids in your store
once ever. Freddy says, "That's cause Some 'Spicious Characters

scare them away!" and he's chasin me out with a mop. I even get band! "You're band for life!" Freddy says. First time Freddy made me band was on accident but now I can make it every time. Got band three times one week, honest. When Freddy's mad enough to put a band he gets red like cartoons and I wait for some steam coming out his ears.

*

I axed Ty at Harvey House why Freddy will be so mad. Ty keeps watching on the TV and says, "Tell you what. Buy some Nicaraguan vampire bats. Release them into Freddy's home, let them fly down through the chimney, and you can't get out because shit there's something blocking the door—I put big rocks there—and the guano is flying, and God there's a bat in your hair and it's like of course the bat's just as scared and trying to untangle but it's hopelessly caught and the leathery wings are smacking you in the face as it screeches pathetically, which just attracts more bats, and what the fuck, seems like these bats got their sonar screwy cause all they do is crash into you, and finally one forward-thinking bat gets the inspired idea to bite you in the jugular vein and hey: that's when you black out." I can't do these fancy Ty things. Where can a man get some bats? I axed him an easier way. He says, "Shush, space shuttle news is on." He's a weird one, but he's trying you know.

*

But like we say, this was the days. Dr. Hal Rockefeller and I, we don't now bicycle together cause of scoundrels that did lock my bicycle and also because Dr. Hal Rockefeller is lost yesterday. I was leaving him play outside on our walk, and what do you know—he's gone. I told Liz, a Harvey House helper lady. "That weasel of yours running around loose?" I says he's a *ferret*. She says, "He's dangerous?" I says 'course not, Dr. Hal Rockefeller is a courteous ferret and with manners. She says, "She'll turn up." I says it's a he not she.

*

I was showing people my only picture of Dr. Hal Rockefeller. Of the doctor in his bike basket and me steering. People say nothing or else "I haven't seen your rat" or suchlike unhelpful things. Dr. Hal Rockefeller most of times is coming home before long, but he was lost for a day now and I hadn't ever missed him so awful much as this. Could've looked for Dr. Hal on my bike if not for scoundrels! The police says last time I had no ID and never no bike. Police Ed goes, "Who would give you a bike? You'd just hurt yourself." My bike is a gift to me by one Henri Acton, who has the absolute best music band (that's different from Freddy's bands from the card shop) all by himself, with zero backup, on the little piano. He says I'll enjoy it more and I'm his biggest fan, and that L president-hey of the Henri Acton fan society has important things that needs modes of transport. But now! I had to be on some searches for Dr. Hal with no bike no help, even though I axed Ty. Ty says, "This government is soft on crime." Not as soft as Dr. Hal Rockefeller, you be sure, I says, but Ty is a meanly shout, "Quiet for *America Sings!* And P.S., the rat-finding expedition is a no-go." On TV some guy, singing, and wow, was he somewhat loud. I says that guy would make good at a baseball game announcing.

*

By the tracks where I can be taking breaks from searches I watched some big wooshy trains. They were fun and neat. I seen trains lots and some littler with pretend towns suchlike Henri and I were playing at times ago, in Harvey House around the Christmas tree. It has littler pretend people to be waiting for the train and it's fun cause I'm like a giant at them, but a friendly giant. I was too close to a regular train and in a shiny woosh it blew away from my arms some drawings of Dr. Hal Rockefeller I wrote for passing out. Flying and I can't catch them from the air. There's a man with a hat who I catched at on accident. "Whaddayu think you're doing, throwing those all over the platform." I says I was catching only and no throwing. "Don't let me see you at that again." He gives his dumb hat some touches and is stepping on the train. I have only been once inside of a train, when I was a kid and having a nosebleed. Thing is some ways I'll do a nosebleed, but no biggy, just for a usual. Dad though was shouting cause I was eating of the blood to get it back in. "Stop!" which is a word I know is on red *octagons*, and he was crying at me, but my blood were like funny candy. Henri taught me octagons and others of crazy shapes. Nosebleeds nothing, Henri was like to say, Dad still loves me, it's his job.

*

There's a whole buncha people that I talked at for the Dr. Hal Rockefeller-finding expedition, the word I learned from Ty, and all standing like dinner line-up. They were getting at train tickets, obvious. My stomach was growls because some criminal had a delicious hot dog and my stomach was thinking bout Texas Wieners, a tip-top restaurant, only I can't ever remember where it is and when I try a map it just has lines of colors and it can't work. Criminal for sure. Ty says all niggers are interested with one thing: crime. "Nigger?" I was saying, to practice. "Nigger? Who? How do we spot the nigger," I ax. "That," Ty points at Ernie, a cleaning Harvey House guy. "O, a nigger is a cleaner guy!" "No!" Ty says, "with the *skin*." "O," I'm shouting more, "a nigger is a guy with cleaner *skin*!" "*No!* A nigger does not have clean skin … they have dirty skin. So dirty it's black." "O," I'm whispery, "am I a nigger?" "Idiot," Ty grumbles like dogs, "a nigger has *really* dirty skin. You're just *kind* of dirty." "O," I says, "now you're understood. I'm just *kind* of nigger." "Yes," Ty says, "but full niggers are criminals, not like you." We watched on TV an animals show where a baby walrus was rescued so he could grow big. Ty kept on saying "Just die," at the baby walrus, but boy was I happy the walrus didn't. I wished it could've sat with me suchlike it was my baby.

Then they make the walrus go back to his real wilderness home, and zoo people are having a cry?—hello, it's a *happy* ending! "Ty," I axed, "a criminal. How do we spot a … criminal?" "Just look for a nigger," Ty says.

*

I'm going at the line-up people and none want a chat, not even the criminal with his Texas Wiener. They just move up the line with toys in their ears and talking to the back of someone else's head. The train-ticket guy in the jail was frowning a lot and says, "You, come over here." I was too afraid and looked around. "Yeah, pajama pants. Come here." But here's what: everyone is wearing pants and can sleep in them, which means we're all wearing of pajama pants. The train ticket guy is just more frowning. "Get lost," he goes. And there are moments too soon! Cause right there in a wall hole on the side of the jail is some tail. "There!" I shout to the line-up, and diving for Dr. Hal. The tail goes in the hole so I stick my arm all in too. The line-up people say stuff, but I don't hear so much cause I called at Dr. Hal Rockefeller to come, and was promising some cheese—his favorite kinds, which is monster. My fingers in dark can feel at rocks and a box with soft pills in it. I felt a moving. I grabbed it and found a tail to pull, which I was sorry to do cause you know it hurts, but when Dr. Hal comes out he's not looking like himself and his tail is naked and gross suchlike nothing else, not ever. He's dangly and bitey and I say: "Hey, you're not the doctor," because for certain this thing is not. He's squirmy and try to bite again, and then some line-up people saw. A lady screamed, and others making big fusses for nothing. "Don't be worrisome," I say, using a Henri word, "Only a rat, like *Ratopia* on Animal Channel," and brung it closer to show how harmless, but these people are screams. The criminal holding a Texas Wiener has a surprise and dropping his Texas Wiener and that darn rat wiggled out my hand. He took a chunk from the Texas Wiener on the ground and runned out so fast, you have no ideas.

*

The train-ticket man came out of the jail and with a mad face. He says, "I told you, get lost," and pushed me, and went to give the screamest lady some touches. I was crying but pretended I wasn't cause the line-up people were looking, and hey, a cry is for little kids. But it was too late to not have a cry and I wiped at my crying, and I go downstairs to sit by the ice cream place but not wanting some and crying still. Who walks out with some ice cream in a sugar cone, my favorite, but a police name of Bert. "Why you crying, Grady?" "A cry is for kids." He's licky at his ice cream and says, "Why don't you hang with me, Grady, take a load off?" I yell, "I don't take what isn't mine!" and runned off, boy. Runned and runned. Runned in a tunnel under the train tracks and runned smack into some boy kids. One boy shouting: "Hey, watch where the fuck you're going!" I tell that swearing is for bad people, and he goes, "I am bad." It was darkful with the tunnel but I can't leave. Another boy is saying, "It's that guy! I know who you are." "Cause I'm famous?" "Yeah, a famous loser." "Famous," I says, "wow." And then the boys are laughy, and I'm laughing but the laugh is making more crying come out. "What's wrong with you," says the bad boy. Dr. Hal Rockefeller is gone. "Who is that, your boyfriend," goes the bad boy, and the other boys are laughy again. No, I says, he's my *ferret* friend. "I have an idea," says one boy, "we'll help you find it." "What?" says another boy. "Are you retarded?" "Shh, dude, trust me." "This is stupid." "O Jesus," goes some others. "Yes please!" I'm yelling, "you have to!" and the boys are almost scared. "I was needing help." And I wanted to cry some more, but holding it in to be brave. And one boy, who is so gosh-darn familiar, looks at me and looks away.

*

The boys are walking into Harvey House with me to help with a sign, a sign with real words. Amy, a helper lady, says, "Oh you've got some new friends there, have you," and smiles. I smile. I got

a poster thing at the arts and crafts room that Ty always calls arts
and farts, and I laugh for it. Ty goes, "You don't even know what
a fart is, do you." I says no. He tells, "A fart is when white stuff
comes out your weiner." I was so laughy at this, maybe most ever.
Ty is looking bad and says, "That noise. What is that stupid noise
you make?" The boys draw words I told for the poster, about Dr.
Hal Rockefeller and his personality, his favorites of cheese. I tell
his color and softness, and the boys were making the fanciest
words. "It's done?" I keep asking. "Almost." In a bazillion years
it was ready, so long and fancy! "It's the best," I say, and the boys
was smiling, but one boy not, and he's looking same—this boy
is like Leo. He says, "Grady, don't use this sign." Other boys say,
"Shh." I say: "It's perfect." The boy says again, "Don't use it," and
catched at it to rip! I say "No! Please don't! Please." And before
you knew I was crying again at the Leo kinda boy but more cause
I was needing the sign so much. "See," says the bad boy, "he likes
his sign, it'll work great." He takes it from the Leo boy and give
it at me. "Grady," he says, "I have a feeling this sign will make
you very happy." And the little Leo putting his chin on his chest.

*

I was walking with a sign so beautiful. Up to the trains for the
line-up train people to see and tell me clues. And sure you bet
sure some people talked at me. Of most, people were looking sad
at me, prolly cause it is so sad when animals get lost. The talky
people, surprise: they knowed nothing about Dr. Hal. They give
me free dollars like the Harvey House helper ladies give dollars
for Ice Cream Saturdays. It was riches for me! At the first, I was
giving dollars back and axed about Dr. Hal, but these people just
was talking bout other things. One goes: "Can't your worthless ass
get a better job than this?" I say my weekly chore job is organizing
arts and farts table at Harvey House. He says to shut up. I axed
if some information 'bout my ferret, but again he was saying to
shut up, and is calling me Simon. I ax who Simon is. He is saying,
"My worthless ass son," and leaves.

*

More yelling at the train tracks. More dollars. Some peoples throwing dollars but not yelling. What about Dr. Hal Rockefeller? Nothing. One guy is yelling bout his girlfriend that is sexy but making him nuts. I was laughy cause he's saying sexy, a laughy word. I had a girlfriend one day at Harvey House, helper lady name of Jessica, except o boy is here the kick: her favorite Jell-O being *orange*! And since mine is lime green which will be of course a superior flavor of all time, we must be calling it grits, which for usual come the day after Jell-O Night. I told Henri bout my love life once, and he says, "Irreconcilable differences." Sing it! Cause I say that also to Henri's music—they say it too on Sunday morning singing TV with criminals.

*

A train stops once for long. Sad and sadder faces in it.

*

One guy is going, "What do I want to rant about." He's looking at my sign and says, "Boss, that's good," and then was yelling bout Mr. Price someone. He's yelling into a while, well, other peoples want turns. He says, "We need more people like you." I says, "Tell Dr. Hal I'm here, if you're seeing his furry behind." Just then I heard my name and there's good old Vince! He goes, "Grady, what's this racket?" I says it's cause of wanting to find Dr. Hal. He reads at the sign. "I'm sorry," he says. "Somebody played a joke on you." And even though I fuss he wouldn't hear me explain and says he has to take my great sign! That was the most sad, so here I was to cry. Again. He took the sign. "Grady Grady Grady" is Vince's words, and he is fold of the sign. I am not a kid forever, but sometimes just like the Harvey House helper ladies say, you can't help it. Vince is not mean like this, I think, and the people waiting in a line for talking at me start leaving cause of Vince! I try no more crying and yell, "Dr. Hal Rockefeller is alone plus to that prolly scared!" But my crying is making the yells blubby and I know I still look like big stupids, cause I am. "Trust me," goes Vince, giving me a touch, which I am *hating* now and want to say but so ugly a word, suchlike a thing always they tell at Harvey House to Ty, they tell that Hate Is An Ugly Word. So true, cause I feel an ugly in my guts. So I runned, I runned. And downstairs of the trains, even worse! The bike locked up by the scoundrels is not locked up but gone! The criminal unlocking my bike finally, but stealing it, the frosting on a fate worse than breath. I runned again for Harvey House and a phone: the police given me a hotline to a detective. He is Larry and at most times sleepy on a desk, but other police are telling me don't let it fool you, don't judge a book by his sleepiness, cause he is extremely detectively.

*

Only it's lated. I runned past the creek for telling me the way back to Harvey House and look and my precious bike is sinky in the crappy brown water! All bent. All crappy. And I don't swear like Ty but jeez is it crappy now. And the crying, like a dumb baby, but Vince was mean and criminals broke my bike and Dr. Hal is lost and Henri doesn't play me songs or come visit even and nothing is fair, so I lie in the garbagy grass and let the cry cry.

DH /// ANDRONICUS, FLORIDA /// LAST FALL

*DH Forsyth and Leviticus Van Vetchen sit dozing in their renovated
ice cream truck until a clanging at the rear door startles them.*

LEV

Open Sesame.

*DH obeys. A rangy, tanned man with a torn white shirt and faded
Miami Dolphins cap climbs into the truck and stands, hips thrust,
facing its owners.*

DH

You with Endless?

LEV

Yeah, are you?

TOM

F'ize with Endless, I'd be dressed better.

DH and Lev share a look.

LEV

What can we do for you? (*scrutinizing*) Facelift? Not gastric.

TOM

Name's Tom. Want the VV.

DH

Who said we—

LEV

Five hundred.

TOM

Shit, son, I only got but three. Ball'n'chain doesn't know I have *that* much. Won it on the ballgame today.

DH and Lev share a look. Tom pulls a crumpled brown bag from his jacket pocket, flinging it onto the operating table. He produces a second brown bag and drinks from it.

TOM

Suppose I need to be a damn sight drunker to not feel the cut and all.

DH

Actually, we've got the gas.

Lev smacks his forehead as Tom's eyes drift up to the shelf of silver tanks.

TOM

Make me manager at a MexiLickin'SurfHog. I don't believe this.

LEV

Tom, I would love to perform VV on you, for your own continued safety and blah blah blah, but Hallaxor gas is expens—

TOM

Okay. Cards on the table. You give me the VV, I can direct you toward a high school car wash. This truck hasn't met much dirt, but there's a little firecracker working there you'd get along with nicely. My daughter. They're all in bikinis; she's the only one in red. Babysitter hair.

He takes another swallow of booze.

DH

We'll do it.

LEV

"We."

Lev starts rooting around in cabinets for his tools.

DH

Can I ask why you want the procedure, Tom?

LEV

(*Head hidden*) O, yes, let's not forget the survey.

TOM

Sad story, but sure. New baby died, couldn't've seen it coming. Wife said it was the crib death, something infant death syndrome, crazyass thing I never heard of. Thought that up on her PMS and plus she was half stupid from losing the baby on top of being half stupid to begin. But a doctor said no doubt about it, H12. A professional said. Wife and me at risk, he said, and we can't afford the surgery, not the real thing. But I was at the bar watching the Little League World Series and got lucky and heard about you all, so here I am.

LEV

We're the real thing.

TOM

Are you, now. They said a mobile center wouldn't hit this neighborhood for another couple months. Maybe I need a new calendar, hnn?

DH

What about your wife?

TOM

What about her?

LEV

Lie down already.

Tom gets on the table and shuts his eyes as DH pulls down a Hallaxor tank, attaching a tube to a mask.

TOM

I can drive home after?

LEV

More or less.

Tom laughs.

DH

What?

TOM

Forgot I sold the shit car to get the money to bet.

Lev rolls his eyes, fits the mask over Tom's nose and mouth. DH twists the tank valve.

LEV

We aren't responsible if you're allergic, but we'll dump you at a hospital if anything happens.

DH

You've got to breathe deep. You're going to feel sleepy, but you will not be asleep.

LEV

Sure won't.

They roll Tom onto his stomach, and DH draws an incision line with a marker. Lev pours half a bottle of water over his lucky scalpel and slices the back of Tom's neck open as DH watches with growing unease, knowing he's already cut too deep.

AIDAN /// IVYLAND, NEW JERSEY /// THIRTEEN YEARS AGO

Henri swings stubby legs under the bench, ratty catcher's mask locked in the raised position so he can chew and spit sunflower seeds. He musters inhuman gobs of saliva'n'shell fragments that absorb dugout sand, clotting into putrid buttons you can feel through cleats. Henri playing catcher not because he's the best at it; Stanley just figured that's where the fat kid goes.

"Kilham! On deck!" Stanley yells from the other side of the dugout.

Coach Stanley. A next-level alcoholic. Guy who clarified what it meant to be one right as his species went extinct. Never without this shiny film on his face, as I only saw him in Jersey's swampy late spring and early summer, and the sort of gnarled gray hair and creased cheeks a Jack London fur trapper would sport in his twilight years, squinting beneath the brim of a crappy mesh hat. Yes, Stanley, pride of our suburban little league circuit, was the inevitable byproduct of volunteerism. Henri'd finally put his foot down on the hide-his-flask trick we always played, saying the man's life is already too sad, an excuse that annoys more than a flat refusal.

"Sean's using it."

Stanley does like he's having an idiocy-related aneurysm.

"Well take it away fromm'im!"

"But he's batting now …" The protest disintegrates.

"Use mine," Henri wheezes through a repellent mouth,

seeds sliming out. Sean hits the kind of pop fly that's an easy out for anyone but little leaguers. It's caught, though, and a lone Hawaiian-shirted weirdo in the bleachers claps twice. I take a few cuts with Henri's monster bat.

"Ou godda behd yr deez," Henri garbles, mouth even fuller than before.

"Bend my knees. Don't act like you made that advice up, butt nugget," I tell him. Henri guffaws, seeds chuckling forward. I laugh, too. "You have like an infinite number of seeds in your mouth! Your head is just a sack of sunflower seeds! Look at you!" Now we're in hysterics, headed toward full-body laughter I won't be able to shake by the time I reach the plate.

*

"There's one."

Game's over. I struck out looking, team lost again, Stanley urinated on the pitcher's mound and thereby salvaged a kernel of pride. We're trolling the neighborhood on bike after ditching equipment in my mom's minivan. The house I have in mind is a sad shade of mustard and sits atop a hill cluttered with trees and overgrown bushes. Henri pushes sweat-laden bangs away from his eyes, panting softly as I jump off my bike and prop it against a telephone pole.

"I don't want to." I find and throw a pebble, which can't help hitting him somewhere in the chest. "I told you to stop. They're home, anyway."

"O my God, Henri. Like anyone cares."

"Easy for you to say. Not all as skinny and agile as you. Someone *did* come out, you'd be a block away in no time. Whereas I'd have to bend over and rest after running like ten feet." He swings a leg over his bike's crossbar and puts down the kickstand with his hand, a dumb method in my opinion.

"I'd stay with you."

"BS."

"*You're* the BS." I toe a crack in the sidewalk and attempt to pry the concrete slabs apart with my foot. Henri has his hands in his pockets. "Are you coming or not?"

"It's weird."

"What is?" No answer. "Nothing else to do."

"Get some bottles and play Submarine."

"I'm bored of Submarine. "Come on, wienie-puff." I absently karate-kick at the waist-high grass along the curb, pausing every few seconds to tear crumbly caps off of the blades and flick the powder at Henri.

"Would you stop!" he pleads, unable to suppress a giggle.

"Weenie-puff, weenie-puff," I chant, like he's stepping up to the plate. He really can hit.

"You can't make me. So far, too." He's not exaggerating: probably about seventy-five steps to the top, and steep ones. "This is so stupid."

"That's why we do it. Stupid kids. Weenie-puff."

"Pish-posh."

"Pish-posh? Are you, like, the Queen of England now?"

"'Pish-posh' is a perfectly acceptable term."

"You saying 'pish-posh,' *that's* the pish-posh."

"I'll go up if you stop saying 'pish-posh.' "

"Deal. After you." I jab my index finger into his spine to get us going. The steps have wooden frames but are filled in with gravel. I occasionally grab a handful and toss a gentle spray at Henri.

"What is it with you and throwing things?"

The lawn is drier and pale as the hill stretches upward. When I start to listen to him, Henri is saying something about how human waste that ends up in septic tanks is sold as fertilizer once the solid waste and pathogens and stuff are filtered out.

"That why you're always shitting on your lawn?"

"Said you have to *filter* it."

"Could you walk any slower?"

"Told you this hill would suck."

"Fine, stay here."

I shove Henri aside and bound up the remaining steps, leaving him next to a fat pine near the top. When I arrive at a crumbling brick stoop, I notice all the creepy paraphernalia of a person who tried to fit in but failed spectacularly: a battalion of lawn ornaments dot the crest of the hill, many with parts designed to spin in the breeze. They're motionless, rusted in place. Wooden wind chimes, maybe a dozen sets, bonily chatter from freestanding steel rods. The first floor windows are caked with dust on the inside.

"Henri?" I turn to hiss. There's only a rustling. Out of a desire to get it over with, I tiptoe up to the door and find the mailbox off to one side, turn the old-fashioned red flag thing up to the 'got mail' position. Pointless, really. I start back down two steps at a time.

Behind me, from the house, comes a definite thump. I veer off the path, twist my ankle on tilted ground and go down in a cloud of limbs. Scrambling with hands and feet, I get behind the pine Henri had been waiting near and peek around it at the front stoop. There's a screech as the screen door swings out savagely, then a snort as the man who opened it steps outside.

Wet, yellowish skin: looks like he sweats potato-chip grease, but every third day it's gasoline instead. He rocks side to side on filthy feet while surveying the property from his stoop, dressed only in a stained tank top and boxer-briefs the color of old paper, with a pistol jammed in the elastic waistband.

The raised red lever on his mailbox registers at last; he flings the tin thing open and slams it shut in one motion. He stares at the closed mailbox like he's trying to meld minds with a higher life force. Then he punches it, leaving a crater. The sound coaxes a woman's voice from inside the house—can't be made out, but the inflection is of casual worry.

"Supposed to get a check today," he yells in. "Dickhead mailman is playing *games*." He wrenches the red flag off and hurls it down the hill, then brandishes the gun, asserting its realness, and disappears inside to answer a follow-up question from the female voice. I crawl under the low-hanging pine branches and find Henri a few feet away. He's sitting between two pricker bushes and pulling up grass by its roots.

"What happened?"

"Shut up and go. Not the stairs."

"Fine."

"And shut up," I remind him.

Henri shrugs, gets up and starts threading his way through the overgrown vegetation with the expediency of a dying turtle. I can't leave him. I kick him hard in the ass instead, and he wheels around with an expression of silent indignation.

A gunshot punctures the air above us. I shove Henri to the ground next to the shrubbery lining the stairway and topple onto him in the process. We roll apart and tense up. A drop of sweat bleeds into my eye. Henri's heartbeat mingled with mine. Mine faster. We keep our eyes on the one stair visible through the brush. Two bare feet drop onto it and shift around anxiously.

"Still here, aren't you," the guy shouts. "Good. Long as you're trespassing I can still kill you." We wait a long minute and hear him spit. "Fuck it," he says quietly, and the feet withdraw.

"I think that's old man Clafter," Henri whispers.

"Listen to you with the old man shit."

"You know, Leo's dad."

"You didn't even see him."

I raise my head and spot the man up near our pine, parting its branches with his gun to look for a climber. We get to our feet and move as silently as boys could ever hope to, slinking through the last clusters of bushes toward the street.

"You know why he went crazy, right?"

"How would I?"

"Cause their other son got all messed up from VV when he was little. You know, the gas? He was allergic—stopped his brain from developing."

"Such a liar."

"Yeah-huh, Leo never got VV, the gas is too risky if there's a family history. And his older brother—"

"Leo doesn't have a brother."

"Then why'd he beat up Jack for saying it? Anyway they bought him twenty years guaranteed at Harvey House and that's why Leo's too poor for school lunch."

I glance back up the hill in time to notice that Mr. Clafter or whoever is crouched like a spider on the front stoop and calmly training his gun on us. A shot goes wide, burying itself in the lawn with a queasy *thunng*. I gasp as though it passed clean through me.

We drop into a gravity-assisted sprint. Every breath stabs at shredded lungs. Joints are pumped fluid. Another shot. Henri, a few feet in front of me, is running like he's forgotten his body, running so fast that he can't compensate for the last bush in our way and catches the side of it with his shoulder, knocking a whitish football-shaped bees' nest out of its niche within.

Buzzing dots unfunnel from the papery ball as it tumbles downhill with us. Tearfully I barrel through the swarm, taking dozens of stings in my forearms, the only shields I have. The sound gooey terror, a living chainsaw. Henri tramples the nest as it rolls into his path. Pop and hiss of two more bullets. One for each of us. Bone grinds. Vision is a stain. This is what it's like to regret something, I have the weird coolness to reflect. We should have played Submarine.

We make it to the street, but it's not good enough: I look back to see Clafter struggling to reload atop the stairs. Red welts flame out like mutant chicken pox. Henri's giving his kickstand a rapid-fire series of kicks to get it to swing upward, too panicked to realize that he's kicking from the wrong side.

"I knew he was crazy!" he shrieks. "I knew it!" He gives up and starts riding with the kickstand still down. My hands grip rubber, igniting bolts of pain from stung palms. We ride, Henri's bike limping is how you might describe it, kickstand periodically catching the road and grating along asphalt till he regains his balance. I pedal furiously, not slowing even as I pull needle after tiny needle out of my skin.

When we reach my house, I coast straight into the backyard. Instead of slowing down, I simply let myself fall sideways onto dry, sun-beaten grass, the bike toppling onto me. The chain grease is cold on my leg. Henri stops, pushes his bike aside and crumples.

"I hurt everywhere."

"Same." Could count, but it's easier to call myself one giant sting.

My mom's semi-concerned alto floats out of a window, across a sky silver and veined like a dragonfly wing.

"What are you boys doing?"

"Nothing," is the answer, in unison.

We lay there, reptile-still, replaying action and reaction with awe. Some spoken, some drifting through brains. Through mine, anyway. Leaves overhead ripple at a calm boil. The waves of surreal memory crash without direction. To and fro. In and out. Points of debate are exhausted. Certain blanks fail to be filled. One or two tortured what-ifs haphazardly examined. Apologies come, awkward and quiet. Our stings quietly throb, but the breezes are balms. Blankness creeps up on us.

At last, Henri, attempting a conclusion, offers:

"We should've played Submarine."

"Should've played Submarine."

PROFESSOR FLEER /// IVYLAND COLLEGE /// ONE YEAR AGO

The students give me hope when they do not open their mouths too wide. But this little season has seen slack-jawed awe in the main, and the shrouded inner walls of throats refract things miserably. A quality—let's say coherence—escapes in muted gasps, slipping serpentine toward sunnier rocks. It's humbling to remember humility.

To doubt the primacy of our species, I mean.

He's leaning over my desk, asking for my wife, when I notice. (Truth be told, I have no answer, confirming healthy levels of marital trust.) I can barely snatch a word between the oaf's intimidations. His tie is oddly textured, fish-scaled. Full Windsor knot wrenched as though in pain; it reminds me of a sculptress who worked metal into corkscrewed shapes to strangle and drown her adulterous father in history's clouded stream. One can't recall, sculptress, whether your art ever pitied mom instead.

"There's a caterpillar on your shoulder," I interrupt, pointing. The detective sneers and crushes it with thumb and forefinger.

They are simply everywhere—the word is *biblical*. Too many warm winters, buttressed by this muggy spring, have yielded a bumper crop of the yellow-speckled creepers. Our campus is their extra-leafy Eden; a formal armistice alone prevents them from wresting control from the deans. Yet I let them feast at Azura's honeyed insistence, will never maliciously kill one lest she catch me in the boyish act. My vermiculate office spider plant is holey testimony of that appeasement, swarming with the busy plague.

"Are you hearing me right now?" the detective blusters, apparently vexed. "You're to help me find certain responsible parties."

I tell him I'll draw up a list of moral relativists in the department.

"Funny. I'll ask again before we go downtown: Professor Azura Carcassone."

My wife … crime of passion … exits rising to enable. Sixth floor. She pushes the elevator button with sweet impatience. Inuit cinema to teach. Sylvia, a fiery if cipherlike student of mine, is already descending. Sixty feet below: safety, the ghastly gift shop of Ivyland College Museum. But no. Doors whine open. Four too-similar eyes are locked. Sylvia, my wife shrewdly concludes (and is it any wonder with this quicksilver Sherlock? I blame her sense of noir), has just enjoyed my favorite exhibit, "Gauguin in Tahiti," which fills the seventh, uppermost floor. Glorious flattening of space, Gothic complex of rilled drapery boiled away to one dimension. Would that I lived within such mazes.

Azura can't help but see her chance. Perhaps a Sylvian tic is prologue. Formalities dispensed, a ruby-encrusted butterfly knife—Christmas gift—enters her at every angle and erogenous zone. Azura alights on the second floor and ecstatically cartwheels en route to fire escape. Ding: doom spills into the lobby. Hot blood folds over the precipice between elevator and gleaming wood floor. Some clerk, lobotomized townie, ratchets up a scream. Sylvia's slender fist uncurls from the knuckle-crack that announced her fate.

Is what I'm guessing happened.

And tenure was so close this time.

I start shoveling Žižeks, Kirkegaards and Lacans into my briefcase, bare essentials for a portable library. I sprinkle some William James on the pile for good measure. Call my temperament pragmatic. A dusty edition of René Thom's squirts out of my hands, falls open to the butterfly catastrophe. $V = x^6 + ax^4 + bx^3 + cx^2 + dx$. I kick it back at the bookcase in a mounting fit, wishing I owned Dalí's merciful last painting instead.

"Uh," says the chuckling detective, whom I'd quite forgotten. "Going somewhere?" The dreariest impasse.

"Coxswain duty. There's a meet against Rutgers today, and I'd hate to disappoint the girls. They've rowed *so* expertly this season."

"Do a lot of reading on the boat?"

He gestures sardonically at my open Samsonite, overflowing with dense critical thought.

"The proper passage never fails to galvanize an athlete," I smile, casually holding up a copy of—O, dear—*Discipline and Punish*. I drop it like a catty footnote.

"Did I mention that I'm a cop? And that your wife is wanted for questioning as regards senseless criminal acts?"

"Senseless?" I laugh. "Don't be ridiculous."

O, double dear.

*

Azura always orders what the fattest man in the restaurant is having. Often with archaic zest. Watch her struggle to not say *Je voudrais*. Adore it when she fails. Thrill at the articles studding her syntax: "It is easy as *a* pie," she'll insist when begging a favor. By now she's wise to the hiccup and executes it with flourish.

"I love you so much I could cut a off homeless man's nose and catch the rainbows streaming out," she whispers as I unmoor myself for sleep.

"Let's call that a mistranslation."

We are exhausted from the day, a visiting artist's new exhibit: "Justice/Mutilation and the Reversed Con," photo galleries of unknowing dark faces with ghoulish epithets written under skin, liminal smirks of thieves whose ruses have gone all 8-figured. They are African sources of fraudulent e-mails, phony princes and supposed heirs, here made to believe someone has fallen prey to the scam. Only, trust must be established. Our artist teases with the promise of bank-account codes. The signs of good faith are obscene facial tattoos, in baffling, vile English idiom. Strange but irresistible trade. They uphold their end, photograph themselves after hours and days spent under a needle. Of course the numbers never come, but the faces we see are fully expectant, sadness unassembled, inked hate glancing off cheeks and through the gritty lens of a cell phone camera.

"I don't see where material trickery can dovetail so with physical cruelty."

"Live to breach faith; your faith is breached. What could be simpler than Hammurabi?"

"Don't deserve *that*. And the circuit is false—artist gives up nothing. Can't show her subjects in the days of gathering comprehension. The reversals go unrecognized."

"Naturally," Azura says, "the prelude is all that counts."

She runs fingers through my hair and bites an earlobe.

"If I can't have you, no one can."

"You have me, Azura."

In spite of everything, she does.

*

Detective York smiles, knows I cannot escape, splay of a reproduction of Pollock's *Cathedral* dancing fractally beyond smug teeth. And just as I sense the first flex of thigh, divided between fight and flight, my office door flings open, its knob barely missing the detective's gut. Laura, my dourly dressed editor, steps in, clutching a paper that has clearly inspired anxiety.

"*This* is your blurb for Reynolds's new Kant translation?"

"Really can't tell when you crumple it like that. Don't quote."

"Uh, ma'am …" the burly detective says.

" 'Reynolds has untangled the putrid knot of Kant's phrasing and therefore renders unto us a document of masterful inaccuracy.' Really?"

"Some knots should stay tied, Laura."

"I'm sorry, miss," Detective York says, "but we were just—"

"Readability? Is that a crime?" Laura interrupts in a monotone shout, putting a hand over the appalled detective's mouth.

"Readability a crime," I laugh. "It's not even a word outside of focus groups!"

"You're going to have to excuse us," Laura says, pushing York's reddened, disbelieving face—and by extension York himself—into the hallway. I rush over and lock the door just as he realizes I'm going to. A kick comes, splintering the wood. He kicks again.

"How'd you get on this guy's good side?" my editor asks over continued battering.

"Laura, I would love to discuss the fusillade of Kant's grammatical gaffes and their bearing on the Critique's success, but I, ah, how many police vehicles are outside?"

"Couple. Why?"

"Really should be finding my wife." I throw my briefcase out the window, straddling the sill. The detective's boot punches a hole in my door and struggles to yank itself back out.

"We may need to thrash things out," I explain.

"Women. Bonnie's estrogen levels really fuck up our relationship at times."

"Why, Laura, I had no idea you were a homosexual," I marvel. She shrugs.

"She and I have our weird way of resolving things, I guess."

"Bless you for that," I say.

And jump.

*

When I dip toward sleep but spasm uncontrollably, screaming about the vampire bats who've shadowed me since childhood, soft mangy things that doze under blankets where feet plunge into warm black mist, waking to flutter upon clammy limbs, Azura holds me with tenderness I certainly do not deserve. She tells me it's just a thing, this spasm.

By which she means: it happens to everyone.

By which she means: it's nothing.

But she is constantly forgiving me, which is nice.

*

I land on one of the pulsing orgies caterpillars prefer, maybe millions thick. Have to admit I'm embarrassed to murder so many for convenience's sake. I pull slime and fine-haired carcasses off in gobs.

Other pockets hang together on benches, buildings, bushes. Writhing chain mail. Rappelling on invisible wires from the tattered leaves of trees. Azura is considering a cycle of poems on the wretched creatures, and the contagion of her focus can madden.

"Consider," she said last night atop the peeling old observatory, "their manners."

"Yes, they bow to greet each other." I grabbed a dark handful from the balcony handrail and flung them into cheap-smelling night. "Almost Far Eastern?"

"*Religieux*, essentially. The cocoon *une sorte de purgatoire*— they trust in an afterlife. Paradise." She lets one squinch along the length of her finger.

"And can it be that the caterpillar who sees a butterfly sees an angel?" I ask in the teasing voice men save for their worst moments with the women they love.

"Who says they'll be butterflies?"

What I know:

- I made the deplorable mistake of reading my wife excerpts from Sylvia's term paper for Philosophy of Psychosexual Criticism.
- Azura masturbated to Herzog's *Lessons of Darkness* right there in her seat when it premiered in Berlin in '92.
- I can remember Sylvia's scent, but any sense-record of the act is torched *ex post facto*.
- Azura can climax without even her fingers; I've learned to

notice when she does it—the micromoans, the muzzled hummingbird pulse after I seem to have punched in for my shift of night terror.

- Regarding Herzog, we agree: There is something unhappily erotic about wastelands.

What I suppose:

- It would be facetious to say in ill-fated Sylvia and predecessors I see an other to Azura, simplistic to say I see a sameness (for Azura is above all blessedly dissimilar to the world), approaching fact that I see a spark of *potential* Azura that must be fanned, for Azura's mortality is more horrific than mine.

"'Every discipline,' I recited, "is secretly anchored by its articulation of Lacanian lack.'"

"A lack that by definition is where nothingness and catastrophe fail to be articulated," Azura replied. She took off her shoes and examined the space between tanned toes.

"'Literature finds the female vampire, a monster whose fanged orifice in Stoker's hands is the paradigm *vagina dentata*.'"

"I wish this girl would realize," lamented Azura, "that the mouth is not a substitute vagina but something worthy in itself." She dipped her bare feet in a pool of caterpillars and laughed lightly at their ticklish touch.

"'Astronomy's black hole, meanwhile, is a fundamental expression of phallic illusion, the ultimate void amongst countless protrusions.'"

She saw a painful erection trapped in my slacks, but I didn't follow her gaze, didn't look at myself, just watched her face while she stared a stare that trumps the uncanny, and when it was over I'd written sideways in the margin of Sylvia's C+ paper:

But the black hole isn't a void at all; it is a node of unthinkable mass.

*

I shred through the silk threads festooning our campus, feel caterpillars in my hair and heart. Singeing, sticky strands and hot spring sun. I stop to lighten my briefcase, tossing less worthy works into a dumpster behind the steamboat-shaped dining hall. How had *Korean for Beginners* made the cut at all? I look up, trying to remember why the hell I bought it, at a tropical sky that sighs Azura's name. Perhaps I'd simply needed a new book—any book—and, being a city boy, liked the menacing glow of Seoul on the cover.

Her Algerian-born parents, Azura recounts, found her newborn eyes resplendent as the Côte d'Azur, moon-baked site of her conception. But protean blue became earthly brown—a sea-change to acquaint her with despair.

"Didn't they understand your eyes could change?"

"You see the blue, buried," she prompts me from bed.

"I know it's there."

There's no expanding on such shaky claims. Besides, I'm busy. My class is looking forward to a lecture on the perversities of David Koresh, his branch, his ranch. The research solders my senses together. Babies sinking in blue dark pools. Brides of Israel anointed early and often. Flock painted, drenched, in their own lambs' blood. Did he figure it for the new Masada? Did the alignment with Passover bubble cheerfully in his flutes of marrow?

"*Regardez-moi*," Azura pouts in periphery, nightgown waterfalling off.

To recognize the God-sent Cyrus? They say he'll ride a milk-white horse.

"Much better," she purrs when at last my hands explore her maps.

"Do not tell others our special ways," a would-be messiah begged his girls.

"Your skin," I whisper, thinking: *who can hear topologies?*

Outlanders rose against his prophecy, unaware they fulfilled its word.

"Are you cross?" she asks imploringly.

The Babylon beyond will judge.

"I am never cross with you," I say.

As sinful men will always do.

*

Choppers, mutant toys, jackhammer overhead. Not for me—they drop fist-sized silver irradiation (or whatever, I'm no scientist) orbs to kill the bugs. They fall like so many New Year's novelties, too slow to believe, settling easily on the boughs of Norway Spruces. In the deafening thrum of mass murder, I collide with Aidan, a preening milquetoast of a student who's worked up the courage to say he can't wait for the annual open house tonight. Whose? Mine and my wife's, of course. Hosting duties, honestly, are a casualty I'll never mourn.

"Might there be a more appropriate event?" I ask, panting, massaging my ribs. "With grain alcohol punch and ritual humiliation of the sub—er—unconscious?"

"I'd rather continue our debate on fragmentary analysis," he admits. "It's more … personal."

"Aidan!" I chide. "Young man, theory is anything *but* personal."

As he tries to digest this witless comment, I take off running once again.

*

My wife and I once took a cruise, just us. Borrowed a colleague's yacht that neither of us could manage. Were all but capsized in a storm off Cape Cod and decided that was that and started screwing the hell out each other up against the enormous steering wheel, which dug into your back reassuringly.

"I love you," I said.

"I want to come when we start to drown," she answered.

But the very idea went rocketing through my blood so ferociously that all I could do was come right then and ruin the final lovemaking of my life, which it wasn't. Some sea nymph stopped us from listing as I withdrew, and I said as much with a facile grin.

"Of all the times to mention another woman," she mumbled, truly hurt.

When we finished all the food but couldn't find land for days after, we had a starving contest.

*

I stop in fitful shade, the churn of departing helicopters a failing breath, and crunch the odds. I move again, steps bent toward Jerry Godforth's office in O'Hare Hall, its clock spire ever ready to inject the heavens with time.

Azura, naturally, has beaten me here and barricaded herself in Jerry's office. I wait as she drags the furniture away from its ignominious pile on the door's opposite side. Soon as I squeeze into the disheveled room, Azura turns back to the window, cradling the WWII-era Sturmgewehr 44 assault rifle I bought her last anniversary.

"You know that was for your private enjoyment," I say, when really I meant to say nothing at all.

She turns her head, smooth wave of hair a deliberate dig, expression cool and careless. She signals with her eyes to Jerry, who is struggling and making what noise he can. I take the spitty gag out. He licks his teeth.

"And Azura, how would you respond to that?" he asks.

"*Exactement*," she tells the glass, "No gift *sans* conditions."

"Tell him," Jerry reminds her.

"If you wish to give me a gift, it must be a true gift, to enjoy on my own terms. *Mondieu.*"

"When did your terms stop being formalist—or don't you remember that raving manifesto you sent me from Prague?" Jerry twitches his nose at this.

"What did we say about trying to ground our thoughts in a less theoretical place?"

"*We* didn't say much on that matter. *You* did. And Prague is very real."

"Don't hide behind the joke."

"What I want to say, Azura, is that I buy you these gifts because I know your attractions … but I can't stand by while innocents suffer."

"Better," says Jerry, who squirms in his ropes, slightly rocking the chair in search of relative comfort.

"And I certainly don't see why you have to treat our mutual friend and peer, who has been kind enough to counsel us though he no longer practices, like a common hostage."

"*Quelle surprise*," says Azura with alluring sting, "trying to make an ally."

"Azura's right," Jerry concedes, "don't make me a talking point."

"*Merci.*"

"Is it fair to suggest she treat others with a dose more compassion?" I ask. A beam of giddy romance slices through Azura's face.

"May I show him?"

"I think you should," Jerry nods. "I think that could be very cathartic with respect to the conflicting feelings we were discussing."

"Come," says my wife, gesturing with the Sturmgewehr, and we leave the office.

Jerry grants me a wink as I pass.

"Where are we going?"

But Azura says nothing, leads me up the hundred stairs to the top of the clock tower. To a pair of bells made from molten Civil War swords on orders of Ivyland's pacifist mayor—two weeks before Appomattox. We look out over the South Quad. She points with her rifle at the grass.

"There."

It's Sylvia we see, alive, a stretched, overpale thing on patchwork blanket, body flinching now and then as she flicks away invisible pests. A face-flushed and ridiculous odalisque.

"I would have. But look. Just look."

She's standing now, a stupid white stalk in the blaze of perfect green, an awning of fingers above her eyes as she scans the clock face. For the time, not us. And now I know Azura's point. This creature is no threat to her.

"But, the detective—he said."

"No," she says, watching Sylvia. "More important women to destroy. A certain Lady Liberté? Ever watch the news?" Erupting with a quaking glee adults are supposedly drained of at thirty.

Sylvia cocks her head, bewildered, as police cars surround our tower, sirens scribbling out the afternoon. Corpses curled like commas rain from trees. The bells chime four, bringing students out of classes, into soft hail and extinction. Through silver oases of silent demise, littered like dew drops, sunbeams boomeranging off.

But Azura. Azura. Criteria of goddess-ship, work of Fauvists to the last: bodies hum. Perspective a myth. Her halo spins one hundred miles an hour.

"Tahiti would be nice," I say, and she kisses me.

She shows me the only caterpillar poem so far, a joke, scrawled on a napkin and untitled, as megaphoned demands beat silence raw.

I can put aside their feel
Milky clasps of muted hair
The way you rear on blades of grass
Cast your heads about and there
Look for what you cannot name
Yearning just to greet and bow
When you find the one selfsame
Mismatched friend to show you how

Neither needs to play the game
And not one will wear the crown

But I have to say, it's so unfair—to make them human, make me care. Give them eschatology, and revelation they can spare. Hell is a Paradise you can't share.

The Lambs are ready: let them dare.

"Are you cross?" she asks in stained-glass glare.

*

What I like to do before "Gauguin in Tahiti" is study his last Continental paintings, from just before he abandoned his family, and contemplate the savagery to come.

"The Yellow Christ" is our museum's best. Crucifixion scene set in thick cloissanist lines, a harvest countryside. Breton women weep for jaundiced Jesus. His beard in that pointed French style Gauguin himself wore. An unnamed man steals into autumn hills—logically he's Gauguin too.

Hang my yellow coward's corpse with nails, leave it out for carrion birds. I will still get away. There's no need to go, to skulk offstage. These bells will ring as long as we want. Wherever, whenever our cells slow past thresholds for life, we'll pluck the fruit of true solipsism. Our world shades over into private apocalypse. Yours soldiers miserably on.

CAL /// NEW YORK, NEW YORK /// SIXTEEN YEARS AGO

We went to the Thanksgiving parade. I'd seen it on TV, of course, but the promised remaking of rhythms and colors in a city's throbbing heart, no medium to pale the joy . . . was tempting enough that I demanded it, and my parents were happy to comply.

Years of elbow warfare as we pushed toward the train. Glances exchanged with smaller children being dragged through the forest of adults. On board, every seat was taken; people shoved from car to packed car in denial. It was a third-world train, lightless and dank. People clogged the aisle, gripping luggage racks overhead. Babies' voices curdled. A crazy man dressed in garbage bags bit the air and foamed. Maybe H12.

Mom and I were somehow split from Dad and Aidan. We glimpsed a three-seater that looked empty, save one well-dressed man staring out the window. Shoving closer, we discovered a woman in a black silk dress lying across the bench, her head resting in the man's lap. Even I could tell she wasn't sick, that this was some fixed possessive posture, a sculpted warning. His finger made circles in her hair. Mom pointed and said: "Here."

I wouldn't sit. I wouldn't say why, and I didn't know how. These people soaked into me like acid. I said, "Let's Go," and Mom said: "Don't Be Ridiculous, Cal."

"Is this seat taken?" Mom asked like she didn't know. I came undone, looked down, trying to muzzle this panic.

"Sorry?"

The man's finger froze mid-circle. Jutting bones in his cheeks that dreamed of escape. Dirty smear of passing smokestacks and bald trees on the other side of glass.

"Can my son sit here?" Mom asked.

The man glanced down at the woman, who sat up. She wore dangling icicle earrings that swung with indignation. She flattened straight brown hair against her skull, slid over and mauled us with her eyes.

My eyes bored into the empty seat. How a child's private shame evolves. Standing there, near tears, convinced my precious agony could kill. Mom sensed hesitation like only mom could. She said, "Sit here, I'll stand next to you." With a hand on my shoulder I obeyed.

I moved my body against the aisle armrest, away from the couple. The metal on my skin was cold. . . yes, that would work: take stock of the million discomforts. The train smelled like wet garbage. Floor was sticky. Babies kept crying. But these two invaded even my litany. They spoke in stage whispers. I caught what the woman said, sotto voce.

"Can't believe that bitch."

She said it to the man but threw burning glares at us, and said it again, "That bitch." Mom stared straight ahead at nothing. My hands got clammy and tight. The woman kept saying it every so often, muttering "That bitch, that bitch." I wanted to sink, slip down between the seams. "That bitch," she said, "that bitch," and always waited till I'd almost put it out of my mind before saying it again, a bit louder each time.

Mom would later claim she confronted the woman, shut her up. "If you have a problem, we can get the conductor," that was the line. Really, she shuffled her feet. I examined and reexamined my shoelaces. We tried to lose ourselves, to make our deafness plausible.

*

I'd been to one other parade, as an only child. In misting rain on Saint Patrick's Day, my birthday, we stood on Fifth Avenue and watched a river of people stomp by. A parade expressly for me: it was simpler to say that, my parents reasoned, than explain sainthood. I'd waved, sitting on Dad's shoulders, to drunken redheads and bagpipers, thanking them for celebrating with me. They knew that green, with its numberless natural shades, was my favorite color. I cheered at banner-waving policemen and towering floats and shamrocked ancient immigrants. It wasn't strange, their generosity. I was lucky that way.

An odd icon's death day. Banisher of snakes. I never discovered the lie because it never took root. Hearing the story, memory stalled. The sole impression: sitting high, squinting at pins of water. The crow's nest. Dad's hair. It silvers in my hands.

*

I stayed off Dad's shoulders this time—too old, I decided. Aidan enjoyed the view instead. I heard snare drums, boots slapping pavement. Sounds dulled by walls of flesh. Wind clawed at the streets. A nor'easter's wind without the storm. Parades aren't something to cry at. Even so, there thousands stood, weeping at the sight. Bladed air extracting tears. Below its wrath, my eyes were dry.

This was when the balloons rebelled. The weather proved too much for their handlers, who yanked desperately at ropes meant to control the sagging characters. Spider-Man swiped the face of a silver office tower with extended fingers, then turned to kiss it. Bits of a window washer's scaffold popped loose and fell to the street like a handful of toothpicks. Woody Woodpecker could hardly stay afloat— he folded as a knifing gust put his beak to the street. The Cat in the Hat, piloting a fanciful Seussian vehicle, tipped a street lamp that flattened some woman, we heard. The papers, already bankrupt at that point, followed her coma for a week. Garfield swooped low, collapsing on a pocket of disbelieving spectators before teetering unsteadily on. Ambulance sirens boiled out of the distance. Santa Claus concluded the carnage. Blood, I thought, could be happily lost in his red velvet stuff.

*

We trudged back across the blood-drained island. Featureless skies began to spit—water flung off a fish gasping for life. I said nothing to my family; they tried to pretend this misery had been worthwhile. Mom asked if we loved this or that and wasn't it neat to see so-and-so. We passed a nest of shivering hobos.

"I always feel worse for the homeless this day," Dad said.

Near Penn Station, we came upon a group thrusting pamphlets and petitions at passersby who sped along. They had a wall of posters displaying Asian people—some badly hurt, some dead. People on the sidewalk were imitating the pictures, pretending to torture or be tortured. I asked. Mom explained. "They're protesting these people being cruel to other people in China because of their religion. They're asking us to notice."

A woman lunged out to hand me a flyer. My left eye rumbled in its bed. I snatched the paper, dropping the crumpled result in the gutter, and walked on. I saw a man sitting cross-legged on a mat some yards away, eyes closed, meditating. Untouched by surrounding noise and grime, the picture of serenity.

Maybe, I've told myself since, I wanted to remind him what trouble lay all around, and that is what tilted my reason askew, scraped my insides, hollowed me out. But consider all the dropping you'll do in your days. See if that stops it. Take the worst thing you've done, and the best. These are two people with nothing in common.

Accelerating toward him, hanging wetness sprinkled me urgently. A vanishing crack as fist met nose, sincerely fusing. Cells in my knuckles and his startled expression interlocked, dragging each other out of place, bits of us both suspended in rain. I struck him again, trying to break the face. I couldn't. He clutched at my arms, refusing to fight back—maddeningly—and rolled onto his side. Hands over his slick red features. His bloody hair stuck to the mat. My parents tried to pull me from him, this grown fetus, but my feet lashed out and found his spine.

*

I didn't speak anymore that day, as much as Mom stormed and swore. This was the first time I heard her say "fuck," and I saw Aidan's ear twitch at the curse. He sensed how different this was and wanted to get out of the way, seized the first chance to run upstairs. "What if he'd pressed charges?" Mom asked. "Where do you get this from?"

Dad: "And do you have anything to say for yourself?" As if I could talk the logic of hate into them.

I didn't come down for Thanksgiving dinner, and Mom gave up calling me after two tries.

*

By the next day, I'd resolved to stay in my room. The needs to eat and eliminate did not seem obstacles, mysteriously. I woke early out of habit, sat up and stared at the wall. In an hour, Mom came in without knocking, puffy-eyed, same as she had when Grandma died. I was lying awake then too, and waiting. Now I tasted the menace again.

"Cal," Mom said. "I don't know why you did what you did. And I don't think you'll say. You are a determined young man, is all. That's why you'll go far." She was crying. I didn't try to stop her. "I know that you want what you want when you want it," she continued. I knew the blanked guilt of missing desire. Exactly what wish had left me? "You've always known exactly what you wanted. I remember once, when you were little—you know Duck Soup, *that Marx Brothers movie you loved? 'Hail, Freedonia?' " I gave the slightest nod, saw its slow and certain shadow on my blanket. "Once, I know you didn't mean it, but ... I thought of this when you ... One day, they didn't have the video to rent. Someone else had taken it out. I'm sure you don't remember, but when I told you we couldn't get the movie, you hit me. Just hit me in the face. And that's what I thought of yesterday, because you ... it felt like a slap in the face again ... "I listened to her sad sounds and swallowed dryly. "You didn't mean it then, and you didn't mean it yesterday. Cal: You're so good and smart*

and wonderful and you know we're so proud of you, but maybe it wouldn't be a bad idea to see someone who—"

I was atomized. I would never own these deeds. A thousand clashing points of dark, dead but reassembled well. Mom's eyes searched and with a blink confessed. Her love could not disguise me. No love could make me good again.

AIDAN /// IVYLAND, NEW JERSEY

Opening the fridge door, I see Henri's economy-size box of popsicles has found its way onto my side, crowded over by soggy Fong Friday's containers. Sorry, but isn't it common knowledge that frozen things go in the freezer? The purple puddle collecting at the bottom of the crisper says no.

A note on the counter reads:

Think I clogged the sink.
It doesn't have a garbage disposal, does it?
Sorry again about last night, must not be sleeping enough.
   xoxoxoxo,
                   H

Has to be more than nocturnal habits: what coincided with our accident was an unmistakable fit. But I don't wander to the topic of his health these days, no matter how plainly it fails him.

As for the garbage-disposal query: a thousand times no. I reach into the drain, grasping a handful of ominous mush. There's nothing to account for Henri's ignorance here—he practically grew up in this house. Inherited, along with money, from his grandfather, who subjected it to a barrage of amateur carpentries that give each room its funhouse angles. Yet Henri somehow lacks a muscle memory of that wonky raised step as you exit the sunken living room, or the dimmest idea of where one might find the fuse box (don't think I haven't shown him). I'm grateful for a bed and roof, but if I weren't around, it's doubtful this stack of rotted shingles would still be standing.

A postscript to his note, scrawled hastily:

P.S. Do you have that dictionary of trucker lingo or know where it is??

Just what I need: the CB radio version of Henri, except instead of chatting up actual truckers, he's pestering me, and after every bit of jargon he asks, flush with undue enthusiasm, "Know what that one means?" I eat a stale bagel over the sink, making a mental note to hide that dictionary as soon as I get home. Beneath Henri's memo, I scratch:

No, no and no-er. Call tree guy. Get life.

I run up to his room and knock on the door. No response. Inside, the place is stuffed with boxes from an online pet store. Tremble to think what that's about. Then I recall that Henri started sleeping in the third floor bedroom a couple days back.

"Henri," I'd said, "why could you possibly be moving to a smaller, hotter room up another flight stairs?"

"Because," he began. Then he tripped coming out of the living room. "I always forget that's there," he explained.

I take the rest of the stairs up, stepping carefully on the groaning wood. This has got to be the only house I can think of with such an impractical staircase: narrow, spiral, smack in the middle of everything. I knock on his door, and Henri grunts on the other side.

"What's up," I say. "You doing okay?"

"Thinking about … religion."

"Don't waste your time. Maybe you could stop by the Second Chance office and look for non-philosophical employment instead."

"I think you have to have *had* a job and lost it to qualify?"

"Call about the tree, then. You'll have roughly all day to get it done. Left you a note in case you forget. Bye, champ."

I head back down, stopping off to grab my crumpled tux. Reception last night was abysmal. Father of the bride paid for two extra hours of party, and Phoebe kept dropping shrimp into my pockets.

I gulp water in the kitchen and open the dishwasher. Someone's put dirty dishes in with the clean. I throw the cup in the sink instead. Turning to leave, I whack my head on the open cupboard door and ask why. Two peeled ceilings overhead, Henri shouts curtly. Probably wants me to pick up junk food on the way home. I think he'll live.

*

I expected the few usual nuts and Anastasio, but their enthusiasm must be spreading after all: some thirty people are milling about, a few out in the street, admiring the Virgin. An alarming pair of camping tents is set up on the lawn. An approaching car does a sustained honk, the unshaven driver coasting easily into rage.

"Fucking Christ-lickers!" he screams through an open window before swerving around the crowd and squealing off, his license plate dangling by a screw.

I pick out Anastasio immediately, talking with a few other guys it seems he might be related to. Or I'm just racist like that. He sees me too, and we converge at a spot in the middle of the crowd.

"Good morning," he beams, much bubblier today.

"What is this?"

"What is what?"

"This ... this!" I gesture at the tents, like: *what else?* Anastasio opens his mouth with honest surprise.

"I've contacted a few friends in the state about making pilgrimages to our miracle here."

"Are you kidding? This is nothing, a fluke, a dumb ..." I'd been expecting something more convincing, or at least coherent, to come out. Anastasio folds his arms. He's about five foot six but can look shockingly regal when he wants to.

"But this can't be legal, can it?" I ask. "Our property ... can't have you camping out on the front lawn."

"I spoke with your friend Henri," Anastasio says with a hint of indifference that confirms he has this angle covered. Nothing good could come from an interaction between these two, and I grimace accordingly, law enforcement X'd out on my list of possible allies. "He was most gracious to have us and said we must remain."

Most of the growing clan is gathered around the tree's burnt shell. Two young girls kneel on its bulging roots, which must actually *hurt*, jet-black hair grazing their hips, lips moving silently. What harm am I thinking will come of this? I can't quite let myself relent.

"Henri said that? When?"

Anastasio shrugs, glances at a bulky digital watch. "An hour ago. He is the house's owner, yes?"

"He. He is, but I sort of ... yes." Sounding dumber by the minute.

"Marvelous," Anastasio grins. "We would be honored if you wished to attend the service tonight. I have invited a priest from our parish."

"I have work." My hands fumble, searching for an unneeded gesture. Finally they fall to the side in defeat. "Yes. So. I have to get going now. Work."

"O. Have a nice day," Anastasio bids.

"You too," I try to say, but vocal cords aren't vibrating, and Anastasio is gone already, to supervise the raising of a third tent, which forms a diamond with the other two tents and the tree.

*

"Phil looks like he could use another drink," Phoebe pities from afar as she sets a table. Phil, a Chinese waiter who is by unspoken agreement always slotted to work the sushi station, is getting an earful from the bride about the wedding band setup. The rest of the family shuffles into the ballroom cautiously, avoiding her line of sight.

Mike, the curly-haired amateur magician working bar tonight, is wadding a napkin into his clenched fist, oblivious until I rap the counter with my knuckles.

"Watch this," he demands, then opens his hand, dropping a crumpled napkin. He scowls at it.

"Yayyy," I drone, clapping mindlessly. "Give me a cranberry juice. For the bride, so feel free to dress it up." Across the room, she squints at a towering floral centerpiece, then begins to either rearrange or wrestle it.

"Guy doesn't know what he's in for," Mike laments, mixing the drink.

"You married?" I ask, not actually interested.

"What do I look like," he says, head rearing back, "a fucking gay?" He slides the fake cosmo over to me, winking. I respond with a weak thumbs-up and snatch the glass away.

*

Cocktail hour goes smoothly, discounting the elderly woman at table eleven who makes a habit of pinching my arm when I ignore her, much to Phoebe's amusement.

"Now you know how it feels," she taunts, smiling perfectly.

"Who said I didn't like it?" I counter. I pretend to adjust her crooked bowtie, but really I'm studying her flawless face, the hazel-yellow eyes that flit nervously down when I touch her clothes.

*

In the kitchen, Roy heaps a vegetable medley on plate after plate, as he's done forever. Dewlaney, this kid whose first name no one seems to know, watches as he works, shoveling steadily.

"You notice that's always his job," Dewlaney says in a low voice, smirking. "Check out that pimp chain." A plain gold necklace swings from Roy's neck, the cross cutting with glare through wisps of steam.

"Heh," I shrug, "what a player."

"Yo, Phoebe," Dewlaney shouts into the humidity. When Phoebe, on her way back out, turns around, he taps his lips with a middle and index finger.

"Not now," Phoebe yells back, pushing through the door.

"Fuck her, anyway," Dewlaney says. "Coming to Heat-22 tonight, Kilham? Those strippers take all my money, but it's worth it. Whole frat's going."

"Shit. Can't tonight."

"Yeah, you've got somewhere better to be," Dewlaney prods, placing metal covers over his dinners. On the other side of the counter, Donald narrows his eyes at us, peeved about whatever makes him so constantly peeved. "Your loss," Dewlaney relents. We take up our trays again and leave the kitchen together.

"Thanks," Phoebe sighs when I reach our station, "Pinchy Grandma was about to *bite* me."

*

A break finally comes following an argument over the phrase "medium rare." The bride, for her part, torpedoed that whole debate by amending her husband's steak order of "rare" to "well done." I listened to the toast: this guy was in the *Marines*. He has an unconvincing glass eye and is very friendly with the maid of honor.

"Cigarette?"

"But I thought … Dewlaney, he said about the, uh."

"You don't really think I'd waste my break on him," Phoebe says, and wrinkles all her features together irresistibly. The sentence carries implications I may have invented.

Over the past year, though it doesn't immobilize like it used to, I'd been caught off guard now and then by her loveliness, and paranoid that she used it against me. Can't stop the infatuation creeping back sometimes. I barely even fight it now.

In the cool dusk of the parking lot, she holds out a pack of cigarettes, making me choose. I snatch one quickly, obscuring its origins. She pushes her already-lit tobacco to mine. The metal door punches open, and Phil drags himself from the outer fringe of misery into the night, retrieving his flask from a jacket pocket.

"Time for a drink," Phoebe says, making him start. He steadies himself and politely agrees.

"Oh, a drink, but yes, good night for a drink, drinking, drink …" he singsongs, moseying away from the spot Phoebe and the other smokers seem to prefer, his cadences following him into the buggy night.

"Where does he even buy his booze?" Phoebe wonders.

"Hope he makes it back," I say. A rogue wave of nauseous guilt crashes over me, formless, disconnected from Phil or Phoebe or work. "That marriage is destined for greatness," I add, waving limply in the direction of the party.

"Honestly," she says, blowing rings, "did you see how he wouldn't let her do the garter thing?"

After a while she releases her cig's butt and toes it till it goes dark. My body goes prickly and torpid at the display, excited and unresponsive. *Scratch your chin*, a frantic quadrant of brain keeps shouting, hysteria doubling each time my hand fails to execute, but finally something loosens and I scratch casually. Phoebe's leg pivots back and forth on her toe, heel swinging. *Perfect moment*, that panic-stricken corner of my brain is yelling.

"I think … " I hear myself putting on an affected voice, setting up for a bare and moving line that does not, will not, could not exist. Our eyes meet and for once I am not ashamed to be caught looking. This contact is without the tension it always coaxes forth, and I'm finally sure that such anxieties do not arise because the eye is too expressive but because two pairs of eyes aligned will make a tensile bridge that buckles as the stare persists. Soon the bridge demands every bit of attention, threatening to give way in a nervous movement. Gazing down the fragile connecting nerve, focused on maintaining it, you bore clear through the other end.

"Yeah?" she says, and I swear I can hear imprisoned music rage inside me. Everything clenchable clenches. A halting countdown takes place but starts over every time I finish.

Phoebe senses it right away, but of course she leaves me in the lurch. I locate a rock on the ground and wing it down the sloping hill of the lot, remembering too late that Phil is still wandering that area. I hear no expletives from that direction and decide I didn't hit him.

"How's Henri? Haven't seen him in a while."

"Fine," I say, "Mostly sedentary but manages to be a pain in the ass." An anger anyone else would call volcanic but Henri would term *Vesuvian* is flooding my lungs, and I detect the alien desire to pummel someone. "Guy's like a parasite, won't even pitch in with day-to-day stuff. He's a waste."

"This is your best friend you're talking about, right?"

"Might be the free rent that's keeping me chained to him."

"Don't say that. That's terrible."

"He's terrible." Already dug myself a hole, better make it plenty deep. Phil staggers into view, making erratic figure-eights a dozen parking spaces away, then sits, exhausted by the journey back from his drinking spot. His sushi-chef hat is torn and muddied.

"What happened with you two? You used to look after him." This choice of terms isn't helping. Phil's head makes the quiet 90-degree arc to meet slick asphalt and rests there. "Wasn't that the whole reason things went weird with you and Cal? When's the last time you spoke to *him*?"

"When's the last time *you* did?"

She waits a while before suggesting we head back in.

I stand there alone, wondering what happened to instinct. Phil startles awake from a broken reverie and collects himself, patting down the wrinkles in his tux and preparing to stand. I stall, then flick my long-dead cigarette and walk over to offer him a hand, which he's overjoyed about.

"Thank you: thanks," he says a few times, loopy sounds of gratitude.

"What happened to your hat there?" I ask. He gropes the tattered thing without taking it off, raises his eyebrows suspiciously. Then memory kicks in.

"A dog tried to take it! I fight him, boy. I fought for victory."

"May as well have let him have it," I say.

"I lose my drink," he admits, tapping the chest pocket where his treasured flask once lived. "But, my hat … I keep. A private place for my head, yes?"

*

Inside, the night's winding down. Donald is furious that I haven't refilled water glasses. The dance floor is barren but for two women trading seductive moves. I spot their husbands consoling each other over cake. A bridesmaid nearly catches fire when the palsied maitre d' does his banana flambé bit. Phoebe just works.

I call Henri. No answer.

*

Phoebe offers to drive me home. Nice of her, but even this late, traffic on the one remotely safe highway is a special horror. She says a word or two but no more than necessary, nixing small-talk until I stop trying to initiate it. The headlights of cars across the divider bathe her face in white triangles.

Drivers ignore signs warning that the road will narrow to one lane, instead zipping as far ahead as possible on the right and cutting in at the last moment. Phoebe has none of it and gets flipped off accordingly one, two … five times by various Jersey denizens.

The mall parking lots have been converted into skeevy hangouts, ghost-lit stores and frosted mannequins the only signs of civilization, an odd shaft of light cast down by extraterrestrial streetlamps capturing baggy skateboarders mid-ollie. Bushes alongside the road rustle fluidly, morphing with weightless ease.

A cluster of pines ahead expunges a doe that soars perfectly out of hiding and lands in the gridlock, its muscles giving off a small aftershock when hooves meet pavement. Black eyes search out friendly soil; she slips between stuck cars and vanishes among Viking Putt's burnt plastic skeletons. Always more of them, always less afraid: they ignore the fact that they've nowhere to go.

Henri, years ago, was in the car when his parents hit a buck that took out their windshield. It struggled and bled on their hood for ten minutes—they watched its ears twitching. He missed the whole next week of school, but I could never figure out why. He wasn't hurt, anyway. I brought him homework, all the subjects he aced without trying. He and Cal both made it look easy. I wish Phoebe would rescue me from this, aged questions that slide past each other like eels, stealthy, deliberately strange. Covert dreads run together.

On the side of Route 22, just past the cooked mini-golf course, is a post-accident tableau. Cops standing by their cruiser, chatting over 40-oz. Adderades. Cheap sedan and SUV sitting twenty feet apart, bumpers mangled. The SUV holds a man with salt-and-pepper hair and a younger woman riding shotgun, bare feet propped on the dash. The other car has a guy slumped over its open passenger door, shaking his head. Ahead of it, an ambulance prepares to depart, sirens winding up.

Everyone slows to a lewd crawl, inching by to study the picture like penniless window-shoppers. Past the scene, the traffic breaks, and an actual road opens up before us.

"Glad this whole thing was for a worthy cause," Phoebe says, smiling sarcastically. We drive for another half-hour and take our exit before she adds: "Sorry."

"Are you apologizing in case we crash?" She laughs as tastefully as one can on the subject.

"No … whatever. I have shitty days sometimes."

"*Sometimes?*" making a face of ugly astonishment.

"Stop!" she says, punching me. "Trying to be nice."

"And I'm not letting you off the hook."

"You already have," she says. "I mean it about Henri. He's the nicest guy, and you love to shoot him down."

"Yeah, I'm an asshole. So be it."

"No you aren't. You're just being one because you think it gets girls all wet."

Talk about a call to arms. But there's no time for rebuttal—the scene on my lawn as we pull up is an automatic change of subject.

"God."

"You guessed it."

A few dozen points of flame hovering in the night, candlelit faces gathered around the miracle tree. The neighborhood is otherwise dark—our block's power must be out again. Heads bowed, the group chants together, voices sometimes stretching beyond the frayed edges of unison. Anastasio stands closest to the tree, facing the group but not leading it. He holds his candle to one side, illuminating the face of an old man in religious robes that I recognize from childhood as the local monsignor. Sweat rolls in bulbs along the jagged lines of his neck, the crowded air and insects endured. Shivering light ignites gold flecks in his heavy getup. Phoebe is spellbound by the congregation but leaves hands on the wheel, anticipating a getaway. Lowering the windows, we can hear the monsignor speaking in a fine plastic voice.

"Jesus is always there, not just in our time of need, but in our minutiae and our ecstasies, errors and triumphs, ever vigilant and sure. But he is nothing without the promise of renewal. What is the forgiveness of one sin if no one absolves us of the next? What is the first lesson without the next? Humanity's greatest thinkers have insisted our education is never complete. In God's universe, we are always children, always learning. Likewise, even an ordinary life requires ongoing salvation. The crucifixion is Jesus's absolution of humanity captured in one crystalline, timeless gem, one enduring image and act. Yet this is only efficient summary of his sacrifice. Neither is any litany of His miracles meant to convey His entire goodness; they are the fleeting accounts of an eternal savior. Every Christmas, Jesus is born again. Every Good Friday, He dies on the cross. Every Easter, He is resurrected. The Gregorian calendar is marked with these days, Christian festivals replacing old pagan ones. Christmas takes place on one of the year's shortest days—we make it a celebration of light and a conquest of the dark, as people did a generation before Jesus, and a generation before that, and so on. Easter's date is determined by the lunar phases that so occupied the imaginations of nature-worshippers.

"Do you see that the dates are of no significance? That all could occur consecutively, that the progression of holy weeks could be reversed, and it would have no ill effect? What we attach to these days, that sense of repetition, gives them their power. In each *annus domini* the promise that Jesus will be born, live, breathe, and die again is what sustains us. It is in the pregnant womb of the Madonna, the Virgin Mary with child, that our promise dwells. The beauty of that picture! An icon of perfect joy. The mother, the son, old creating new, day by day, before our eyes! Jesus is reborn instant to instant, renewed with each supplication, each confession, each cry for guidance, salvation. All His glories converge at the present. How terrible our lot would be if Jesus was born but once, how lonely and remote we'd feel, at such a remove in time and space."

He broods on this alternative, steepling his index fingers as glittering eyes sink into the grass. Anastasio shuffles his feet. The narcotic drone of cicadas strings the night like a handful of beads.

"But this"—the monsignor gestures at the gutted tree—"tells us that we needn't fear that fate. That if the divine has not revealed itself, *one day it will*. That it may hide in the womb but will break forth and make itself known. That the world will crack open and reveal a holiness inside. Revelations are unique to each; hope's path is open to all.

"Some condemn so-called 'blind faith,' and would have you believe our convictions are inferior to those adduced empirically, in labs. This friction is not as black-and-white as evolutionism or creationism, pro-choice or pro-life. Those are empty and symptomatic distinctions. No, conflict between the religious and the irreligious boils down to that villainized phrase: blind faith. Many cannot accept the fastening of spirit to a presence that cannot be scientifically sensed."

The congregation grows restless now, sensing a climax. The monsignor strains for a second in the mindless heat, placing a hand on the tree. Anastasio quickly inserts himself between the old man and the blackened trunk, which slinks invisibly upward, its twisted half-branches bleeding out into sky. But the old man straightens.

"We should rejoice in the message borne by images—the message of knowledge and good and redemption that can shape the heart—not the image itself. In the absence of Heaven, even in the absence of belief, we must have faith that belief will find us. The agnostic, the atheist, anyone can summon it. It serves as our point of contact, the common thread that binds us all. God needs faith. But faith does not need Him."

Even the cicadas hush at this dénouement, exposing the soft cricket song they'd overpowered. The congregation waits one robotic second before moving its lips once more:

Hail Mary
Full of Grace
The Lord is with thee;
Blessed art thou among women,
And blessed is the fruit of thy womb, Jesus.
Holy Mary,
Mother of God,
Pray for us sinners,
Now and at the hour of our death.
Amen.

"Hm," I say. "Thanks for the ride, then."

"Yeah," Phoebe says, descending from a different plane. I slide out of the car and see she's parked with one wheel up on the little rock wall separating yard from driveway.

Out-of-focus colors of a congregation dissolving in midnight, walking to cars parked along the street or continuing down the sidewalk to wherever. The talk subdued and churchly. One or two attendees stay to speak to the monsignor, beside whom Anastasio, unflappable, remains.

Phoebe's car slushes out, and her panning headlights cast their weak beams on Henri, who is moving stealthily into the house, holding something that appears to be struggling in his arms.

"Henri!" I shout. Phoebe's lights realign with the road and he's lost in the darkness of the house—I can barely see now that the candle-holders have dispersed. I hear the front door slam as I move carefully up the front walkway.

"You are looking for Henri," Anastasio observes from behind me.

"Actually— "

"He attended a bit earlier, our prayer meeting, but seems to have left. Is he ill?"

"Ill?"

"Ah. Aidan, I would like to introduce you to Monsignor Diavolo. From my church," he says. And only now do I truly remember him, this craggy man with smoothed edges, features that absorbed a lifetime of incense. Between memories of tone-deaf Sunday sermons that enumerated the effects of leprosy or chastised the parish, sinning machines all, there was this man, with his out-of-place eloquence. Talented. Despicably so. And a face that shone weirdly in the dark, I discovered.

"I must thank you for your hospitality."

"You're welcome, but the hospitality isn't mine."

Anastasio makes a mild choking sound but seems okay despite it.

"Nevertheless. You have been most gracious."

"Is Henri inside?" Anastasio says, "So the monsignor may

express his gratitude also to him?" I'm getting sick of manners. Lacking an excuse, I invite them in, the monsignor's age turning the front steps into an arduous five-minute climb.

I light candles in the living room. Combined with Anastasio's mentor here, it looks like I'm setting up my own damn chapel. These men are too imposing for the worn, faint home, and stand statue-like rather than settling on our dingy sofa. They clasp and unclasp their hands in the seizuring light.

"I'll get him," I say.

Henri is cooped up in the second floor room, his old one, with the door locked. I can hear him puffing and clattering about inside.

"Hey. You've got visitors."

"Can't."

"You're not leaving me to fend for myself against these people." The clattering resumes. A swear sneaks through from inside. "What candlelit work are you doing that's so fuck-all important?"

"Please. Don't make me come out right now."

"When have I made you do anything?" I catch the inexplicable fear of being compressed by the hallway, the house closing in. In this dark, who knows, it might be. "Henri? Why can't you come out?" I expect an irreverent answer, a one-liner, anything but what I get: a climactic thud. This wasn't worth it.

I start down the stairs. *Stop*, I hear.

"Henri?"

I look up. He's squinting right down at me from the third floor landing, like I'm an artifact under a blanket of ice or I've blended into the walls. His face is pushed together, hands on the banister. Not the usual joke, I don't think.

"What is it?" I ask. He shakes his head to clear something from it and retreats from the banister.

Back in the living room, neither Anastasio or the monsignor have moved, and their faces are pulled with exhaustion.

"White Whale can't come out to play. He's sick. Sure you can come back and jam some other time."

"I know you," the monsignor says. "Your family. You don't attend services anymore, then?" The lack of hostility in his voice makes this all the more annoying. A snort jets through my nostrils. Anastasio is on the cusp of interfering, but the monsignor beats him to the punch.

"You are angry," the old man intones.

"I know."

A dry click, and the power comes back on, every light in the house firing up.

"So many grow up with God in their life only to shun Him."

"I don't shun God. And I'm far from the worst in the family." I flop onto the sofa that they've both ignored, blowing out the nearest candle and kicking off my ratty black dress shoes. Really need new laces.

"Saw your brother's name recently, is how I remember," the monsignor explains. "You really do resemble him."

"Why are you still here?"

"Have you been following his mission? He will walk on the moon, it said."

"I read this also," Anastasio chimes in. A stifling gravitas settles over the room. It never dissipates.

"Yeah, the Vesta 1 thing? Got bumped from a backup team, I think."

"You have not seen it on the TV?"

"TV?" Anastasio echoes. Both of them place the accent on *V*.

"It takes one of real spiritual fortitude. I understand they are having some communication issues," says the monsignor. "But NASA is still promising success."

"Then I'm sure they'll have it. Listen, sorry about Henri, but he's incommunicado recently. I'm honestly surprised he would invite you people to camp out here."

"Religion can be the last refuge of the desperate," the monsignor says, and it doesn't read as an accusation, but the fact that it could've bothers me. The wick of my torso is ratcheted, half-crazed. Upstairs, Henri sounds to be stomping or grappling with an invisible wrestling partner, which—let's not even ponder such scenarios.

"Go ahead, talk some good religion into him."

"I wonder," the monsignor says, finally and carefully positioning himself on the easy chair, whole room ripe with his smoky scent, "why you shut yourself off like you do." A creaky hum builds from the basement.

"Here it comes."

The power drops back out.

Yes, I have doubts. More than that, I don't have beliefs. Don't see how they could help. This life so far, I've looked at competing options and zoned out. It's a step short of even indecision: nothing presses me to pick a side. Why can't such a thing's pure shittiness stop me from embracing it? The monsignor nods from within his yellow aura, understands, but that's all. Raw comprehension. Unseen walls protect him from the dismal conclusions that shoot up around me like weeds. I'm just a member of that delicate new caste, the generation least prepared for a nation's backslide and nonetheless assigned to halt it. The one that wrings small pleasures out of each day, feeling bad about some abstract contribution to the state of anxiety at large.

"I've enjoyed talking with you," the monsignor yawns much later, subsonic vibrations of power lines still not buzzing in bones and our candles long spent. Anastasio says he'd love to continue this dialogue. I remind him that lying is a sin.

"Maybe we will talk again, and Henri, too," the monsignor says with a smile that takes grace to muster.

*

The room he was working in is a mess, cardboard boxes and blue plastic tubing spread out on the floor. Up another flight of stairs, in the pre-dawn weirdness, he's locked in.

"Henri? You all right?" Then, "the monsignor seems to think you're desperate." "What does he know?" Henri's voice surprises, chuffing across the bolted slab of wood.

"Don't make fun of me, but I'm actually worried about you. What are you making downstairs?"

"Why would I make fun of you?"

"I don't know, for being … I have no clue. You wouldn't, I guess, is what you're saying."

It was something the monsignor mentioned about Henri being distressed, "afraid to be alone." Alone, with a capital *A*. The phrase tunneled in, tied organs together, and tightened. Henri coughs and speaks again.

"Some days I slip up, Aidan. Small things, little tricks my mind plays. Thinking I heard or saw things that weren't. Smear of color or movement. And I know right then that I'll go crazy. I'll snap."

"Come on," I say. He'd never talked like this before. Henri's problems were always less than real; now I sensed their crushing grip, the way each phrase struggled to the surface. Yet I find myself ill-equipped to explore the shifted terrain, or unwilling. "No history in your family, is there."

"I'm not just weird," Henri says. "Another aspect. I can't guess what."

"Sleep on it," I tell him weakly, the dumb advice chilled and catching in my chest as I start, off-balance, down the stairs. With any luck I can forget I said it. But when my eye is level with the plane of his floor, the power comes back, blaring mutely. Light spills out from under his door, and he's standing just behind it, the shadows of his feet two dark yawning bars on pooled white wattage.

HECUBA /// IVYLAND, NEW JERSEY /// TWO YEARS AGO

One hangover-blasted Wednesday, Hecuba dreamt she was asleep at the wheel, lead-foot subconscious running her route. Eventually she admitted to herself this was no dream and hooked an instinctual right to avoid entering at 60 mph a drive-through ATM tube that would've shaved the top off her jitney. Squealing onto Maple Ave., a treeless one-way street, she bore down on an SUV headed in the opposite direction, swerved, popped her last hubcap off into spinning shine on the air as a pothole's grace note flickered underneath, and sneezed.

It was a bus of the undead she piloted, seniors being the only passengers with a life expectancy not drastically shortened by her driving, and she circled the urban prairie of Ivyland four times daily, like a clump of hair that flirts with the shower drain. Courseless though she seemed, Hecuba did have a navigational approach: she drove toward the colorful, trying to outpace unsaturated hues that pervaded Jersey's suburbscape to the point of conspiracy, this dumbly guillotine-blade sky. Her cargo didn't care, content simply to stay in motion.

"Pardon me, miss, but the rec center is in the other direction," one zombie had the gall to pipe up. "Worked there, actually. Thirty-two years. There when they put in the new wing, supervised it. My grandkid—little angel—she's got a piano recital, and since it's the next stop, and normally you never stop there, not that I'm criticizing—"

"Shut up now, please," Hecuba said when she could take no more. She puked discreetly enough out her window, tried to blame Tequila Tuesday. Lenny Marx, who owned Viking Putt MiniGolf on Route 22 and kicked his dog as though he needed a creature to pity, never failed to goad her into it. Tequila Tuesday at Sipwell's was his Sabbath, his booth a shrine. Afterwards, they'd usually screw. But Hecuba hadn't held out hope on that front a few Tuesdays back when Lenny'd won two hundo on a scratch ticket and vowed to drink it. He'd fade into brainless neon fuzz, reemerging with a smile and twin shot glasses of amber venom. At last call he'd rushed the bar while Hecuba coasted on a perfect fog.

The glitchy jukebox played some albums too loud, and Lenny had memorized which, so when a Celine Dion single suddenly cut the din, Hecuba's suspect list was one name long. Lenny, across the room, held a handsome leer up to frail light.

"What faggot put this on?" this grease stain missing an eyebrow roared. Lenny jabbed a thumb at the backs of two planetoids disguised as Collars. *You were my voice when I couldn't speak*, Celine oozed.

"You," eyebrow yelled at the neckless duo, who turned away from a South Jerz girl they'd been feeding umbrella drinks. One pointed at both his platinum blonde sideburns, like: *me?*

"Yeah, you. Are a fucking. Faggot."

Flesh hit flesh, toppled tables broke glass. Lenny settled next to Hecuba as the carnage erupted, scratching her shoulder with his stubble.

The jukebox yowled, *I'm everything I am.*

"Not that you needed a reason," she began.

"Jumped me in line. Manners are all we've got." He drowned his grin in beer as a guy who'd been tossed once already that night sprayed the brawlers with a fire extinguisher, filling the bar with a nasty white smog. Hecuba threw back her head and laughed so hard that a Sipwell's lifer dozing in the next booth, eyes still closed, asked if she was gonna be okay.

Recalling the bloody tooth that splashed in Lenny's mug shortly after, she laughed again, meaning to suffocate on arrival the uninvited image: opened pink-and-white box. On her toilet, days after the fact. Leering the pretty way Lenny did.

Ivyland was smug as she blew through its crowded vacancies, past gutted beauty parlors; the offices of injury lawyers Oppenheimer & Glove, which used to be a car dealership run by local ad loony Unami "Uzi" Cloudfoot, and with its dorsal-finned red roof seemed an overturned sailboat; strip malls offering party favors in bulk and used vacuums, while brass-knuckled guys sold powerful Adderade cocktails in forever damp back lots. The scenery singing *you got a little too used to this*. Remembering to take a shortcut, she cursed—did adapting to a swamp mean you were unfit to leave? She knew the wonky light on Fairfield stayed red for six and a half suicidal minutes, that the dead-ending maze of McMansions up past Floods Hill was so like those assholes' sense of humor, and that JFK Junior High let out at exactly 3:13, would-be gangstas and goths, seeds that might never break the surface, tumbling out in knee-length white T-shirts and clip-on nose rings and re-stitched backpacks. Kids she used to bus to school, who threw crap at her jitney when she slowed down to see if any might recognize her.

She had two children of her own—adults, technically—the elder a daughter who'd eloped with a geneticist given to dressing like Elvis. He actually dreamed of cloning the man, wore a ring set with his synthetically duplicated DNA, was once sued by the licensing company that owned The King's image, had been rebuked at Graceland countless times for you-don't-want-to-know what kind of reconnaissance, and hoped to snag the bio-copyrights to some less untouchable celebrities, probably a comedian. Hecuba identified parts of the obsession both pathetic and charming.

The son, DH, had been living under her roof for twenty-eight consecutive years, discounting a short window of foster care and various weeklong benders that stranded him in Atlantic City jails, the Filthydelphia sprawl, and once even the Pine Barrens (sand from the Jersey Dunes collected in the corner of each eye), rarely with an inkling of how he'd arrived. Hecuba pictured him sleepwalking up and down the Turnpike for days at a stretch. Lenny casually sparked these episodes with a game of crass allusion to the long-disappeared father, who'd worked a job in South Woodbane's septic quarter apparently too humiliating to describe. Lenny was given to claiming that anyone with a son like this would be a fool *not* to ditch, whether they came home smelling like shit or no. Then a wink at Hecuba. DH, by contrast, was committed to a fantasy he'd perfected out after seeing a special report in sixth grade: poisoning by tainted spinach. A senseless tragedy. No one's fault.

DH's boggling and childish insistence on this point unnerved Lenny, who occasionally feared karmic payback for the hazing, and what would be more poetic than death by toxic vegetable? Any gut-ache was cause for alarm, and as he woke on Wednesday, one pale shade of consciousness dissolving into the next, gut was where the first ache bloomed. He recognized the mangy green of Viking Putt's sixteenth hole, the mead-toting valkyrie statue, both of which reinforced the worry. What'd he eaten? That suspicious gyro. What'd he drunk?

Lenny rolled onto his back and stared at the underside of Nidhogg, an apocalyptic beast set free from the Underworld, jagged head raised in a mute roar of celebration. Or maybe pain: a child-size golf club dangled from the dragon's eye, jammed in a hole where it'd been used to whack through the brittle plastic. Thing wasn't worth fixing, Lenny concluded. Neither was the Viking Putt itself, with its garbage-filled water hazards and defaced mythology factoid signs, sandwiched between Fong Friday's—always on the health inspector's shit list, never shut down—and a guitar store where kids loitered inside wishing they could buy something while Sal lurked in his dusty back office wishing the same.

Lenny blamed kids; he always did. Blackout as he'd been,

there was no way he'd scaled Nidhogg's spine, hadn't done so since the Wall Street riots a few years back, when he'd sat on the dragon's head with Hecuba, sipping Beam, and with ancient binoculars watched the cracked ash-globe of downtown Manhattan smoldering across the river. Above gray wake, the atmosphere pulsed blue and clean and indifferently bright. Easier than ever to believe the skyline was a mural. Someone had put a thumb to wet paint, pulling detail into a monstrously beautiful smear.

Seamless segue from ambient dread to ambient disaster. You didn't want the dust settle and prove the wound. He recalled DH that night when he'd gone to check on Hecuba again, complaining how school wasn't even dismissed early and that their geometry teacher made them turn off the news, plowing ahead with a lesson on vectors. Mainly the way kids dealt with it, Lenny guessed, was pretending they always knew it would happen.

*

For Hecuba it boiled down to this dirty truth: Lenny made her laugh. He was one of those dangerous, high-wattage crazies you get close to so they'll train their evil humor on someone else, nobodies you wanted to hate anyhow. And in case they spill a drop of way-fucked genius. His shit with DH was a joke gone too far, she knew, one that set off her own pangs about Kurt, the stoically meek man she'd married, who had had the strange dignity to wear one of his three bright seersucker suits to work every day in spite of what lowly, unmentionable and foul-smelling task awaited.

But if she could withstand it, Hecuba reasoned, then her son could too. It was a small price to pay for a decent lay or guffaw now and then.

However uproarious his cruelty was, it made her unlikely to attempt *any* serious conversation, forget the one they were headed for. She found herself pulling into Viking Putt's parking lot with a pre-defeated sigh. He could be negotiated, maybe. A few seniors got up when the bus stopped, but Hecuba shouted them back into their seats. A small plastic frog was glued to the dash; she chucked it under the chin. Taped beside it was an index card that read:

NORTH AMERICAN CRYING FROG
Amphibia Lacrymosa Americana

Lenny called her that when she cried—minus the Latin, which he added for show.

"Cheer up," she told it.

Lenny, in the pungent office that doubled as his living quarters, was watching a sassy TV courtroom judge berate a couple with haircuts ten years off-style. His mutt walked in and blocked the screen, prompting Lenny to pitch a shoe at his head.

"Fuckwad, *move*!" he yelled, and the mongrel, strangely enough, obeyed. Lenny's sneaker hit the TV and flipped the channel, bringing *Jeopardy!* to the screen. Hecuba entered with minimal resolve.

"Len."

"Hec."

"Problem." Lenny hacked a cough and wiped the result on his dog.

"Who is Manute Bol. DH?"

"No. It concerns you."

"What is Elba. Should have to say, 'Where is Elba,' really." He glanced up at Hecuba, who for an instant thought she might will his head to explode and was relieved to remember she couldn't. Lenny shifted in his foul bed, revealing a familiar stain. "This … I just so hate how the money isn't real. It's abstract. I hate that."

"You *hate* that?" Hecuba asked.

"On principle," he said.

"I'm pregnant," she said.

"You're not being abstract?"

She fought a snorting laugh and shook her head with the gravity that confirms, yes, I'm un-abstractly pregnant.

"Pill," he said, slumping back and smacking his head on the usual part of the windowsill. "What is a Möbius strip," he recovered, unwilling to admit it hurt.

"Too late."

"Late? Who are 'The Mamas and the Papas.' Do you say 'are' or 'is' for bands?"

"Way late."

"What is—how long ago was—unhgod*dam*mit … he chewed through this wire." Lenny held up a mutilated power cord. "Should that kill you? Shithead?"

"I can't tell if you're talking to me or the dog. You know, most people have a dog voice, or like an animal voice, and you can tell the difference."

"Not changing my voice for the fucking dog."

*

Back on the bus, Hecuba didn't notice she was missing a few seniors, because she tried to never look at them. Roaring into traffic, she thought of her children again, wondering what remote locale she'd soon fetch DH from—a chore less hateful than his absence. She loathed being without him, ever since she'd made the Mistake that her mind revisited each day without permission.

Hecuba, when a newly single mother, had taken her squabbling kids out to their dinky front lawn, tied them to the kitchen chairs, and hosed them till purple crept into their lips, hoping to impart some morsel of wisdom since forgotten. A neighbor outright threatened to call social services; Hecuba retorted that it was only child abuse if you used hot water, and doused the nosy bastard before aiming the icy stream back at DH, who squealed and opened his mouth, trying to drink it.

And when they came to pluck him from Hecuba's arms, he bawled something fierce, still shivering, not understanding in the slightest why it had to be so.

*

Lenny was prepared to find DH himself when he detected young
voices in the vicinity, assuming the boy had once more suggested
Viking Putt as an oasis where he and his entourage could sprawl
out in their popper haze. Instead, he found unfamiliar kids piling
out of a skunky station wagon and told them to scram. We were
going to play, they whined.

"Were," said Lenny, unlit cigarette dangling expertly.

The mutt stared in through the screen door as he yanked
out each desk drawer. Tequila escaped his body as sweat, more
poisonous than ever. Finally he found two bottles of lighter fluid
under a stack of unopened credit card statements. He patted his
thigh and felt a book of matches, doubtless from Sipwell's.

Strolling around the rigged-to-be-unsinkable eighteenth, past
the peeling Odin statue, Lenny whistled. Here was the Ragnarök
sign. Gods do battle, most die, fabric of existence is torn a new
one. It'd make a good Saturday morning cartoon. He struck a
match and held it to the sickly green turf, which wouldn't burn.
Struck another and held it to a plant, but it blackened and curled
and didn't do much else, so he doused the area with lighter fluid.
How much did an abortion cost, anyway?

Two old harpies and an ancient man in a porkpie hat
appeared, asking when the next bus would come through. Lenny
had to laugh. His dog stalked over, ropy drool stretching for the
ground, and sniffed the seniors apprehensively. Upon analysis, it
fled.

"Won't be for a while, folks," Lenny said, smiling for the
first time that day as he caught a drop of rain in his palm. "Say,
you wouldn't mind helping out while you wait, would you?" He
handed one of his bottles to the old man. "Gotta spray this whole
area, uh, jitney stop, with disinfectant."

The old man squinted.

"It's these kids," Lenny added, eyes knifing toward the
poppers he'd turned away. "No hygiene."

The old man nodded knowingly, sniffing the nozzle.

*

Something like actual disinfectant hissed out of ventilation grilles and settled in clammy layers on the rest of Hecuba's passengers, who studied the skies as she ranted to herself. Too old. Too stupid. One condomless Tequila Tuesday fuck.

"Storm's a-comin," wheedled some zombie woman. "My arm's swelling up." Hecuba cracked her knuckles. Dopplerized wail as fire engines raced past, towing sheets of rain in their wake. Her next baby didn't have a gender but she knew it would be a girl, like young DH had always wanted. She touched her belly button with a pinky and flipped wipers and headlights on.

"Quite a rollercoaster," a bifocaled thing behind her said, and it brought Hecuba back to school-bus days, when the kids, spurred at the sight of an appointed serpent-arrow sign, would daily begin their cultish chant: *roll*-er *coast*-er, *roll*-er *coast*-er … and Hecuba, laughing, would put her yellow monster through the S-curves near the wooded reservation at breakneck speeds, hugging concrete barriers like a bobsledder as the kids screamed, got thrown against each other and walls and windows, spilling into happy heaps in the aisle. They'd barrel down the other side of the slope, back toward town and responsible speeds. But for a blessed weightless moment, as they crested a sylvan hill that still belonged to deer and birds, they floated above their seats, free of Ivyland's gravity. Freed by turbulence and yes, the generous odds of spectacular death. Yet there persisted an agreement that the bus and its kids were together invincible, that Hecuba absorbed all risk.

She couldn't ruin another child, Hecuba realized, curtains of water melting her view. When things got this bad, she told herself Elvis-boy had taken her daughter far away; she imagined their honeymoon and the one-story glass house they had in the starry southwestern desert, nobody else around. But if she's divorced, diseased, dead, Hecuba thought, then I'm to blame.

"What the hell," she sang. The old folks wanted a rollercoaster … she crossed the double solid strip and swung back again, horns streaking by. Crazy, but Hecuba sensed her daughter pitch forward inside her. The town bled light. Tracing a wave, running all stops, she gained speed so gradually that her passengers took no notice, except for the bifocaled dingbat—she giggled in Alzheimeric delight. The tires rose up on pillows of water. They lost the road. And the second before Hecuba's jitney hydroplaned into a streetlight, she asked aloud, but not bitterly, whether she'd had a choice in the matter. She saw a dark figure in the darker sky, falling.

AIDAN /// SANDPIPER, NEW JERSEY /// SEVEN YEARS AGO

I can practically smell the booze, hear the dim laughter it's unlocked. Regret ringing the doorbell soon as my finger slides off.

"Damn, I wish you haddina rung," Henri moans, "I was just gonna suggest we bail."

"Nothing better to do."

We notice a clicking and turn to find Phoebe making careful progress up the wonky flagstone walkway. Weak waves all around.

"Swore I wasn't going to wear heels, then I did."

"Well worth it," Henri says, mustering all the elegance one possibly can while wearing an orange sleeveless tuxedo.

"Cannot believe you had the sack to wear that," Phoebe admits, reaching out to hold the heavy lapel for a second. He fidgets with delight. "I'd say we dateless wonders managed to … well."

"Make some memories?" I suggest.

"Always do," DH suddenly there, leaning in the doorframe as he lights a cigarette and scratches at facial hair that underscores his advanced age. "Glad you made it, A-bomb, just getting started." We stall in the foyer, letting him disappear into the back of a shore house rented under some disinterested or recklessly rich parent's name. Probably Ryan Danke's. "Can change in the bathroom there if you want," DH yells from down the hall.

"I'm keeping this on," Henri immediately warns. "I'm getting my money's worth."

"Who's stopping you?"

"Society."

"I'm changing," I say.

"Me too," says Phoebe.

"After you."

The sounds of laughter and a spastic coughing fit beat against muffling walls while Henri and I wait. If you listen closely, you can instead hear Phoebe's simple red dress pooling around her ankles as she slides off the second strap, the silk stuff bunching in flowery folds. So needlessly good-looking, and in some stage of nudity, and right *there*. Bet she didn't even lock.

"Did you try the calamari?"

"I've heard your opinions on the appetizers."

"But did you have the calamari?" Henri presses.

"I don't remember."

"You remember."

"Nope."

"I remember."

"I know you remember," I snap. "I had it. It sucked. Too rubbery. The end."

"You must not have had it with the sauce."

Phoebe emerges at last. She's wearing tight, *tight* jeans with colorful patches she's sewn on herself and a dark blue jungle of magic marker doodles covering most of the denim. Black tank top. I'm a goner.

"You're changing, right?" Phoebe asks. How long have I been staring? I hurriedly nod and go in, locking the door behind me.

*

We venture into the den as though dragged there. Apathetic hellos directed mainly at Phoebe. Ryan Danke is already passed out in a corner, puke crusting his pillow. A spacey band I don't recognize is quietly issuing from a stereo.

"Sit," DH says.

"Is he okay?" Henri bleats instinctually.

"Mm? O, no, no he's sleeping … drank too much, but he's sleeping now," DH mutters, momentarily taken in by the unconscious pile of Danke. He laughs, remembering it all, eyebrows flexing as he inhales deeply, then blows air out. Phoebe tugs at her pocket. Henri clears his throat with importance. This kid Ed, sitting with DH on the clam-shaped loveseat, starts to talk, gurgles, giggles at his gurgling, and promptly goes blank once he's finished.

"I, for one, have not haven't … had … enough Belltruvin," DH posits.

"Nice English, pillhead," Jack snipes from an easy chair.

"Fuck you, douche cocktail."

Everyone laughs, for different reasons. Somebody whose name definitely starts with a *B*, something nerdy—Bernard?— gives one sharp laugh and returns to near catatonia in a striking imitation of Ed circa thirty seconds ago.

"This guy," Henri jokes, pointing to the blank B-named-kid, but I can tell he has no follow-up. Doesn't stop him. "He's like Buster Keaton, only the great *stoned* face!" Which is worse: the silent film allusion or the pun? The party teeters for one hushed second on the brink of cardiac arrest.

"What about a drink?" Phoebe maneuvers, prompting a chorus of agreement that zaps us back into functioning order. I grab a rank light beer for myself from an ice-filled garbage can. DH pops *Easy Rider* on for ambiance, and we're off.

*

"What'd they just take?" Ed, possibly more acned then when we arrived, asks with suspicion when the film reaches a fragmented sequence. In a shadowy corner, Henri and Phoebe are talking, sipping their drinks in unison. Phoebe laughs—a sound that should intoxicate, loosen you up. She's hot enough to make you deranged with other people's bad ideas, shoulder-length, darker-than-brunette-but-not-quite-black hair, hazel eyes flecked with *yellow*, for God's sake, and yes, I worship every inch of that perfection. But right now I'm not smiling.

"Acid," DH reasons.

"DH," Jack breaks from a conversation cluster to say. "Show us how you can shimmy all the way up one of those streetlights."

"Not when I'm this gone," DH laughs. "Not ever."

Now Henri, slanting with inebriated confidence against the wall, laughs, chokes, then laughs at himself post-recovery. Phoebe pats him on the back, laughing along. Just having a fucking blast over there. The sliver of Phoebe's hip covered by neither shirt nor jeans is unfair. Henri's voice peaks elsewhere in my awareness, grandiloquently: "*Bibamus, moriendum est!*" he cries, fetching himself and Phoebe more beers.

"Hit this," says B-name, passing me a bottle of Jack Daniels. I do my damnedest. "And your sights are set on?"

"Mean who am I ..." eyeballs lurching back to Phoebe.

"I mean, college, work," B-name mumbles, taking the whiskey.

"Ivyland College."

"Dumb. All the jobs'll be gone in four years."

"Yeah?"

"That's why me'n Jack and Danke and Ed got ourselves into police academy."

"Really."

"Cruising, shooting. Set for *life*."

"In Ivyland." But B-name is up on his feet, getting someone else's attention, leaving me to consider my own depressing plans. The trick with Phoebe is to say something you're too chickenshit to say, an unctuous inner voice whispers. Henri's still got her cornered by the kitchen. Can't hear what he's saying, but the man must be spitting game like there's a surplus.

"Henri," I shout, holding up the bottle B-name left wedged in the couch cushions.

"Don't we have any mixers?" he whines.

"It's easy," Ed is assuring someone, pulling on a cigarette, blowing a ring, and a smaller ring through that.

Holly, lately denied the title of Prom Queen (due to student council corruption is the rumor), makes a well-timed entrance. The party cobbles together one of those drunkenly smeared but jubilant "Eyyyy!" noises to acknowledge her.

"Talented man." She finger-guns at Ed and his smoke rings.

"Pup-tent, Ed?" Jack shrewdly inquires, tickling the back of Ed's neck. The answer is a swift punch to the shoulder, Ed's other hand remaining a strategic groin shield.

"Rednecks," DH says as two motorcyclists are shotgunned to celluloid heaven by some good ol' boys. The movie was about fifteen minutes long by my inner clock. Phoebe whispers in Henri's ear, and they're atwitter. He takes a massive swallow from the bottle.

"What's so funny?" I slur.

"Nothing," Phoebe teases, pointing her beer can vertical.

"Damn, girl," Holly admires. "Aidan, come here, I've got something to show you." The words are replayed in my head, garbled, twice, meaningless. The DVD screensaver is too verdant to be true.

Phoebe's gone. Henri's gone. Shit.

"Dude, you made my life," I can hear DH gushing somewhere, and then there he is, holding aloft a bulbous bottle half-filled with bluish fluid, jabbering lowly, a shine on his eyes.

"New Adderade cocktail," he's saying, "best so far, this guy drops all sorts of goodies in there that're still prescription. Can't believe we ever tripped on cough syrup," he laughs. DH starts passing the bottle around. It finds its way into my hand. I scan the room for Henri and Phoebe again and, coming up empty, allow myself a mouthful. It tastes like a shitty diaper, but I wash it down with more beer. I sink back into a beat-up chair that angelically appears at exactly the moment of need, then somehow vacate it, up again, forcing myself to stay in motion.

"Endless ... fucking tight," Ed says in a pained voice after he drinks the stuff.

"They made people who glow in the dark," says Jack.

"Such a lie," says a half-alive Danke from his pass-out corner.

"Why would someone *do* that?" Phoebe agrees. No, not Phoebe. Holly.

"Cause you can."

"Cause they get off on it," Danke says, suddenly part of the conversation.

"Come on." An impeccable manicure meshes with my own ragged fingers, pulling me away. People knowingly snicker.

"Be good," I hear.

"Any more Belltruvin?"

"Yes."

"Me too."

"Right here, big guy."

"You guys ever tried gas?"

"Do I look rich to you?"

"Did you guys see the video of the Michigan bridge collapse? The Winnape or something."

"Two in one month? And the same place ..."

"I *know*."

*

It's Holly who leads me. We wind round a spiral metal staircase. The world keeps spinning after the stairs. We're in a blandly nautical bedroom, lampshades with seahorses and anchors.

"Had something I didn't want to share," Holly confides, reaching into an impractically small purse.

"Not a good sharer?"

She removes something that looks like a giant bullet, sleek and silver, and attaches a length of clear tubing with a valve to a nozzle at the top.

"Hallaxor? You ... "

"Sit."

She pats the covers. Her top is cut low, and if she doesn't notice me staring at her tits, she's blind by all definitions. She scratches me under the chin, calls me cute, puts the end of the tube in her mouth and opens the valve, sucking hard. The giant bullet comes to me and I imitate. She tips forward and rests her face on mine.

Her breath is wrong, polluted, not what I want. Not Phoebe's. We kiss, Phoebe's lips replacing Holly's. Same for hair. I clutch a shoulder and pretend, shutting my eyes, body charting the earth's rotation, falling through the sheets and the floor and the ground and everything below it. A knocking filters in, maybe imagined, so we don't respond. A click and a creak.

"Oop, sorry. Aidan?" says Phoebe.

"You guys were holding out on us!" Henri booms as he stampedes into the room, snatching the small canister. Phoebe, just as trashed but a smidge more tactful:

"Can we hang out here?"

Holly is more generous with a lungful of gas, and we all sit cross-legged on the bed, Henri's corner sagging.

"Whose room is this?" he wonders, but it's a rental house, so what a dumb question.

"You know what shotgunning is?" Holly asks the group. She takes another hit, then pushes her mouth against mine and blows it in. Henri is rapt. Phoebe watches the ruinous transfer in the corner of one eye.

"Now you do her," Holly instructs, indicating Phoebe.

I give everything away. Phoebe's eyes dart in radiant shyness, the yellow firing out from hazel. I suck on the tube, and Phoebe comes in. Fingertips graze ribcages, trembling with mute gasps; I feel the small of her back heave under my palm, my shirt tighten as she clasps its collar and draws me in, unrepentant. I see only her closed eye and the wall beyond it, expanding and contracting with supernatural life, the floor cresting and breathing, dotted with wiggling amoebas locked in tailspin.

"Give someone else a chance," Henri butts in, defiling

everything. To my horror, Phoebe sucks gas and shotguns Henri for a split second. She's just that drunk. It's only a game. Lights are twinkling differently now.

"I feel it," I mutter.

Lights are twisting. A funhouse of wild shifting angles. The bedspread is self-aware. The room sighs. Lights are goddamn twinkling differently, and I rotate my head to see the starry points of white spin back-and-forth, back-and-forth ... they twist now, and are they doing that on their own? Stop rocking your head from side to side, but can't. Or I do, and the lights keep twisting. *Stay out.* What?

"What?"

"What what?" Holly asks, amused. Phoebe is prone ... sleeping?

"Did you say something? I thought. Well, even so." Senseless. "Didn't you say something?"

"I don't know," Henri says. *Just the same.* As what?

"Aidan."

"Hm."

"I feel it," Henri tries to say.

Blue, a blue muted but like diamond splinters that rocket through heads leaving holes and fissures, filling them with buzz till I look at my own should-be blue eyes in a bathroom mirror and see only wet black gaps yawning back, stains of ash, irises devoured by pupils that are islands in tired off-white oceans.

"You need to go home."

"I can't," says the mirror. I want to reach through and throttle him, the mirror me, steal his fucking easy life. All he has to do is comb is hair and brush his teeth, maybe floss, but only if *I* remember to. Rest of the day, he's asleep or soaking in the bath. Likes the water the exact same temperature as me, curls into the same position I do under the blankets.

"Fetal."

"Stop saying everything that pops into your head," the mirror

says. The bathtub is melting and I can take it in stride by singing
a little kid's playground rhyme:

Little Bob Squeazy
Got his VV
Then he went to bed
But he woke up dead

Big Dad Squeazy
Sued the doctor E-Z
Won a ton of bread
Then it went to his head

Sad Mom Squeazy
Wanted baby Squeazy
Couldn't bring him back
So she killed herself instead

Knock at the door—no. Me bumping the cabinet shut. The
bathtub may be melting, but it's also filthy. Dirt oozes down
the drain ... spirals, fractal waves that surge upward helplessly
... in the bathroom with me now is a person, a girl, kissing
my burning cheek. It's Holly, and she mutters sentences full of
blanks: "You'd never believe ... I'm gonna ...," volume varying
as she moves up and down my neck. In the mirror, I'm staring
out of this embrace, trying to find blue in my eyes, doubting it
was ever there. Studying the cartoony floral wallpaper to calm
things down, counting each petal and then each line within each
petal where they do this jumping, things so criminally patterned.
My skin tugs upward with each kiss. I look down at Holly, but
now she's Phoebe, or always was. Water drips from the faucet
in heavy balls, *dyooop dyooop*, submarine sonar pings. "Phoebe?"
She's not listening, but guides my hand up her shirt. She's not
wearing a bra. My hand is torn between ecstasy and panicked

claustrophobia, but I force it to stay, make it follow those full shapes and caress them in what I direly hope is expert fashion. I stagger backward, sit on the sink, accidentally turning the faucet on. The sudden gush is deafening after minutes of only muffled whispers and sighs, and I jerk forward.

"Let me ..." I say, maybe talking about the faucet. Phoebe grabs my belt and feverishly tries to undo it. *Wait wait wait wait.* My legs are jelly, and they crumple. "I want to ..." Phoebe says, or I imagine. When she moves her head it leaves a trail. The lurch of blood in my ears, prickle of every surface—each piece of air bouncing off. I have a hand under Phoebe's shirt again, on her back, and she's sweating.

Now the blood-red thing dawns on me, saying *Cal was here,* defiled all. I shouldn't care. I swallow the truth with difficulty, drown it in saliva.

"You're high," I protest for some reason. My other hand is sunk in a bathmat and can't stop groping its ropy mildewed fibers, which seem to make a squeaky sound. "You hear that?" I ask, meaning the squeaking.

"No," Phoebe says, silencing me with a messy kiss.

"This bathmat is squeaky," I announce through the side of my mouth. "Stop." This time, I push her off. "I just need ... wow ... okay. Fuck!"

"What's wrong?"

I stop short of crying and crawl to the door. A towering white four-sectioned monolith. Still lying down, I reach the push-lock and snap it open. Through the sliver of space at the bottom I see the amoebas swimming and two shoes. I recuperate for a second and reach again, pushing the door, push—push to close—pull it open. And there sits Henri, somehow abandoned to listen to teenagers sloppily fondling each other. His face can't be understood. Seeing me, and past me to Phoebe, woozily recumbent against the bathtub, he stands.

"Aidan."

"You aren't mad, are ... are you mad?"

"I respect you," he says, taking the time to get his line right. "I respect you, and you're like a brother, but I can only respect so much." The amoebas are magnetically attracted to his feet, I can see now, and they swim into fuzz circles that rotate softly, clockwise and counter, little combination locks. I pet one.

Henri's gone.

I leap to my feet with a frazzled energy I didn't think I had, running out through the bedroom in pursuit. Behind me, Phoebe too is clattering out of semi-consciousness into action. In the hallway, Henri is moving as fast as his legs will carry him, toward the deck and the ocean. I struggle over a rug that slides on polished wood, scrabbling at the walls. Henri throws open a glass sliding door, luckily for me—I would have plowed right through. The din of a raging, oblivious party and *Fear and Loathing in Las Vegas* in the other room (*You took too much,* I hear) slams me for a second as I remember where we are and briefly recall my dad showing me this photo, saying, *Here's me and my friends with Hunter S. Thompson at a talk he gave. He never did figure out what to do next, except for in the end with a shotgun.* Situation surges back, injecting fresh adrenaline into rubberized muscles. A nearby A/C rattles psychotically, no, honestly, as if it really does belong in some grimy asylum, and surely at least not here in a painfully standard beach house where on the salt-blasted deck I clip my hip on a bin full of rancid garbage whose funk is so pulverizing that I sort of pass . . . out but keep running.

Practically a footgasm from my toes sinking into the cool dry fluid of the sand and movement becomes a joke. Henri has slowed down, too, I can tell, but as I sense the gap closing a weight hits my back, locking my knees and planting me face-first in the sand. I flip over, say something immediately disqualified as language. Phoebe is straddling my chest, a lurid grin plastered on her face. Even in spare light the fiery parts of her eyes move, contort, scary/sexy. She glows star-colored, lit from within. I give in for another moment till she comes too close and runs a perfumed hand through my gritty hair, another keeping me pinned. I clench my teeth when she kisses my earlobe, too, too intense and one-of-my-legs-can't-tell-which jiggers insanely, thumping like an overexcited dog's. Air exits my mouth in a delirious hiss till my tongue pushes against the back of my teeth to stop the sound. Weight lifts. Phoebe is missing. I'm paralyzed, back arched, tendons taut. The galaxy overhead moves in streams, flowing calmly, the moon absent, and I instantly weep full ancient sobs, tears glazing the sky, rolling out of my eyes only when enough water has collected to pour sideways over quaking skin and into tiny divots where the sand claims their moisture. I count to three, shut my eyes and quell a tremor that insists I'll never get home. A star river even on the back of my eyelids, searing greens and purples.

Henri is sitting there, I realize, looking skyward.

"Do you see that?" he asks, choking on the question. I sit up with ease and touch his shoulder. This suffices for the moment, before I remember to say I'm sorry. I wish I were blind, deaf. I bite my fingers raw.

"I don't know where we are," says Henri, answering the question I hadn't yet asked. Phoebe lies a few feet away, a surface of vomit or a beached jellyfish gleaming by her head, mouth bent in a wan, sleepy smile. She could be alive or she could be dead. Hendrix died thus. Dad went to Woodstock, but for all my investigation, his story ends there: How old were you?

Real young.

How the hell did you get out there?

My mom's friend drove us and dropped us off. It sounds ridiculous in retrospect.

And it was cool?

Of course, it was Woodstock.

"1969."

"69?"

"Childish."

We cannot nix the dread that some malfunctioning mass of

neurons won't flip the switch from CHILD to ADULT. And if we have nothing of value to offer. Then. Am I meant to apologize for my time? Enjoy and not reverse the end? It's true we can't spend our lives in trances, with perfect TV-related recall. But who's to judge. Schedule me. I am highly trained and helpless. I assumed there was a plan.

"She's breathing," one of us says, paroxysms in lungs: the X of paroxysm floats before me, stretching until it's X'd out everything. I crawl over and stick a trembling finger under her nostrils, pretty curls of heated, even breath. I sniffle, feel sand in my nose, petting her and now hear this, it's like one sad album played on repeat, guitar reverb soaking up moonlight of foreign song cycles, familiar melody ringing when Cal held my hand that day and took me home (though I'll not get back), took me from a deathscape of blood on ice, an ice transparent but not fully so, played with my blood, took me back. The moon that ice. Uncharted territory, says Henri, and I've found the moon again, the night is not without one, though it is bloodless—it is clear and cratered and a steady shiver and here we sit in love with immobility. Cal was homesick no matter where. In hearts. In the game of Hearts you shoot the moon, do everything wrong to be saved at the end. Henri picks up a stick that's hollow at both ends, holds it like a telescope. "Why can't I see through this?" he asks.

Zeros spinning in the sky. Wheels, gears, interlocking in pairs and pairs of pairs, scrolling mosaics, transparent geometries brushing vision. Veins bulge and snake as if charmed. Henri speaks and he gestures in rainbows and does not inhale once so far as I see with *you could have her without trying, and I'd charm all night and never, never like she wants you, not just that way, I'm saying, but wants you and to be with you, God this is fucked up, I want it to end, I mean not like my life, don't get that idea, but with Phoebe*—the name lingering even as he continues—night making his orange tux gray, little amoebas breathing on the tie he borrowed from his dad: they've seen your parents how you never will. What do these people refuse to say? They lived through worse, and it made them stronger? Or they were simply born with something, let's call it virtue, or *arête*, if Henri is to have his way with classical vocab: *arête* is a *hexis*, habit. A *hexis*. Virtue is a hex on us, and onus too. Might so much deserve my rage that I can't begin to rise in anger, frozen, my hundred wills all grown this cold? Henri stammering on, *it's like, like, like she's ahh she's a home, a home with good thoughts*. He's tracing his hand, thumb, finger, finger, finger, finger, and back again, pinky, ring, middle, index, thumb in that kindergarten Thanksgiving turkey way, just so in the chilly sands that boil with scars of violent holidays. There's been nothing in my life that could … I was born knowing this.

"I'm sick," Henri says.

"You're fine."

"I'm sick and I'm going to die," he insists.

"You're not going to die. Don't tell me that."

Thing being, we're not far from the house after all: I see faces moving at windows. Drunk and happy, collapsing into the reckless headlong narrative of dream while the mind paces alone and calculates its disaffection. A home you can't get back to. First Circle of Inferno for us uncaring pagans, more Purgatory Forever than Hell. When the last comes and things break, you don't repair them, you squeeze what's left out of the shards. Trying to fix things, you ask: *What was this supposed to look like?*

We trudge in place through the edge of that world and back into our own. Phoebe stirs. Trees near the street decked with leaves or dangling metal mobiles that move and catch scant warmth of distant suns. An ambulance streaking by is unusually profound, a wailing vault encrusted with glittering jewels. One that came for Henri years ago … When it happened, I was sure of the worst, never shook that certainty. He needs to stay. I need to stay … we stay awaiting zodiac rays. A car squeals past, following the ambulance. "Where's that guy think he's going?" I mutter, making Henri actually laugh, the sound so alien in this place. The brush along the road rustles knowingly, its serenity throwing me for a minute as our surroundings conspire to a higher purpose. But the glass nothings pass, impurities colliding with space again. Fraught voices pierce us from the house, and a bird chirps, not waiting for dawn.

Belltruvin float, now airborne. The cop hesitates, smelling the potent Adderade cocktail we got in Baltimore. Once he's asleep I'm going to dig some ice out of the cooler and rub the back of my neck with it. Weird to think about masturbating the old way. Can't believe people still do.

"Are you an organ donor?" Lev asks over a clipboard.

No. A bunch of hours longer ago: I'm speeding when we leave North Carolina and going faster when we hit Georgia and a total grease streak after we show up to Lev's dad's abandoned house.

"He can't hide," says Lev.

"Seems like he can," I say, and slam on the gas.

The cop pulls us over a bit later. I haven't gotten to drive since.

"Fast truck you have here," the cop says, chewing his moustache. "In a rush?"

"Yes."

"Why's that?"

I look at Lev, who shrugs.

"Humanitarians," says the cop, admiring the poster we stole from a harvesting clinic and plastered on one side of the truck. JERRY GODFORTH WAS A PIONEERING PSYCHOLOGIST, BUT IT IS HIS KIDNEYS THAT BEST SUPPORTED A PATIENT: GIVE TOMORROW'S GIFT OF DIGESTIVE FILTRATION TODAY. With a picture of the creepily smiling guy himself. Where the poster's scratched through you can see some of the old ice cream pictures.

"Who sent you boys on the mission?" he asks.

"One of Endless's new mobile VV units for Rural Protection," Lev says, adding, "also licensed to do coz."

Turns out the cop knows where Lev's old man lives, this same county but down toward the coast, a plantation-style place that never was one. He also wants penile implants, which Lev assures him he can do, despite my silently panicking eyes.

"Suppose these celebrities want some quiet," the cop says. "Didn't know he had a son, Brutus."

When we get around to Lev's first attempt at genital enhancement, the cop's eyes are not focusing. His words drip from the corners of a chemically wet mouth.

"Let's see," says Lev. "Hand me my etherscope."

"He knows what he's doing?" swims the cop's mouth.

"He knows everything," I laugh, forcing his unhinged eyes closed with a gentle palm. "The hell's an etherscope?" I whisper.

"Not real," Lev admits.

A crackling voice turns out to be the cop's walkie-talkie, which asks: why aren't you patrolling, you're one of only two cars in this whole stupid backwater, and here I am staring at this halted tracking blip on my screen that represents your very stationary ass, and if you don't cover your ground I'll come down on you like a fucking bridge. I hit the off switch. Lev pulls down the cop's pants to reveal an already oversized member.

"I'm ethically bound not to operate," he sighs in relief.

We take what we want off the guy and dump him back in his squad car with a sorry-note I scrawled—saying too much of a good thing is no good to anybody—and Lev and I motor off to his father's house by the beach, which turns out is something from a slasher flick, weeping willows and Spanish moss hiding a white rotting portico, like the whole place is trying to grow back into the earth. It's nicer than the first house, though. We walk on in.

Inside erupts the stench of mildew, and I start sneezing when we come to a dark wooden study. A hard object strikes me in the head and I open my eyes to find on the oriental carpet a small bottle of allergy meds that I used to get stoned on as a kid. Brutus Van Vetchen is sitting at the far end of the cavernous room, behind an enormous dusty desk in a pool of dirty sun that pours in from floor-to-ceiling windows, wearing a three-piece wool suit in soul-incinerating heat, cutting something tiny apart with a butter knife.

"Don't bother introducing your friend," Brutus says, and it doesn't sound like a joke. "Can't visit your father without a bodyguard?"

"*Et tu*, Daddy? Didn't even tell me you moved."

"Earthy, yes? A present from Endless for my life-saving efforts. The appearance of life-saving efforts."

"Sure you saved people, Daddy."

Brutus is slicing open pills, tasting the powder. He looks way too young, the lines in his cheeks too sharp, as if he's only ever made one face besides the current. Also, what do *I* look like these days?

"They have orangutans mixing doses now. My old partner Reginald agrees. How is school going, Leviticus? Anatomy still holding you back?"

"Not at all. Got a tutor, it's going great," Lev answers, head tilting at me. "Anyway, Daddy, you want to have maybe a sweet tea, whatever it is they drink down here, talk a minute."

"We're talking now."

"I need the gas."

Without looking up, Brutus pries himself away from the pill project and walks to a cabinet in the corner. He takes out a glass, a capless bottle of Scotch, and a recognizable sleek silver tank, but no familiar symbol. Inside that, the perfect ratios. He pours himself a few fingers of Scotch, drops the tank on his desk with a bang that makes me almost laugh. It leaves a mark on the wood.

"Even with all their legal products," he begins.

"This is legal."

"Not for what you want it for." Brutus sips his warm drink. The whole place is preserved, marinated in some peaty Scotch like that. Creeping vines growing in through busted windows and boggy air. Moss on the unused bookshelves even, creeping up around a lone picture frame laid facedown. I flip it up to find a photo of hard-hatted young Brutus standing with a forced smirk before the skeleton of a construction site. Closer to the foundation, on the far right, is a person cut off by the shot: a seersucker-sleeved arm and a sliver of face that could just as well be mine.

"Had the anger long?" Brutus asks stonily.

"Anger, sir?" I ask.

"It speaks. Anger, yes, the withdrawal?" Here he pulls the tank's plastic mask to his face and turns the knob, inhales deeply. "Getting worse every second, isn't it—have to chew a ton of Belltruvin to stay remotely happy. Is it worse when I do this?" he takes another lungful, his eyes rolling back like a shark's.

"Stop it, Daddy."

"A medical tool," Brutus goes on, spittle stretching down the length of his tie. He gets syruped from doing two hits in a row, but fights it, drinking more, then sucking more. "I can see why you're seduced, Leviticus. Everything reassembled."

"It's for the hospital where I'm doing my residency in Ivyland," Lev lies. "Services immigrants, mandatory VV upon entering the country, and if they don't have the money, they get deported. I want to make it free." True, except for Lev doing his residency there.

"What kind of person believes you?" Brutus asks, slumping back in his chair.

"Please, Daddy," Lev trying to weep. "There's a little boy named Carlos who I'd kill myself if he died of H12."

"Nobody dies of H12," Brutus says. He licks a palm and massages his face with the spit. "Just moved along."

"Because of you, Daddy."

"Because nobody." Brutus paints his spit-sticky features with pill powder. "Indian war paint. The medicine man," he laughs. "They cured some things."

"Daddy."

"Go to the basement."

"We're going to negotiate."

"Useful things in the basement."

"I'm not a kid," Lev says.

"A basement is where I bet Kurt is right now."

"What did you just say?" I ask, knowing it couldn't be what I heard.

Brutus stands up like he barely knows how, shuffles to the window, swings it open and climbs out into rippling high grass.

"I guess let's try the basement," Lev sighs.

We head downstairs and crack open a rotting door to get in. There's a fireplace, fat screwholes within Φ-shaped dust outlines above. Scratches and dents on the walls. I step on something that crunches. It's a fingernail with dried blood around the edges.

"There," says Lev, pointing to a hairline crack in the wall below where the Φ-shaped thing used to be. "Come on, stockpile." He crosses his fingers. We kick in the flimsy panel together.

On the other side, squatting like a nestful of dinosaur eggs, are tens upon hundreds of silver tanks, shelves bursting with pills. A bunker to wait out the firestorm. But the fire found them.

"We can't take it all," I say breathlessly.

"We can take a lot," Lev says, grabbing bottles of something called Pyramil, the pattern-finding stuff we both came to love more than gas. But the gas is good, too.

"How come the tank your dad was hitting had no logo?" I ask as we start picking over the lot. "Can't imagine Endless would ever allow such a thing."

"That was the first one, the free sample they gave him. I'll start loading this shit, just go make sure daddy's not spasming."

So I trudge reluctantly back up to the study to find Brutus carving what look like hexes and crop circles in the carpet.

"You all right, sir?" No reply. "Thanks for …"

"Place'll be less haunted now. And with these."

He gestures hopefully at a set of concentric circles.

"Haunted?" I ask.

"Endless man used to own the house, family man. Kids."

"Sounds like a family."

"At what age did you get VV'd?"

"I. Well. Never."

"Now, with a few years hindsight."

"Mr. Van Vetchen, I'm not sure I know what you mean."

Brutus begins to weep softly.

"Killed himself with a favorite shotgun in this room."

"The family man?"

"The family man."

"And his family?"

FRANCIS /// IVYLAND, NEW JERSEY /// LAST SUMMER

Minute I walk in the door, Wombat says the shower's busted and where's the hose? I mention outside's a bit chill for a hose wash and the Wombat goes well living room it is. I says a hose wash under my roof, uh, I think not. Someone's gotta see to it this house doesn't rot inside out and last I checked, that someone was me, bucko. He tries to throw a tattered piece of Aunt Margot's old robe at me without getting off the couch. It goes like six inches, lands in some mouse turds.

I says to Aunt Margot, "Wow does this place have a woman's touch by the way."

"*Ex nihilo*, whence your great father brought you," Aunt Margot speechifies from the chair. "I suppose you'd prefer he'd left you there." I says more like ex-mooch, that's what you'll be when I kick you out of my shithole, which, being mine, I have the right. She cries fakely and goes: "What would your mother think? Especially given that the cruel vicissitudes and her saintly son have landed her sister in a zoo without so much as a functional roof."

I says you ain't my ma, so shut up with guessing what she thinks. There's a little white moth sputtering round my face. I crush it in a fist and wish I hadn't.

"Looked it up—that's what all those caterpillars were supposed to turn into," says the Wombat. "Few got to, I guess."

The evening tantrum starts downstairs and before she can

stop herself Aunt Margot stomps the floor with meaning. She spins to look at me, all piss-drained terror, so I let it slide this once and drop on the couch. My suggested philosophy is, let's have at least some phony good manners. Long as he's down there listening, we could fake courtesy.

The Wombat's flipping through this stained paperback, *Korean For Beginners*. I says throw that out, it smells like a dumpster, and the Wombat says that's where he found it a few months back, in an actual freaking dumpster, on a stroll through the Ivyland College campus. He fiddles with his filthy glasses. Aunt Margot walks up and down the first couple stairs in her pink robe, chewing fingers bloody.

"Stay still," says the Wombat. "You give me the motion-sick." Aunt Margot comes and slaps the book clean out of his mitts.

"Maybe if you were not the very picture of deadly sin, some young lady would have you for a husband."

"Yeah!" laughs the Wombat, "And Gersh'll be president."

"Cram it," I says, "before I let him at you."

"Francis!" gasps Aunt Margot. "The very idea of him loose in the world." I know, I know. "Sometimes I think you have half a mind to do it," she says. "Honestly." She goes to switch on the little radio sitting on the busted TV, cause she can't hear enough about the first anniversary of the Winnape Bridge or whatever the one in Michigan was called, but she has to seize up and let a big-ass sneeze get through.

"'Djyou know in Korea they ain't even say bless you?" the Wombat asks overhead as I clomp down to the basement, grabbing scissors and needles and rope on the way.

*

After Gersh's shot I take the bit of rope and tie and untie bowline knots while he watches. I hand him the knot and he whacks me with it, so I take it away. I start reading him the only kid's book he hasn't torn up, *Goodnight Moon*. Three little bears, sitting on chairs, is when he quiets down. I take out the scissors, because today is barbershop. Have to trim his whiskers because he snaps when I try the razor. I cut his hair as best I can without waking him, starting with the cowlick that always bothers me.

*

How I get paid is by watching opinionated heads and weak parodies and amateur stunts and pranks gone wrong and yet other videos people upload to the web, to see if their content reflects negatively on Endless Nutraceuticals in any way, shape or form. When it does, you fire off a URL to our legal team and the offending clip is plucked from the ether by lunch. When it doesn't, you move onto the next. Or, if you need to meet the weekly quota of reported offenders, you put it on the shit list anyway. They call it Brand Fortification.

And while you're sorting out that nonsense, Vivian, our pushing-seventy boss who only works here to supplement a nonexistent pension from the Newark newspaper she ran her whole life, will stroll in with a sarcastic pep talk about how we are the gatekeepers and arbiters an oppressive society demands. Plus if we're lucky she'll treat us to a dramatic retelling of a crime-beat ghetto-myth about how a nine-millimeter bullet shot at the sky fell through this guy's ceiling and found his groin during Sunday dinner, at which point it was goodnight left testicle.

Hank "Are-You-Gonna-Finish-That" Figsby goes, "Viv, was that guy with the nuts shot off just you, and you made all this up so you could tell the story but not have us know you used to be a man?"

Vivian: "No. No, it was not me." She takes a hit from her flask and offers. "And it was only one teste. Article never made it to print." She stuffs the refused flask back into her blazer and asks Hank to up the audio for a sec on the babies-injure-themselves montage he's reviewing.

"It's just 'I Got You Babe,' " says Hank. "A cover of it I think."

"That song blows," mumbles skunky Pitts in his corner. Vivian smacks him upside the head.

"The fuck, Viv?"

"Lost my virginity to that song."

Hank chokes on a mouthful of pretzel mash plus a giggle.

"Laugh," Vivian says. "Someday I'll throw you out on the streets with two black eyes and blood in your piss."

"Worse, she'll get us transferred to Brand Extension," Hanks says.

"Don't joke," I warn him.

"Me too?" Pitts yelps even though Vivian tends to make the emptiest threats you've ever heard.

"Especially you," Viv shouts over her shoulder, shoving through the emergency exit to smoke on the fire escape.

*

I buy groceries at a store across from the studio lot, stop off at the pharmacy and pick up Gersh's stuff.

"Keep that balance right," the pipsqueak pharmacist says, handing over a bag of needles, and our fingers accidentally touch.

I drive home in the old Volvo with what remaining paint flaking up off the hood and sticking to the windshield. Wipers go right over it.

"Thank God," Aunt Margot says when I walk in. "Some reason, I thought you'd left for good."

"Ta-dah," I says. Had any sense, I *would* hightail it.

"But your father wrote, God rest—"

"Don't worry 'bout cleaning up all my brain goo in the study? Go to New Jersey, Endless takes care of its own?" I ask. "I see you haven't moved today," I tell the napping Wombat. There's something else eating Aunt Margot, but she's too chickenshit. "Say," I says.

"Gersh's been going bonkers," the Wombat pipes up from the couch, not as asleep as he looks in his dirty gray sweats. Aunt Margot starts looking through the groceries, and I snap the bag away.

"I don't hear anything," I says.

"It was earlier," Aunt Margot says. "You weren't here when it was bad."

"No," I says, "guess I never am." She scrunches her face.

"It'd be safer."

Gersh, because he always seems to get the idea, pounds the floor from underneath.

What you made me do already, I says, is bad enough. Aunt Margot eyes the Wombat's chewed-up ear, the crooked big scar hanging over his lip.

"He's dangerous," she says.

Embarrassing, she means.

"He could really hurt someone if he … he could."

But he wouldn't, if these crap-stains didn't provoke him. If they just tried to be civil. Teach by example.

"Nice cut of meat," Aunt Margot calls after me.

I take the grocery bag down to the basement and slip when the last step gives.

"Gersh," I groan, lying on the stone floor. "Dinnertime."

I push off the ground, put an antique lamp back on its shelf, and tidy up some stuff from the estate that has gotten knocked out of place, paintings of actual plantations near Spectre, croquet sticks and porcelain sweet tea pitchers and the constantly toppling stacks of medical books, the rest of the old family junk Aunt Margot can't stand to look at anymore.

Gersh is already slobbering, straining at the rope around his throat, chafing the scar of a successful but side-effect-heavy VV op on the back of his neck. I pick up the extra rope and start tying and untying bowlines, but with food in range, he can't pay attention to anything else.

"Don't strangle yourself," I says. I slide the bag of meat over and he eats like it's Thanksgiving, the twiggy ribs heaving. I take away the plastic bag because obviously. I watch for a minute in case there's a bone I didn't take out on accident. When he's done I prep a shot and he whimpers.

"Someday you'll thank me," I says. "There's places worse than the basement."

When I stick it he gets a good bite in and I cuss, which I hate to do around him. I calm down quick and show I'm okay. "Someone hurts you," I says, "you got the right to hurt them back."

Good-intentioned hurts we can learn about later.

Goodnight Moon: a quiet old lady whispering hush, and he's done.

Goodnight, Gersh.

*

"Been down there an hour," Aunt Margot says when I come up.

"Ew," adds the Wombat, like Gersh and I have been having a grand sexy time.

"So," I says, "you think I like it in that pit? Anybody fixing to take over, be head honcho," I ask—because that always clamps their faces.

"Wish you wouldn't use that slimy backwoods vernacular," Aunt Margot says.

"Maybe that's why I do," I says.

"Wonder if he's improved," she says, whispering the last word.

"Ain't gonna be none better for Gersh," the Wombat declares. Aunt Margot peers closely at him.

"What's the matter with your clothes? So many holes." The Wombat shrugs and picks up his Korea book. I lie down on the couch, which—speak of the devil—has also got holes where moths probably chewed through while Aunt Margot was off breaking the toaster with a fork again.

The front door practically falls down when someone knocks. Aunt Margot is already up, pacing around, but says: "Can't you?"

It's a small Asian girl who wants to sell me cookies. Says all proceeds go to Harvey House and comes in a ways without me inviting.

"And what is Harvey House, exactly?" I says, following her into the living room.

She concentrates, remembering the official description. "A home for people who had an allergic reaction Hallorax gas when they got VV."

"And it's nice? Can someone with a really bad reaction get in? How much is it?"

"Dunno," she says.

"Are you Korean?" the Wombat asks, all excited when he sees her.

"I'm American," the tiny thing says.

I offer to buy two boxes in exchange for the name of Harvey House's director, and the bitch up-sells me to a three-pack.

*

Viv is trying to narrate an amateur porn video that turned up in Pitts's to-screen list because of the amount of Belltruvin consumed therein.

"Basically, they've … *ho*ly crap," she says. Hank applauds a batshit crazy sex move I'd think twice before trying.

"That's impossible," says Pitts, who you can tell is not comfortable with the idea of human bodies touching.

"It is not only possible," says Vivian in a wacky accent. "It is *essential*. Don't flag this one, the world needs it. You guys got anything else of note?"

Hank has a supposedly entertaining clip titled "Guy Tricked Into Thinking He's High On Hallorax," in which I think you know what happens. Viv is lukewarm. She grabs a package from the front bin.

"The fuck is this?" The envelope has only a Φ Endless logo doodled on it, no address—must've been hand-delivered.

"Haven't watched," I says.

Vivian pulls an unlabeled disc (it's the only thing in there) and pops it on. It's a bald man in a field, wearing a dumb white robe. Behind him is a big dead tree. Color's too sharp, or off: a purple sky, gold leaves. No action, no sound. Man looks almost happy.

"What a crock," Viv says, and fast-forwards.

Night begins in the movie. An orange moon rises. Dumbass is there for like, ever.

I push play. A moth dizzies into frame and lands on the guy's shoulder, blending into the white. Vivian reaches over me to fast-forward again.

"Hilarious," says Hank.

But in the sped-up video, more white moths start showing up, one or two at a time, and they all go right for the guy, settling on his eyebrows and in his hair and the crooks of his elbows, and before a moth covers it I make out the tiny crest on the front of his robe: Φ. The Endless logo again. I'd seen it out of place another time, just recently, but where?

"Oh my god," Viv says. "It's the worst student film of all time."

"How'd they do that?" says Pitts, who wheels his chair closer, broadcasting coffee breath.

"Saint Francis of Assisi," says Vivian. "Head count for poker night."

"Don't ask him," Hank says. "He'll just say he has to watch his kid brother."

Viv ogles me like a vulture ogles something it hopes is dead.

"How old is the bro?" she asks.

"Nine this week," I say.

My screen goes black.

Vivian glares but can't stay serious, and that doofus smile breaks. By then Hank's giggling too, and soon they're both braying like donkeys. Pitts frowns and rolls back to his desk. Viv shakes her head.

It's the pharmacist, I remember suddenly, the fat ring he wears with a Φ on it, just like Dad's. Only Dad actually worked for Endless, and this guy works for a Zanzibar Drug knockoff with way-cheaper product and too many Zs in its sign. I noticed

it the last time he handed me Gersh's injections. He always says:
"Keep that balance right." "Balance?" I'd asked him the first
time.

He said, "Hormone balance," and pointed at the stuff.

"Right," I'd said.

Next time, I think, ask about the ring.

Hank starts up the porn where we paused it.

"She needs to shut up. Porn actresses are never funny."

"Women period aren't funny," says Pitts from the corner
before violently realizing that Vivian is still here, eyes fixed on
my blank screen.

"Pitts," she says carefully, "that's the first smart thing to escape
your mouth unharmed."

"Thanks," says Pitts, actually pleased.

*

The pharmacy is closed early for some reason, so I head home,
where Aunt Margot is topping herself. She yaps, barely even
using words, until the Wombat interrupts.

"When I die and get to Heaven, Imma talk to Elvis," he says.
I says Elvis ain't gonna want to talk to you any more'n he would
if you was both alive.

"Imma talk to Elvis in Korean," he decides. A moth comes
through the window and lands on his shoulder. Soon followed
by a friend.

"And what makes you think a southern gentleman like Mr.
Presley would speak that vile language?" Aunt Margot wants to
know.

"Ain't vile, Ma," the Wombat says, shooing his moths.
"Munna go there one day."

I step into the kitchen to grab food and a shot from the
fridge. Something pauses me at the top of the basement stairs.
I push through it, rush down, and trip on what's left of the step
I broke last time. With my face on the floor, I pick up these
breathy sounds. Breezes blowing every which way. A soft papery

life slides up my arm and explores an ear. Then a screech from
Gersh gets my eyes shaking. I look up.

The basement isn't supposed to be white, or alive. I almost
puke right away—the room rippling, no hard surface. Like
everything's made of them.

Moths. Millions. Blanketing the walls. Spilling out of old
cabinets and crashing in waves against each other. Tornadoing
around Gersh, who thrashes smack-dab in the middle, screeching
louder when he sees me. I crawl over and hold him, try to be a
shield, but we're buried. Ragged lights and breath beat through
nonstop wings. At some point, as a creeping fur of them spreads
inside my clothes, I realize the Gersh-sound isn't a scream. It's his
laugh.

I struggle to my feet, emerging from the swarm just as the
Wombat appears on the stairs, asking if everything's okay. I
almost say aloud: When It Rains. His owlish eyes crank open
behind their greasy lenses now, taking in the portrait: me holding
a dirty, oddly hairy, maniacally laughing nine-year-old with a
rope around his neck. In a swirling cloud of ghostly bugs. Just
to prove things can always be worse, Gersh takes this wordless
eternity to seize and eat a whole bunch of them, chewing open-
mouthed for our viewing pleasure.

The Wombat's eyes get an empty look. A sickness that, as
long as things have been like this, guts me. When Gersh gnaws
off a bloody nail whole, or beats the shit out of his shadow and
raws his knuckles in the bargain.

"He—what'd you?" the Wombat asks.

Please, I says as I put him down on his feet, he won't hurt you
if you—he might hurt you but please know he doesn't mean it,
he's your cousin, just like me. Gersh swings his fists through the
rivers of moth, in a kinda dance you might call it.

"He got bigger," the Wombat says, coming the rest of the way
down the stairs. "How did all these bastards get in?"

"Stop," I says.

"Aht-dut-dut-dut-dut," the Wombat says, pushing me away. He walks past me, into the moths. "This tickles."

His expression turns.

"Hey!" he yells. I follow his accusing finger, pointing through the window onto the backyard, and see someone watching us. As soon as I realize it's the tiny pharmacist, he's gone.

And then so is the Wombat.

I turn back to Gersh, who's biting his lip as he ties to peel a pressed moth carcass off the floor. Hate to leave him, but can things really get worse if I do?

Dashing upstairs and through the living room, I hear Aunt Margot demanding to know what's happening in the basement and why the Wombat threw himself outside in such a hurry. I burst through the front door and spot him shoving the pharmacist into lawn ornaments two houses down. He waits for him to turn over, shouts something not really English but certainly threatening. I haul my bruised ass over, get tangled up with a plastic flamingo.

"Those are my *cousins* you're peeping on, freak," the Wombat is saying as I get to them.

It's okay, I says, kicking the flamingo off. A moth tumbles out of my pant leg in the process.

"It isn't," the Wombat says. "That's my *family*. You ever been head-butted in the solar plexus?"

"Please!" the pharmacist squeaks.

"You did something to Gersh," I says, "the needles, you could've had me injecting him with something new every day."

"Wasn't my idea," the pharmacist goes.

"Then whose was it, friend?" asks the Wombat.

The pharmacist tries to bolt, but wouldn't you know, the Wombat has a stubby little gun and sticks him with the barrel.

"Wom," I says, "you got a fucking gun?"

"Cool, huh?" he says, grinning. "I got this special custom finish on the handle—see how it's that mahogany flavor."

"Uh," I says, "I think he's getting away."

"One sec," says the Wombat, giving chase. Pharmacist goes down not far off with a tackle, the pair getting soaked by automatic sprinklers.

"It has to do with that ring," I says when I catch up again, "I know it."

The Wombat says, "Does it have to do with the ring?"

"What ring?" says the wet pharmacist.

"What ring?" says the wet Wombat, to me.

*

The three of us tear through downtown in the Volvo, me driving, the pharmacist (Reginald, he says) in the front passenger seat, the Wombat behind him, poking his head with the revolver every time I need directions. Directions that take us right to his pharmacy.

"Well, Reginald," I go, "you could have just said."

"Ever gotten really high off cough syrup?" the Wombat asks him. "Cause that's so nuts."

"You know," I says, "they sell better stuff than that now."

"Don't tell me what to like."

Reginald unlocks the door and leads us through a dark aisle (the Wombat: "I can't see where the cough syrup is."), opening a second door at the back. Candles light up a spiral staircase leading down to the basement.

"Kinky," the Wombat says.

"Gentlemen," says Reginald. "This is not some den of iniquity."

"Who asked you?" I says.

"Yeah," says the Wombat. Then he pistol-whips Reginald.

"Jesus," I says over Reginald, who rolls back and forth in strings of blood. The Wombat's already clomping down the spiral staircase, muttering threats. I follow. It winds on for way too long, makes me queasy. Along the walls are paintings of people with organs glowing through their skin, pinned-up butterflies, photos of scales with I guess meat on them. There's a drawing of a cut-off head with a clock face staring out of the mouth.

At the bottom is a great green room with a big fire and drinks set out and three red leather chairs like we had in the old house, plus a man in seersucker for each chair. One really old, and a pair of middle-aged twins. They all wear the fat logo rings, which are creepier on them than Reginald.

"Some nice threads, boys," says the Wombat.

"Mark By Mark Twain," says one twin, sipping brandy.

"You could say we're big fans of the spring line," says the second, standing near this picture of an old-timey boat in a storm, tugging at the moustache his brother is missing.

"That's what we say, anyway," says the old one, who ashes a cigar over the fire.

"Fine, just fine," says the Wombat, drinking right from their fancy glass thing of brandy, wiping his mouth on a sleeve and plopping onto a sofa. It's like he owns the place. Over the fireplace a giant gold Φ is screwed into the wall.

"We assume Horace arranged adequate transport?" asks Brandy.

"He's the help you can't get these days," Moustache tells us.

"Uh, yeah," I says, "Horace."

"Haven't met before, have we?" says Cigar, standing up and flipping a switch next to the fire. A whirring starts somewhere above.

"I look like someone famous," says the Wombat.

"I meant you," Cigar says to me. "Hired you for a different extraction, I thought."

"One of those faces," I says.

A half-dozen screens start to scroll down from slots in the ceiling.

"Primetime," the Wombat goes. The three of them chuckle.

"We might've waited decades for one like this," says Brandy. "An especially poetic fit, considering his origins."

"Has to be tonight," says Cigar. "The mechanics are up to

you." He takes a long drag, smiling as he blows it out over bottom teeth. "Family won't be any trouble."

"Families never are," says the Wombat, taking the brandy again.

The screens snap to life. The first shows Aunt Margot peering out the front

window, all nerves; the second looks like the bathroom radiator's POV, and then comes everything else in the house. My blood gets thick. But what grips like every hand in the world at once is Gersh, or what little I can see of him through the moth-cloud, looking around for someone. For me. Cigar taps the screen with his cigar.

Taps Gersh.

"Incredible pheromone we gave him," says Moustache. "Holding up, isn't he."

"That'll change," says Brandy.

Meaning, it gets worse?

The Wombat's squinting at the screens over his glasses, and I'm like, God, keep him blind a bit longer. And me too, while we're at it, because now I'm seeing what look like human leg bones lining the mantle, and plungers of needles sticking out of Mark By Mark Twain pockets. I'm seeing this … business cult sawing Gersh's head off and stuffing a clock in his mouth for kicks.

I'm seeing Gersh on TV, wailing without sound.

"Questions," says Cigar.

"Francis?" says the Wombat. "Isn't that our house?"

They look at the screens, then back at me, putting the unpleasantness together.

There's one screen all the way to the side that doesn't show our home but a clearing in a forest in daytime, a stump squatting in the middle as an altar of sorts, and Φ is carved in the bark of every tree. Like a ring of pinned-up white moths.

It's when Cigar reaches for a needle that I give up talking this one through.

*

Sprinting up the stairs, we both trip over Reginald.

"What now?" the Wombat asks when we get in the car. "MexiLickin'Surf Hog is still open."

"Wombat," I says, "I don't know how you made it this far in life."

I rip the Volvo out of the pharmacy lot and point it home, praying we beat them there. A white limo pulls into the rearview. I thread a maze of crummy strip malls and do donuts in shuttered gas stations to switch directions. I go down alleys too narrow for either car, but they follow, sparks and squeals all running together.

"I'm tired of this," says the Wombat.

If ever somebody didn't get it, I think, here he is.

"Could be wrong here, Francis, but don't cops handle stuff along these lines?"

Yes, I think, the cops. But Gersh.

"You have your gun," I says.

"Here somewhere," the Wombat says, rooting around in the back. A shot goes off, blowing my right eardrum.

"Holy Fisting Jehosophat!" I shout, trying to hear myself.

"I'm okay," the Wombat shouts, strapping himself back into his seat and wagging the smoky gun in my face. "I'm the real fucking deal."

There's a sharp suck from outside, something that shatters the back windshield, exploding through his mouth and splattering the dash pink.

"Wom," I says.

The crash is something dry and airy, like our bodies floated into an already wrecked car. My face is slick, stinging. I see red splotches on a telephone pole. They keep on shrinking but won't disappear. A body slumped forward against its seatbelt, dripping.

Wom, I think, *which cruel uncle started everyone calling you that? Why were you even here? Why happy to be whatever you were?*

I picture him teasing Aunt Margot and getting me to smile. I see the old house. I remember Gersh gasping with joy when we get to the page of *Goodnight Moon* with the red balloon, and do you blame me for finding a hope there that everyone told me was gone forever?

"Goodnight nobody," I realize, is the furthest he and I ever got.

Cigar opens my door and I'm looking down the barrel of a fancy old shotgun I could swear was Pop's. The one he used to off himself when he realized Gersh was stuck the way he was. Pretty autumn weekends for hunting, he'd leave the house with it 'cross his heart, saying This Is A Day The Lord Has Made.

Overkill, really. They'll get their way anyhow. They could just keep driving, and I'd stay here bleeding the rest of my blood. They could scare the bejesus out of the remaining freak at my house, or put holes in her. They could probably just ask. Do I think he'll be hard to take? With me not there?

You don't need to hurt him, I'm trying to say. That's all I ask. But deep down I imagine that Gersh won't need their mercy. That today's the day he's finally learned, after so many demonstrations, how to undo the bowline knot that's keeping him there.

CAL /// LUNAR ORBIT

Emma: barely coherent. What you'd expect. Extra bitter about sharing her death with me, I gather. Laying blame at the only available feet.

Try any control. Nothing. You'll notice a bottomless click—the gutted verb of sterile circuits. Finger sliding off the gathered moisture of its surface. Made me realize: people don't use the Door Open button in elevators. They stick out their arms. Which confirms the fact that buttons are relatively new and haven't quite earned our trust.

I toured a submarine in port on a school field trip. They wouldn't shut up about not touching anything. So I twisted all the knobs, hit any switch within reach. Saved the fat red doomsday button for last. No torpedoes were fired. The sub didn't launch or sink. I didn't get in trouble, either—a parent chaperone walked right up behind me as I yanked a lever above a row of frozen gauges.

"Interesting, hm?" being all he said before moving on to the next compartment.

You'd like to make the game evolve. Poke the universe and see it bristle. When you can't even screw things up, and the world ceases to balance your wrongs? Or: could be the world's only just caught up, its doomsday button slow to respond.

Adrift, letting things divide how they may. Waiting. I would smash everything in sight, leave myself sore and bloodied. I would strangle Emma, and she might not fight. I would lie back and watch it all fold in. We, me, her, this clunking killer time capsule, are done. So why this prolonged farewell to the senses?

Emma is praying at this point. Of course. Someone who prays only in desperation, only for deliverance. The agnostic-in-peril's tradition: appeal to God for one last chance. I don't bother. I never asked questions. If I end up standing opposite some divine light, I'll have a lone curiosity to express: why do good things happen to the worst people?

"Will you please, please say something, please? Please. Please? Please."

Emma won't quit. She tries to squeeze a note of calm from the jumping throat, but it catches right there. It squirms. Imperfections uncurl, webbing her face. Brilliant within the gritty empirics of math, but in a way enfeebled by her skill, like she saw through overpowering glasses. I count each full pore in her colorless skin, the knotted strands in unwashed hair.

She's sincerely begging. We are darkside, and I cave.

"If it makes you happy," I say.

She turns away, and a few seconds later I notice the twitch in her shoulders. She does a decent job of disguising each sob. I unwrap and start on some freeze-dried ice cream. Emma hears the crinkling, the powdery crunch, and faces me again.

"Are you eating the last ice cream?"

"Looks that way." I lick some from the corner of my mouth.

"I was saving that," she manages.

"For what? The afterlife?"

A response gurgles in her chest, and one rogue tear flits down her cheek.

"Don't do that," she says.

"Ooooo," I say spookily.

"I was saving it, and you ate the rest, so it only seems fair I would get the last."

"Is this any way to spend your last hours?" I ask, offering the half-eaten pack.

She looks away again, out the window. We hurtle through the system for an hour or three.

"I feel sorry for you, Cal," she says at last.

"Me too."

"Being incapable of commiseration."

"Take it. Kill yourself. We're all waiting."

"You don't know what it's like."

"For once, I agree."

She cries again; soft whimpers leak through the shield of her hands. Uneasy with the spectacle, I stare down into my lap, exhausted.

Her sniffles and tiny moans lull me into my first sleep in two days with their strange polyrhythm and muzzled pleas. Antipathy and regret charge my dreams with weird meanings, but I won't recall them. The unrehearsed spasm when weightless sleep drops in. Who knew it'd be the same up here?

*

Head snaps up, pulling my face from a pool of images whose impressions are lost like embers gone dark. Truth is, I've never been able to remember my dreams, not one. When I go hunting for them in the morning, there looms instead a smudge of canceled brainwaves.

We are coming out of the dark, and the curtain of blue is dawning inside.

Emma is asleep.

She's new. The blue plays on her face, reflected in parts and absorbed by luxurious darkness in others, nebula of hair turning like a drugged octopus. Her lids are closed in the easy way that suggests easy sleep. Lips slightly parted. Curved fingers of one hand spooning together in a rainbow.

"Emma," I whisper, wanting not to wake her. The weight of the word coasts from me to her and pushes her head to the right, slumping it shyly into her shoulder.

I turn away, ashamed.

Look again.

And with no time between the second glance and next instant, no interval for actual movement, we meet. Free-floating in this blue, she's a water nymph. Any movement, any breath, is locked in her suit. She's motionless. Eyes wet. Crying only moments ago.

We kiss, and I receive the lingering warmth of kissing someone whose tears are fresh, remnants of hot slick anxiety, a subtle saltiness of lips. Her mouth is faultless on mine, shaping to it. I pull back, dizzy, eyes refocused. Emma doesn't move.

Her other hand has been open the whole time, but I notice for the first time again, with the clarity of film. Fingers unfolding endlessly as she slips from consciousness. A drained and slack-petaled flower, its plastic bubble core coming loose in space.

The bloom droops and stiffens. The bubble is empty. Emma is dead.

Or, life and death no longer a binary, she has started across the spectrum.

I rip a pocket open and find my own suicide dose. The case is tough to open—gives you time to reconsider. I pull the pill's plastic halves apart, escaped white dust like grains of purity that fade into the ship's darkest corners.

"I'm glad," I finally say.

I kiss her again.

And in that moment I see my kiss spun toward its base extreme: one body working, the other simply there. The dry penetration, a quiet contraction of only one set of muscles. Movement of only two eyes. Her body not done shutting down, cells flickering out in domino chains, touching earthly velocities of the condemned. The gatekeeper cell that, when done expiring, released her fully. Finally.

I picture her dead ribs under the suit. She's not a person. She's a skeleton with skin. Her body wrongly acquiescent. Lips dead blue. I picture it against my will, my mouth pressing hers into what I want, a second of warmth in a world of chills. Everything pliant, yielding. Elasticity gone. No resistance left to spur. And in the coldest caves of my mind, I've done it.

I kissed her, and she was dead.

Hard to say if I feel more alone.

It's a decaying orbit we're in.

The moon will catch up.

A matter of time.

AIDAN /// IVYLAND, NEW JERSEY /// LAST WINTER

Normally you'd spot Henri from afar, his oversized aviators glinting like an SOS in the distance, but the dark dulls their polarized lenses as he surveys the stage—well, a vague section of sticky floor that sags less than the rest. Sipwell's never did strike me as a performance space, even before it took down the sign outside and went speakeasy.

Once noticed, of course, Henri sticks out like a gangrenous thumb, stumbling and panicked against a wall of weak neon script advertising the Adderades you probably can't even buy here, trying to look everywhere at once. He struggles to move a keyboard held together with duct tape, leaning it against a wall.

"There he is!" Phoebe says long after I've spied him, as he pushes through the grizzled regulars and recognizable IC seniors and even some professors. She slips a finger into one of my belt loops and tugs me an atom's length closer. A happiness echoes somewhere behind my Adam's apple, contained. I press two fingers on the small of her back; she smiles and downs the last of a crude sex-on-the-beach equivalent.

"How does one pluralize that drink?" I ask, my temples humming.

"Sex on lots of different beaches," she says, grabbing the bartender's attention as Henri appears behind her.

"Audience's a little restless," he notes, more wired on stage fright now that he's dispensed with setup. Someone starts counting into the mic.

"Screw them, we're the ones who count," Phoebe says.

"Glad you could tear yourself away from scholarly pursuits," Henri fake-sneers at me. I laugh. Phoebe kneads one set of knuckles with the other. We both do.

Peals of drunk laughter ricochet through the dinginess, overwhelming the self-introduction of a solo acoustic act. An especially wasted woman, oblivious to the amateur hour, pumps some quarters into the jukebox and puts "The Devil Went Down To Georgia" in direct conflict with Acoustic Boy's strums and wailing woe, and Jesus but you have to admire this kid for doubling down, yowling a whole lot louder, funneling newly minted anguish into his song. Jukebox Lady twists and bops next to the machine, swigging pills from a fat Belltruvin bottle, hip-checking anyone who tries to dance with her or cue up a new song.

"You better be good," Phoebe says. "But I know you will," she adds, terrifying and assuring Henri in one breath.

"Thanks."

"Why are you wearing those stupid things," I say. "*I* can barely see."

"I'm worried Grady won't find me otherwise—he has this thing with facial recognition."

"Who?" I ask. Henri starts to tell me, but I'm busy patting my jeans, trying to divine from the thickness of my wallet whether I or Phoebe paid for the mystery gin and tonic in hand.

" … and he can't like it there, I think he'd be happier with a little more independence," I hear Henri saying. "Not that his family would agree, but you gotta worry about what'll happen to him when his prepaid stint is up." Whatever this is an answer to, I regret asking.

Acoustic Boy is met by a mounting blizzard of boos for his music, followed by cheers at his exit. A sweaty squiggle of a guy with a fifty-dollar electric guitar wanders on, mumbles into the mic with overwrought apathy. He twangs a chord incorrectly and warbles over it:

> *I remember the gang-rape well …*
> *I remember the gang-rape … WEH-hell …*

Sometimes I have a hard time believing Sipwell's, supplier of felonious booze or not, is still in business. Over in one corner sit some crew-cuts from high school, in their matching Endless-sponsored cop uniforms, fittingly enough, graveyard of Belltruvin bottles standing within their circle of mugs. One of them, Ed from the looks of it, spills beer on a guy at the next table, who yells himself hoarse about it till Jack pulls him creepily close and whispers in his ear.

"This guy isn't serious." Phoebe asks. "I mean, am I really seeing this?"

"I think he's good," Henri says. "These songs come from a real place—he's fearless."

"O, that is such bullshit," Phoebe informs him.

"Cheers, everyone," I announce, and the three of us clink glasses. Once in a great while, the worries that drag you down from minute to minute shrivel and fall away. This ceasefire between pain and joy holds a special place, I tipsily decide, not as the happiest but most *satisfying* time I can remember, pleasures obvious and small and easy to come by, all wounds temporarily sealed.

Clouds of unreal colors widen and contract as Sipwell's itself gets fast-forwarded, conversations ebbing and exploding and lapsing into silence on eerie schedules, bathroom breaks increasingly common, especially for Henri, who excuses himself for marathon sessions. Six drinks deep, I miss the bowl completely but correct myself, reliving an intense memory of spewing cocktails in the stalls of a condemned but still-operational London pub the semester previous, or maybe in Paris, a binge winding through three of a few thousand soulless discothèques where pills even the FDA would hem and haw over appeared in glass candy bowls carried by indifferent waitresses.

Following the gang-rape one-off: an atrocious punk band, an equally atrocious pop-punk band, a medievally dressed woman whose poetry reading comes to a merciful halt when a beer bottle sails over her shoulder and explodes against the brick wall behind her and a pair of Belltruvin-addled slobs, who demonstrate a host of intolerable sounds on turntables and bongos.

"There he is," Phoebe suddenly shushes me, if I was even talking.

Onstage, Henri (also a little buzzed, the trained eye confirms) fumbles a bit erecting his synthesizer stand. He heaves his trusted Korg atop the thing, which emphatically collapses, drawing spattered applause.

"Sorry, sorry," he pants into the mic. I finish a drink.

"You keep that up, you'll wake up in a SurfHog parking lot," Phoebe says.

"That's the plan. Slumber party?" She's putting her palm to mine. My fingers curl over the tips of hers.

"Ahem," starts Henri. "Thanks for coming."

He searches the crowd. Even with expression-killing aviators on there is an aura of sheer hysteria building itself up around him, pressure mounting as our night lurches into its logical blackout. Crowd's thinned out. People have quieted down, moved from the boisterous groups into poker-faced or sleepy or fiercely sexual pairs that speak only in body language. Henri taps the mic, already knows it's on. Phoebe's hand tracing my spine up and down stirs the thought: *I wish he'd get this over with.*

He glances in my direction and introduces himself as "Caligula's Horse." The synth makes a tiny pop when he plugs into the amp, and one keystroke brings a drone to life. He adds floating arpeggios. Major chords, nonetheless icy and sad. It's a perfect song until Henri sings, in the defeated voice of a foghorn:

Your twisted thoughts
Made an interloper
Kill himself

The more there are
The louder you shout
To try and drown them out

Your sleeping face
Stillborn
At once unafraid

You lying there
It's your little spine
It fits into mine

I will not run
Unless you want me to
I will not stay-ay-ay-ay
Unless you tell me not to

[Instrumental break, with noodling organ on top of bent metal notes, electric plinks riding precisely up and down the octaves. "Holy shit," Phoebe whispers, not impressed or sarcastic, only surprised. I'd heard Henri's melodic figures gestating in the house over the month we've been roommates, but never foresaw a cohesion like this. I'm not aware of the bar, nor an intoxication, nor the insults people surely must have hurled at Henri, who keys into the measured rhythm of my blinking.]

And when we try to warn the others
They will not part from their mothers
And so we shuffle away
Just you and me again

It's such a stupid metaphor
That I'm passed out on the floor
In my dreams, I sadly stare
I'm just too happy to care

Those little lies
Piling up
Over the years

And now you're shy
Well it's too late for that
It's far too late for that

If you're walking down the aisle
Arm in arm and smile to smile

I will not run
Unless you want me to
I will not stay-ay-ay-ay
Unless you tell me not to

And when the fire starts to grow
Ships will sleep and cease to glow
And so we shuffle away
Just you and me again

Nobody said it would be fair
This never-ending ni-i-ghtmare
In my dreams I sadly stare
I'm just too happy to care

Curtain of electronic burbles withdrawing, the room again surges with grime and beer stink.

"That was … new," Phoebe says. "What was it about?"

"He's probably not sure himself," I mumble.

Around the stage, a few patrons are taking the extra trouble to get up in Henri's face so he can be absolutely sure to appreciate how much they resent his being alive. Henri, docile to the point of duckling-hood, clops softly about, gathering up equipment. I push my already muted applause down to a golf clap, fearing mob-exacted punishment.

One heckler jumps up and down, stretches a pale twitching hand out to Henri. He sports a schizoid haircut and filthy pajama pants. Curiously, Henri doesn't brush away this dude's hand but shakes it, pumping hard.

"Who's that?" Phoebe wonders aloud.

"It must be …" I snap my fingers, pretending to search for a name, as Phoebe gazes stage-ward through the bottom of a whiskey rocks. Henri makes a path to the bar, rubbing his eyes, and orders the same.

"Need a stiff drink, do you?" I grin.

"We thought you were great," Phoebe tells him.

"And I guess we kind of still do," I say, poking Henri in his shoulder and getting an oddly painful shock. Pulling back my finger, a second, smaller charge leaps the gap from him to me, actually visible as a bright blue spark. "Did you see that?"

"See what?" Phoebe asks. Henri chuckles and flashes his worsening teeth.

"He shocked me."

"So?"

"Was a *serious* shock. What'd you do, roll around on a carpet?" Henri is entering one of his childhood giggling fits, but he's phony about it. I laugh anyway, maybe grateful.

"I forgot to tell you," Phoebe gushes without warning, sweeping a bowl of nuts off the bar with her arm. "I got a job! It's at this catering place that does weddings—"

"You told me," Henri stops her, giggling.

"Didn't think I did."

"Fieldcrest Manor, right?"

Our silence is broken by the weirdo that Henri shook hands

with, who pops his head into our circle. It's when Phoebe moves to allow him entry that I see the too-big hands, the major neck that comes with boosted testosterone.

"Henri!" he crows. "You were the best of all."

"No," Henri says, releasing him after a moment's embrace, "*You*. My number one fan! Grady, I want you to meet my friends, Aidan and Phoebe. Want to say hi?"

"Hi!" Grady bleats.

"Grady lives over at the Harvey House," Henri continues, and, unhappy as it makes me, the entirety of my reaction is reduced to: *a Hallaxor kid?*

"How do you like it over there?" Phoebe says, taking it in stride. He grins back. Phoebe tries again: "How do you like Harvey—"

"Harvey House is the tops," Grady tells us. "We can have nicely helpers anytime."

"Good, good!"

"Phoebe … outside for a cigarette?" I ask.

"They let you smoke in here."

But I've already grabbed her elbow much too hard, leading her through packs of old men who nod like puppets as we pass. I glance back. Grady's hugging Henri like he forgot they already hugged.

"Ow, Aidan, let go," Phoebe protests. "Stop."

Outside is warmer than January's ever been in this town, and neither of us actually has cigarettes.

"Since when do you smoke?" Phoebe remembers to ask.

"Listen, what the fuck was that—Henri's hanging around with Hallaxor kids?"

"This what you brought me out for?"

"Partly."

"Can't you be *nice*?" she says, setting needles of high school memories scrabbling along the underside my skull. "I think it's sweet. You jealous of someone?" She sways, eyes closed.

"Okay. Ha, ha, you caught me. Jealous of all that brain damage."

"Come on. You say it like he's a criminal."

"I know, okay, but here's what I'm saying: le dee da, Henri has a mentally not-good friend who yes, I'm sorry, was a victim of tragic medical fuckups. But this guy, it's going to be my house he barges into when he gets some . . . desire to see Henri, which I'm guessing will be rather frequent? You know how they get, he'll obsess with him and shit, and . . . why am I even explaining this? You know it'll be an issue. I mean, how would you like—"

"First of all, it's not your house. It's Henri's. And second of all . . . second is that you're being an asshole. You know who you remind me of?"

"No."

"I don't know what I expected." She starts stamping her foot, then looks at the bottom of her shoe. Henri's face appears in the stained-glass window of Sipwell's door as he opens it.

"Sorry, just on our way back," I have the wits to mention.

"That's okay," Henri chimes, "I'm leaving, taking Grady home. What'd you think of him? I get the feeling he's been really underestimated at Harvey House. His condition actually seems pretty mild. Maybe I can get him a job through Second Chance or something."

"I think you have to have had a job and lost it," I say.

"Not as affected as they—definitely not violent or aggressive," Henri says. "Which is why he's allowed out like this. Not as good with language . . . I don't know."

"You gonna have time to be his friend?" I want to know.

"Someone should give it a shot," Henri says.

"He's jealous that you have a pet Hallaxor kid," Phoebe says. Her body sinks, molds itself to the right angle between the brick wall and sidewalk. Henri sees my expression.

"O, Aidan," he jeers, putting the dumb sunglasses back on, "nobody could replace you." And with that he reaches out for a fraternal shoulder grab, only to shock me badly again, the static going right through my shirt.

"*Dammit!*" I snarl, the drinks fueling it now. "You eat a car battery for dinner?"

"I'm sorry," Henri says. "I can't help . . ."

"Then see a doctor." When I look back to Phoebe, she's clutching herself at the elbows, trembling slightly.

"I did."

"Well?"

"Just whatever, okay?"

"You're the worst."

Phoebe gurgles to life, pointing at the space between me and Henri. "You. You think you're not . . . you're no better," she drawls, and the venom in this near-sentence drips quietly for a while longer.

"Are you done?"

"Brothers. I might've known," she groans, rising, and vanishes around the corner before I can even appreciate that's she's mobile. We consider her departure until my curiosity starts nagging me.

"What did the doctor say?"

"Forget it."

"You get me like this, make me meet your retard friend . . . fuck." The eloquence has nowhere to go but up, but it's been plateaued around nil for some time. "You act like something's wrong with you, and then you clam up because you know it's bullshit."

"I don't. I don't deserve it," Henri insists, face shaking. "I don't have to tell you."

"What happened? I thought we were having fun tonight." I'm par for some hungover regret. "Let's find Phoebe; I'll apologize?"

Grady stumbles out of the bar as though shoved and collides with Henri, who stabilizes him.

"Hi again, you," I try, waving. But Grady's already forgotten my face. Henri pushes me aside, leading him into the street by his shoulder. This early in the morning, no cars are out, leaving the pair free to meander down the middle of the road, passing under a traffic light that sports its cheap red. A clown nose. When they're directly under the light, it flickers twice and is hushed into blackness, a candle gently snuffed in a breeze. Forgetting that Phoebe's already gone, I ask her if she saw it too.

The dead stoplight reawakens as a lustrous green after a dozen seconds of throat-tightening outage, a lonely electric lime nailed onto nothing, its black case blending seamlessly into a bruise that hoods the sleeping world.

Henri and Grady have moved on. They walk, weaving back and forth in the road to avoid roadkill and potholes, through another four intersections. I watch. Until they fade from sight, I let the flawed film unreel. Each intersection, Henri—and Henri alone, I could swear—kills off a red light that returns as a green, creating a plaintive rhythm of red, flicker, black … green … red, flicker, black … green … that aches more with every repetition. Moonlight follows that same path, still touching them when I wipe my eyes and squint, wrapping their bodies like another skin when they finally meet the ink-blotted distance, Henri turning around, one arm still across Grady's back, and examining the horizon to see if I'm there.

*

Grady does come over in the future, but to his credit, I was wrong. He only ever broke one thing, and that was Henri's old pogo stick—who knows how it'd held out so long in the first place. The dusty artifact's spring-loaded plunger creaked with rust when Grady took it out to the driveway, and one of the footholds soon snapped clean off.

Grady mentions later on, or I'm given to understand, anyway, that he had a friend named Pogo as a kid. Henri mouths to me: *imaginary.* He has a new ferret he brings over from time to time, and Henri suggests names for it. They debate passionately, stopping to ask my opinion on "Hal." They ride bikes together in a spring-like February, Henri on his old blue piece of junk, Grady on mine. They make vague plans for a road trip, something neither of their families had ever attempted.

One day it all glides to an end. Henri buys Grady his own bike with a basket, a new helmet, goes with him on a test-run, says goodnight, and never invites him over again.

"Just starting to like him," I mention one frosted morning in early April before heading out to campus, noticing one of those caterpillars that were everywhere the year before. It's dragging itself up and out of the kitchen sink drain. Henri, trying to destroy every functional brain cell by playing online poker nonstop (and nonetheless doing rather well), lets his head drop back over the top of his chair.

"It . . . we couldn't be friends anymore."

"Because?"

"He had this—I hate to say it, but it was too much to handle." I can see Henri's eyes for once, marbles with coal at the center.

"Those sunglasses fell by the wayside fast."

"What, the aviators."

"Yeah."

"They didn't work."

I turn from the door and stare at Henri, who smiles tiredly as it closes, and start laughing for real once I'm alone in a freak swirl of weightless snow outside.

Every third bar, Lev finds a foreigner. This time it's an Australian in a horned Viking hat and what looks to be real, polished chain mail.

"*Was* with a friend. Kiwi bloke, my drummer. Too pissed to see."

"Why was he angry?"

"*Pissed*, mate. Legless."

The bartender paces over to us from the register, where his only other customer is staring into a mug. We are three quarter-lengths of the bar removed from this despondent, oddly familiar man. As the bartender begins to speak, he puts his hands flat on the wood, thumbs stuck out at right angles, six inches of space between. He's done this eight times now, and in every other instance he licks his lips before asking if we want another. We do. The Australian wants two, which'll have to be factored in. Lev is squeezing him for data while I watch the self-erasing Coriolis swirls in grease-prints made by the bartender's stubby fingers. Every time the minute hand of the ornate cuckoo clock in the corner hits a multiple of twenty, Lev slips me another P to take the wooze out of the gas, help the patterns come back. Words waft by.

"What do people down under think of America?"

"Fat, guns. Stupid." The guy is a parody of hammered. "Bossy?"

"I mean the country."

"Is it true that at MaxiLickin'SurfHogs here," (he actually says *Maxi*) "you can get a kilo of chips? And a schooner of cola."

"Sure," I pipe up, 15% more clever when drunk. "But that's a medium."

"Why don't we shut up," Lev suggests.

Over the rows of liquor bottles, there's a plaque with an engraving of a suspension bridge next to a crying lady in a tollbooth and the assurance: *Big Win — We'll Never Forget*. Next to that is a picture of two grayed guys smiling alongside statues of a horse's head and a castle. GREETINGS FROM THE WORLD'S 2ND LARGEST CHESS SET! is the frame's leering gold inscription. The whole room, really, is humming colors that warble giddily, teetering on some brink. Lev ignores it. A green light above the billiards table drones an exact minor third, a musical concept I learned from reading the Johnston kid's unused music theory books, but never quite heard in the wild till now.

Down in Kentucky we saw an old redneck and a black boy hustle seventeen consecutive games of nine-ball, taking in an average of fifty bucks per game, which they split sixty-forty, as the boy had to do all the work of goading the mark and setting up the diamond rack freehand while the man got to gulp bourbon in a corner and act drunker than he was. The boy always sank his last ball in a corner, swaggering with charm the way no white guy can; the old guy sucked the last of a crumpled cigarette before carelessly banking his into a side pocket. Lev and I offered VV in return for their winnings. The elder belched a belch of acid smoke and curdled dairy. He croaked a afterthought-ish sound.

"What'd he say?" Lev asked.

The boy translated: "Says he has a bridge to sell y'all."

The old grifter wheezed and clutched at himself.

*

Leviticus is trying to convince the Australian to come to an actual MexiLickin'SurfHog with us, but the dude saunters off to take a leak mid-proposition. "I know this man," I say, "or his doppelgänger." "I don't," Lev insists, biting bloody fingernails, "know anyone like this guy." Probably the angles of his skull, I theorize, similar mouth-width to chin-width ratio as someone back home. I'm thinking football team—maybe Ryan Danke? That's the P talking, Lev says, it's the Viking getup and your Freudian issues with Lenny's shitty mini-golf place, is all. He twists his head in every direction, saying we'll help him to the truck, talk him into a nose job. I'm like, tell me the difference between that and kidnapping-slash-violent assault, then maybe, *maybe* I'll consider. Lev's ass should be in jail already, but I'm staying lily-white innocent as hell. Just on call while he works. Handling the tools. I wash them, wipe them clean, but that's the extent.

The Australian emerges, fly horribly agape, water matting his Prince Valiant bangs. With notable difficulty he mounts a stool.

"So ... American hamburgers?" Lev beams. "Sexy teenaged wage slaves? Might like you better with a shapelier nose."

"Can't. Kiwi'll miss me: prolly off for a bat." The hulking fake Norseman, having just settled onto his seat, abruptly stands, snatching his unfinished drink off a coaster that might be floating a millimeter above the bar. "Bloody ... thing is. Awaiting. Musn't disappoint." The Viking helmet slides askew, covering his right eye at a forty-five degree angle and greatly startling its wearer. I snarf my drink, beer-snot bubbling out of my nose. People shoot me their looks.

"Wait," Lev begs. His nostrils flare, blood draining from them. That happens when he's anxious. The Australian trips on his way out but recovers, spilling zero liquid.

"Off to throw another shrimp on the barbie?" I say, starting to bark the laugh that Lev says is an excellent argument for euthanasia. The sad other guy at the end of the bar raises one eyebrow and sips an eighth of his glass.

"Not now," Lev hisses.

"Aussie, Aussie, Aussie! Oi, Oi, Oi!" I scream, knocking an empty mug off the counter with a gesture I can't quite recreate, shrieking when it explodes on the floor. The Aussie replies, Oi!, raising his mug in a doomed toast, thinking he's at home instead of piss-freezing Oxbone, Michigan, where barren fields outnumber souls.

"Watch it, you two," the bartender scowls, cheeks twitching. You can *tell* that he beats his children, and I'm about to say as much when it occurs to me that this glittery minefield of glass on the floor is doubtless a replication of the southern hemisphere's stars. I've never been below the equator. But I like to think, even without knowledge of constellations, that I'd recognize a different sky when it pulled together overhead.

"I'm an anesthesiologist, you fucking peon!" Lev's screaming at the bartender, and you can hear in his raspier voice that he hasn't abused our anesthetic in far too long. "I take the pain away!"

"Adieu!" the Australian calls, opening the door to expose snow raking sideways across the dark. He wobbles. The snowflakes in their cone of streetlight leave white wavering trails, sperm striving toward an asphalt egg. Every flake: exactly the same.

"Son!" the bartender yells. "You can't take that drink outside!"

"Awright, mate. I'm lucky." He surveys the room. "Dead set lucky," he assures us all, and with the merriest "Cheers!" I've heard since we last ran into a drunk Australian, he turns and is swallowed by the blizzard.

Our drinker at the end of the bar finally speaks, revealing four fillings, one for each quadrant of mouth:

"Europeans," he mutters.

*

We drive in blankets of snow, and I'm scared, but I'd be more scared if I had to drive, so I'm glad Lev doesn't let me. First he bitches me out for not recording our conversation with the Australian in the notebook. "Notebook," I go. "Don't even know where that shit *is*."

That makes him real mad.

It snows in reverse, the flakes flying from the hood up the windshield as we blow through pearly matrices, pink fringes of northern lights the blizzard's gauzy backdrop. Storm walls bulging and dopamine-flavored. I ask Lev does he see what I see. He says if you mean Inuit spirits playing football with a walrus skull in the sky, then yeah. I open the glove compartment, reaching for the shaving kit bag Velcroed to the inside. Lev wants to know if I remember what we're doing. The new mission he harps about. I know. "But do I *remember*," he asks, "do I get it done."

"Of course I do. I'm very goal-oriented."

"Then why do you keep fucking with me?" Lev asks. "Stop spazzing like Professor Delirium Tremens. Stop provoking people. We need them." His lighter snicks and torches a 100, of which there are two hundred twenty-seven butts on the floor, accumulated since the high school fundraiser car wash and Tom's daughter, the cheerleader in the red bikini. He's angrier since quitting the gas and overdoing the P. Sometimes his chest pops out so hard I reach for a tank, but he says the worst is over.

"We're helping," I say.

"Poor can't afford VV without us."

"And they need it."

"Illegal not to need it. But we've got other tasks to consider."

Seven more butts arranged in a flower on the dash. I did that. Lev talks while I suck gas: You do realize, he says, even you must realize, that with these nootropics in us we need only one pure specimen, one hick or greasy diner or ghost town whose pattern will unlock it all and make the grand plan manifest. One will do it, will decrypt everything about this place, because America defines itself recursively and every tiny part implicates the whole, okay? A grain of sand, the fractal truth ... but I stop listening, because I don't need to hear Euclid invoked in this truck again. Falsehoods sound falser with each repetition.

Patterns fading, I take two pills with the beer. Then two more, with more beer. The cigarette-butt flower is more of an amputee octopus. Lev clams up after mumbling that he doesn't need to spend his time explaining self-evident theory to someone who obviously doesn't give two perfectly spherical balls of beetle shit about it. There's the dull pitter-patter of his asymmetrical index fingers drumming on the wheel, at nine at two. It takes four tapped beats for the windshield wipers to do a full circuit, squealing intolerably on each return trip.

I choke on a breath as Lev's face shoots wide. He rolls down his window—it's colder than a caring universe would allow. A piece of paper clipped to the sun visor, bearing the forbidden quote, is ripped out into the inky void. ~~Art is the imposing of a pattern on experience, and our aesthetic enjoyment is recognition of the pattern~~, it said. We don't impose shit, Lev says. It's *there*. You only gave it a name.

He puts his head out, says take the wheel. I'm uncomfortable with this.

"Stop whimpering. This is important," he shouts over the wind, letting the wheel go entirely, leaning out his window to scan the nothing. There's no telling the road apart from the clouds, the storm, a certain death. Lev's scrubs snap and snap and snap. Double-time against the wipers. One shirtsleeve's cuff is spattered with who-knows-who's blood. Patient. Victim. His own. But we always slip the noose. People wake up a little disfigured, certainly without their wallets. But that's what you get for wanting black-market hair plugs. The main concern is that while I was first being ravished by my cheerleader in the back of our truck, Lev was sneaking around a hospital in Andronicus, Florida, a pretty major one, slipping P to any patient who didn't know enough to resist. The alibi, which he's made me repeat endlessly: Leviticus Van Vetchen, respected son of legendary surgeon Brutus Van Vetchen, was at the National Anesthesiologist Convention in Cleveland when these post-ops woke up and began obsessively counting whatever was available to count. One guy apparently yanked out his IV needle and etched a bloody web of lines between freckles. Connecting the dots.

Lev had burst into the truck, which we'd parked in a lot by an abandoned betting parlor, on what you'd think was the wrong side of the tracks if you hadn't seen the east side first. My cheerleader coated herself with some loose gauze nearby while he blathered on about when they first synthesized LSD, and how all these scientists at the CIA were just dropping it in each other's coffee, no warning whatsoever, to see what happened. I'm of the mind that you can't enjoy or appreciate that sort of thing if you don't grasp what's going on, but Lev will be Lev.

"Why is he bloody?" my cheerleader asked.

"I didn't kill anybody," Lev said, which struck us all as very funny at the time. I asked him why he'd shaved his head (answer: "One. Too. Many. Layers."), and my cheerleader said that growing up around here her mom always used a bowl to give her a mushroom cut that she hated even more than being blonde, and always in a motel or someplace she wouldn't have to pick up the clippings.

We ate handfuls of Belltruvin to that and did gas (except Lev swore then that he was done with it and just had some of everything but) and she and I happily fucked again, with Lev watching, and we all passed out in a loving dogpile. In the night we shifted and I lay with Lev, as close as we could be without touching.

I woke up to Lev driving us, my cheerleader gone.

"Got out to go to pee," Lev said.

"Go back and get her," I said.

"That was three states ago."

I thought hard about what I wanted to say.

"You fucking unhuman," was what came out.

"Stroking your head the whole time you slept," Lev said over the sound of my weeping, tossing a bottle of Belltruvin. His eyes in the rearview saw past me. "She loved you." I opened the bottle. The worst part of this man is he will defuse you.

"Object-lesson," he said.

*

The truck makes a fatal metallic clang and starts to smell funny.

"What'd you do," Lev snarls, slipping back in. "Clutch is cuntified."

"You. I didn't want to drive."

"You're right. Accountability doesn't suit you."

Pulled over, hood up, the smell is much worse. Wiggling my nose, I can feel frozen hairs crunching inside. Lev examines the car guts, eyes doing two full circular sweeps of seven seconds each. He swears and reexamines, one sweep this time.

"Impossible."

"What?"

"Clutch friction disc is toast. Truck only breaks down in states with a Latin motto."

"Minnesota's isn't Latin?"

"Does '*L'etoile du Nord*' sound fucking Latin to you?"

"A little."

"… although … O, good Jesus Horatio Christ."

The wind builds up to an ornery whine hovering in the octave just below high C, rising and falling a few quarter tones in annoying anti-melodies. Lev is opening my jacket, grabbing a bottle of P from the inside pocket, pretty much drinking from it. He shields his eyes and stands away from the car, the snow less dense now, spaced out eloquently, scoping a blank 360°.

In all this, I'm starting to think, only one person seemed to want to help—fishnetted hooker in Dallas. Redhead. Name of Rosetta. I know what America's all about, sweetie, she said, and I'll show you. I believed her and liked being called sweetie. Turned out she was talking about freezejobs, but I'm telling you, she knew, and further knew not to spill the secret to me. It was like we'd found my cheerleader again, all grown up and streetwise and tending a grudge that was damn well deserved. It's been long enough now that when someone on the road treats us like shit, I figure they owed us from a time we screwed them, a juncture we failed to mark.

Lev fixes on something, and then I see it too: a slice of air that sharpens in the sky. Snow in front makes the popped-out polygon seem a staticky movie screen, but the flakes diffuse evenly, steadily across.

"Closer than I thought," Lev says.

There are letters in the colossal, murky rectangle. The vowels are O A E E E. The consonants are W R L D S (then two half-size ones, N and D), L R G S T C H S S S T. There's one apostrophe, and the number 2 also. Lev points out something beyond it, a gazebo with a truncated pyramid on top, and starts in that direction. I follow, wading through white that wetly packs itself into my boots. Parallel streams of red and green glide horizontally past me, and I'm instantly at ease because they are opposites in the color wheel. According to Mom, Dad had the sort of colorblindness that obscures this. Lev set my color fixation out to sea at a lake in the Catskills, towed figuratively by a freed Sullivan, the pet duckling I bought in somewhere's Chinatown for four dollars, which after some market research appeared to be half the retail value and a very good deal. He says no more aesthetic pacifiers. Fine, I told him, who cares about that crap. I don't even miss Ivyland's duck pond.

The grid of red and green gives way to a bloodless one of black and white, sixty-four squares that go light, dark, light, dark. It's hard to see, but the white boxes levitate above the black ones in the ghost-stalked glow of the gazebo. Lev is not surprised by any of it, because he never is.

"Where … are the world's second largest chess *pieces,* one wonders, for the second largest set," Lev says.

"Who has the first largest?"

"Who gives a shit?" He fingers the point of his top left canine, which is not a good sign. I count eight pills from the auburn P bottle and chew them, hoping the bitterness will de-numb my face. The moon is out again, in its arbitrary stage. Lev, a knight, is walking in L-shaped spurts, more and more frustrated. He puts me in a spot.

"Am I a bishop? I like diagonals."

"You're a bishop."

"That's good."

"You're a bishop that took an oath of silence. Move there."

I do.

And still the board refuses to speak.

*

We try to neutral our truck the thirty yards over to park on the board, under the pyramid roof, so we won't have to get snow off in the morning. Lev stomps the gas with me pushing behind, snow flung into my eyes and nose, the clutch's oily smell burning hard, suffocating. The front wheels go over the lip of the road and bury themselves in a snow bank. Like this was ever going to work. No way I'm pushing anymore. Don't care what he says.

All that's left to do is sleep in the freezing tilted truck, on the so-cold-it's-slimy faux-leather front bench, split open from when Lev extracted the stuffing and analyzed its consistency till he'd been mysteriously satisfied.

The news on the radio is all made up. Just stories. There's President Fullner claiming a time of renewal, vowing a return to the moon after pausing to grieve over another denatured bridge. This one in Oregon. It rained red rain in England, because sand from the Sahara rose into the clouds. How many grains of red in a raindrop? Wish I'd seen all that color lifted, seen it crashing down around me.

I think of my cheerleader, because maybe if she's the last thing I think about, she'll make it into my dreams. I try to fit her in somewhere, but as stupid as this sounds, she floats above it all, not part of the system. I can fill in her past, memories she never would've confided—her first kiss in seventh grade when their teeth clicked together, trips to the beach and trips through the boardwalk's haunted house. Cutting her foot on broken glass, and the blood like red milk on kitchen tile. Images that drown those of abandonment … her squatting in a ditch as Lev drives off, an understanding terrorized. Can't say I wouldn't have left her behind. But she was mine to leave. I would've told her not to learn from it. I would've said my first romantic thing.

Lev can't sleep either, is just writing page after page of notation, drawing chess boards and ripping them up into equal-sized pieces that he piles in a cup-holder. The little square pieces of paper circumscribed in the cup-holder are nice, somehow. I open the glove compartment and remove the shaving kit bag, shaking it. Some pills rattle inside, but not many.

"Conserve," Lev says, sketching another grid, "There's no more where that came from. Till the official product launch, of course."

"Do you remember your dreams?"

"Never."

"Wonder why that is."

"It's all in binary."

He smiles the am-I-kidding? smile. Must be scared of what he's begun to see in sleep, as scared as I am of what I see. I fall from a bright black tower. My heart explodes a thousand times, and I still can't die, and I don't wake up when I reach the ground. I put my chin on a scarred chopping block. A masked executioner swings his axe, but it's not enough, and I can feel sinew and nerve cling stubbornly to my head, gory tears all stung with shame. Lev in the crowd, same expression as anyone else. He's here for the show. The axe comes down again. Again.

I re-count the cigarette butts on the floor of the truck. Thirty-two more than I thought. I would detail this discrepancy in the notebook, but Lev is monopolizing it, jabbing himself repeatedly in the temple with the eraser end of his pencil in a way he's never done before.

"We're stuck, aren't we?"

"We'll just leave tomorrow, walk away," Lev says. "Truck's dead weight. No worries."

"Cops'll find it. They'll know where we are."

"They won't."

"They *will*," I'm yelling. "They *will*, bastard fuck! They will, they will, they *will*!" I punch him hard in the chest now, starting to cry.

"Stop! Stop," he shouts. "We'll take off the plates."

"It's not enough." I put my hands on his throat, but I know I can't.

"They aren't looking for us, you ape-shit freak," he gargles.

"Why not?" I yell, pressing harder. He won't answer, so I make crazy, like I'm really going to. "*Why not?*"

*

Outside, everything is crisp and even, except where the snow has yet to fill our footprints. My fingers slip off him when I realize. To be caught, someone has to care. And Lev doesn't know any better than me why no one seems to notice.

"Done?" he says. Like he was never scared. "I'm passing out. You're not going to bludgeon me?" Of course not. He climbs into the back and sprawls, leaving me alone with the cold. Through the rear glass, Aurora smiles down with inverted rainbows.

I wonder, if we sailed off a cliff tomorrow, what Lev would say in the gut-sick second or two we had. Would he be afraid like a human, or buckle his seatbelt for one last gag? Cover his eyes and apologize? Never. Or, he'd confess no more than the smallest cruelty—something petty and dumb we'd meant to forget, made raw all over again—and fade like a bruise before I could laugh.

IVYLAND, NEW JERSEY ///
THIRTEEN YEARS AGO

AIDAN

Dad's New Year's Day Hike through the Res was an openly hated tradition. Cal could be relied on to throw fits, smashing puddles of ice with thick branches and examining the fragments before smashing them further. The world was gray and fallen—though it must have been sunny once or twice. You couldn't walk far without finding odd islands of junk scattered along the way. Strange things to find out there—computer parts, unused lumber. Crude steps carved in the hills took you to the crest of a frozen waterfall. A turret of dripping bone stalactites that hung from black stone, impossible to picture ignited come spring. Cutting winds discouraged attempts

CAL

Dad in his well-meaning way figured the first of January would be a symbolically grand day to drag the family through a forest. All of us tired. Mom justifiably hungover. I livened the trip up any way I could. The sun never shone on any hike and the sky was only ever one color. Dad would tell me not to rip the needles off pine trees; I listened but continued unconsciously. I always found garbage sprinkled on the path, hubcaps, shopping carts, and once even a refrigerator. There was a way to reach a frozen waterfall. Always ghostly white, a proud torrent caged. If I ever saw that waterfall thawed, it did not make an equal impression. I'd stand at the summit of the wind-stabbed at the summit, but Cal didn't much care, making the climb every year. We'd wave up to him. He'd act like he didn't see. Always more deer than last time. Innocent footfalls sent them dashing into denser forest, but Cal seemed to scare them on purpose. They were regally afraid. Strong cowards. Hikers passing the opposite way nodded greetings but rarely chatted for long, preferring to move aside and let our trail-spanning family pass. Dad would have me on his shoulders when I was smaller—I could take my eyes from the path and look skyward into a web of tree branches like veins and wonder how a tree branch in our own backyard had grown through chain-link fence to become a fused knot of metal and wood. Henri joined us one year, at my insistence. Cal didn't quite register him but never felt circumstance till the moment he chose to erupt. We piled into the minivan, and I talked softly with Henri in the way-back about nothing too memorable or funny. Everyone was sullen

cliff. The family stayed below, their words just soundless shades of mouth. Deer moved noiselessly near the trails until Aidan did something clumsy to frighten them off. Their muscles worked under bronzed velvet, rippling or marvelously still. Their ears pricked at frozen leaves whispering along the ground. Dad would stop to shoot the breeze with other hikers—Mom crossed her arms while Aidan rudely stared. I'd sit on a rock or rotted log and mope and sigh importantly, scratching figures in frosted mud. My body cold and craving movement but denied. Aidan once brought this sad-sack fat friend of his. Henri was his name. I was enraged. I didn't know what else to be. I loathed him but meant nothing by it, and everyone hates this way. Aidan and his lackey laughing in the van's way-back was almost too much to bear. Not that I planned to do something about it. The kid had slept over and downed most of the sparkling cider that we had when adults drank champagne. He'd snored deeply, too; I felt each labored inhalation through our house's ancient heating ducts. I didn't

and sleepy but Dad. I said to
Henri: There's Condensation
On The Windows. Henri
in a mock-dumb voice said
Condensation? You Mean
Like When Two People Are
Talking? I laughed and drew
a smiley face with my finger
on the fogged-up window.
We reached the Reservation,
pulling into a gravel parking
area emptier than the moon.
Cal hopped out of the car, and
I followed. Henri came out
last, but Cal slammed the door
shut a moment too late or too
soon: There was a tripping
echo. And the impersonal click
of things snapping into place.
I saw Henri's head get swept
horizontally by the sliding door
and nailed against the frame.
The door bounced back open;
for two seconds Henri stood
swaying on the car's rubber
foothold, the white toes of
red sneakers hanging over the
edge. Cal didn't move. Henri
fell face first and did not put
out his hands. His knees dove
into gravel. The gravel bit back.
I turned to Cal. He hadn't let
go of the door. As our parents
rushed to Henri, we stared at
each other from a vanishing

*try to hear what they said
now. I could've if I'd cared. We
reached the Reservation quickly,
jolting to a halt before a gnarled
woodscape that jutted out in
depressing Gothic proportion. I
slid the door open, jumping out
first. Aidan came out second.
Forgetting there were three
of us, I heaved the van door
sideways and connected with
Henri's emerging head. There
was a tripping echo, chased by
the laboring crunch of a metal
part coming loose, two impacts
like one musical slur and a tiny
shudder felt in the door handle.
I watched Henri float and falter
at me as the door rolled back,
but I couldn't force myself to
move. His hands hung helplessly
at his side as he toppled, mouth
agape. His enormous stomach
hit home. The ground soaked up
none of it. Aidan spun toward
me. Mom and Dad swooped in
on the bloodied idiot and dialed
911 on a cell. I didn't excuse
anything. There was no one to
hear it. Only Aidan and Dad
got in the ambulance with him.
I can't imagine what was said
as they drove to St. Barnabas.
I was calm as I raced through
odds, and Mom shook her head*

distance. He oozed the fear
of all possible consequence.
When the ambulance came,
Mom and Cal went home in
the van. I can't imagine what
was said, though I suspect Cal
maintained his stoic silence.
Henri had a plastic mask over
his face, I think to help his
breathing, which left only a
pair of almost-closed eyelids.
One socket visibly swollen
and purpled. A high forehead
and moisture collecting in
subtle grooves. Dad told me
Henri would be fine despite
the ambulance's swerving. The
paramedics were two women
with the same severe haircut,
and they spoke to each other
in nods. They were in love,
weren't they. I sat in the waiting
room for a while. Dad called
Henri's parents and right as
he hung up a doctor came
in and told us to go home,
saying they'd handle it from
here. We asked how he was
doing, but the doctor fiddled
with his Φ ring and simply
said: Blood Relatives Only.
All I saw were Henri's glassed
eyes, fake-looking, brimming
with trapped tears, a blue
spark surfacing in dull brown

*saying God My God Please Be
Okay, whispering not to me
but a space directly in front
of her. Maybe she'd forgotten
I was there. At home, the first
thing she did was make me
tomato soup. I accepted and
consumed it. She told me to play
outside. I sat in icy wind atop
the wooden fort Dad built years
earlier and looked at the dirty
creek our backyard fell away
into. Remembering the secret
entrance in the chainlink fence
farther downstream, I bet myself
it could still be pried open.
But somebody could've noticed
and fixed it. I climbed the tree
that'd grown through the fence
and listened to the water, thinly
sonorous in its rocky rut. The
kid was probably dead. I figured
the worst was yet to come. I
played it over, not knowing how
I'd missed him. I'd gone to close
the door and the kid was just
not there. How could anyone
believe he'd turned invisible in
my sight? I tried to warm up my
body by shooting some baskets.
I was making measured free
throws when the car turned
into the driveway. I imagined
they'd leave me to stew in the
guilt I planned on faking. But*

iris as he briefly floated. The image of Mom picking specks of gravel off Henri's face had wafted in and out of view as the howling ambulance wound its way up the mountain. She fetched us from the hospital and didn't ask. Her reckless driving said it all—afraid but angry, running red lights and once hitting the curb on a sharp turn. We pulled into the driveway to find Cal hurling a basketball at the backstop. I strode soundlessly from the van. Seconds before I placed my hands around his neck, he turned and smiled nervously. His nostrils flared; he toppled backwards on pocked asphalt, writhing—laughing—as I asked if he'd tried to murder my only friend. Darkness bloomed where I pressed my fingertips to his throat. But my body betrayed me. I slashed a hand across my face to swipe away snot. I was ashamed, and he wasn't. Nothing to say. I was damp with sweat, pale with the rest. It wasn't an accident. He did it on purpose. He left. Dad helped me up and led me inside. I noticed Henri's pain in my own head.

Aidan came straight for me. He tried to choke me, screaming that I'd killed his only friend, but I held him back easily until Dad pulled him off. Dad spoke as I regained my balance and let the first tear go. I covered it instantly. I was ashamed, and he wasn't. We were a frieze, the three of us. Contorted, still, and the picture of strife. Rhythm of three boys with jagged breath. An accident to make me finally unsure of movements, which were mine and which someone else's. Someone who needed to be sure. Don't stick yourself with a needle to discover the dream; a dream needle will seem just as real. I broke away. I went to the garage and got my bike. I saw them together, drifting up the driveway. Then I rode off, around the backyard. I steered into the road without looking, hoping to be hit by a car.

AIDAN /// IVYLAND, NEW JERSEY

TV wakes me up. The news. From next door, wafting through an open window. If I strain, I can hear an update on Cal's mission.

"… officials have remained tight-lipped concerning the progress of the latest bid to put an American on the moon—the first mission of its kind in decades—but that hasn't stopped a young generation beset by a struggling economy, crippled infrastructure and sky-high unemployment rates from rallying around what some are calling a long-awaited renewal of patriotic spirit. NASA has cancelled a widely anticipated videolink interview with Vesta 1's two astronauts due to unspecified technical issues, but we are expecting to see the duo's first images from the lunar surface early tomorrow …"

It segues to some person who sounds my age, probably being interviewed on the street.

"It's like, this real return to the glory days, you know? Space Race, all the things our parents grew up with. Now people our age are trying to do something."

I have to laugh. Cal as redundant pioneer. Fame would only drive him nuts. Maybe had already. Imagine the press conference for his return: Cal turning a moon rock in his hands, asking it the secret to survival. Hard to believe where he is, where he's going. Harder to think he might be different.

The curtains play in a light breeze, the sun climbs, and I lie stubbornly in bed, hearing the TV across the way crossfade to the chatter of a few early risers in the tent commune out front. Spanish, a language I'd never bothered to learn. Yet understanding would ruin its spell in this moment. I don't want to know what they're saying. The sounds, the cadences are all I want. For a moment I'm almost lulled back to sleep.

Then there's a shout, and sharp flurries of words. I get up and pull dirty clothes on. Down the hall, I try the door to Henri's old room. Locked. I can hear him grunting inside, hard at work.

"What is it I'm not supposed to see in here, Henri?"

"Not now."

"I know about the pet stuff. Got some gross animal, didn't you?"

The work stops. Only heavy breathing now. The room must be stuffy and hot—difficult to be alive in.

"Might do you good to get outside," I say.

Again, muffled ugly sounds more felt than heard, like a thrashing heart that broadcasts its seizure through bone.

"It'll get away," he yelps.

"Henri, let me in, you don't sound good."

"Too many. I thought it would help."

"Let me in, I can help."

"Get them away."

"Get who away?" A tart jangle of breaking glass downstairs brings the voices outside into sharper focus.

Downstairs I find the front window broken. An innocent first stone sitting there on the rug, dumbfounded at its role in all this. I pick it up, weigh it in my hand, sympathize.

Outside, there isn't a speck of grass visible under Believer Town and its agitated citizenry. The group doesn't notice me burrowing through it to the scene of the incident. Anastasio is holding two young men back from a bathrobed neighbor of mine, the one who'd been watching the Vesta 1 story. He spits in Anastasio's direction.

A girl pulls on my jeans pocket, holding out a pellet of charred bark.

"Want to buy part of the miracle tree? I cut it off at night when the guard wasn't looking."

Oh boy. I push past the girl, who makes a haggard face that I guess is supposed to be mine and goes on to hock her artifact elsewhere, the pellet turning to ash in her palm. At last people create a channel leading to the center ring of the circus. Anastasio turns around and sees me, appears relieved.

"Morning, Aidan."

The riled-up pair in Anastasio's corner might be his sons. Looked older from a distance. And as much as their father may have urged them to walk away, I catch a flash of pride around the firmly set mouth: his boys do not take this lightly.

"Who can I thank for the renovation?" I hold up the rock.

One of the young men Anastasio is holding in check points at my frazzled neighbor, whose name I'd long ago forgotten.

"He was throwing this," the maybe-son says.

"This your place, yeah?" my neighbor asks. I shrug. "It's my fault, I'll pay for the window. But you gotta do something about these nuts."

The boys tense up again, but Anastasio holds his ground. They could easily get past him—respect for the outstretched arm does more than muscle could.

"I don't need an Armageddon Woodstock next door," bathrobe guy says. "I could get you all arrested."

"I'll take care of it," I hear myself say.

My neighbor takes a last look at Anastasio's family and the larger throng, considering the offer.

"You better."

He turns to leave and gets a few steps before adding, "Sorry about the window."

One of the boys says something in Spanish, and a few in the surrounding swarm chuckle. Anastasio just shakes his head.

"You can't catch joy like you catch sadness."

"I'm sorry," I say. I should be off the hook at last. Instead, the dread snowballs.

"Please, Aidan, we are the ones who should be. You must not apologize."

"Because now I have to call the police."

A murmur snakes its way through the onlookers, translated, re-pitched with grief, repeated slowly, as if never finishing phrase might postpone its reality. Anastasio alone stares earthward, silent, knowing I'm right. Over his head I see the souvenir-selling kid peeling more bark off the ruined tree and stuffing her pockets while everyone's distracted.

This whole affair was self-cannibalizing. Nothing could sustain it. Not Henri's generosity, not Anastasio's faith, not my apathy. But what Anastasio says next surprises me. Neither a flat denial nor a rallying cry. The words simply hang there.

"Then we must make our case to them."

I shuffle back up the steps and inside. Infuriating. That Anastasio will convince his congregation to stand out there to the bitter last is sick. The broken screen door flaps glumly behind me as a wind picks up and whistles through the punctured window. These people stay any longer, the house'll end up condemned.

I find my cell on the kitchen counter and dial 911. It rings once, but I hang up. Should give them time to move, let only the diehard few lag behind. Less trouble that way. I dial again, reminding myself that it'll take cops just to get the exodus going. It rings for a healthy while before a staticky voice says:

"Officer Larry Moody speaking. What is your emergency?"

"Hi, yes, my name is Aidan Kilham, and I wanted to report a … mm, a disturbance on Meadowbook Lane."

"You mean Estronale Avenue?"

"Sure I do."

Hank hums the specifics as he taps them in.

"Oops, I'm supposed to ask," he says. "What is the nature of the disturbance?"

"Cult."

"What?"

"Just … there are a bunch of people on my lawn who won't go away. Can you do something about it?"

"All our officers are out on calls right now, but later today we can send someone by." Click. Good enough. I sneak back up to the front window to get another look at the yard. Virgin Mary merchandise, figurines, T-shirts coming out of duffle bags and off the back of pickups. Navigating the crowd in a daze is the woman Henri was convinced was our old bus driver. I'm guessing she doesn't know we live here.

Henri yells from upstairs. Forgot all about that. Have to break the news without sounding too excited. I get up to the second floor, but before I can open the door to Henri's old room, he yells again.

"Up here."

I take the next flight of stairs and stop on the next-to-last one. The narrow doorframe is weirdly scarred, lines like claw marks etched in the jamb. He's lying face-up on the wooden floor, near an open window that looks down on the front yard. Nearly catatonic. A sunburst of marble journals strewn out around him, pages peacock-fanning in the breeze.

"Try to remember …" his mouth moves weakly. "It's me."

"Henri. I'm calling a doctor."

"No." Sudden strength in his voice. I take the last step up. "Don't worry!" he cries, gripping his head. "It's worse when you're worried. Please. I've seen a doctor, I know what to do."

"Well do it already, you look awful."

In reply he points vaguely at my feet. I see an envelope on the floor with a name that defies all sense.

"Take it to him. Harvey House."

"Grady?"

"Get out now, please. This isn't your problem."

"How can I ignore it?"

"I can't be so close to you."

And Henri forces his muddy eyes open, mustering a control that, like Anastasio's over the worshippers, cannot be maintained much longer. His hands move off his face and clench next to his hips, hopelessly clutching at whatever it is that will escape someday, grip tightening in anticipation of release. Grasp the piece of ice that melts, these hands say; embed its shape in palm, its architecture in skin. Condescend to save an imprint. A ghostly hollow in the matter. One force shifting loose another.

I think for one grave moment that Henri is crying, but it's a light drizzle slanting through the window that illuminates his face. Seems to bring him some relief.

"Tell me," I say.

The urge to not hear it tears me in half—how can we continue without our absences, and the answers smothering hope? But Henri must see that my resolve is weak or cracked, that I'm not to be trusted, because he turns his face to the window, and his eyelids flutter against invading flecks of rain.

"I promise," he says. "Now close the door."

DH /// IVYLAND, NEW JERSEY ///
TWO YEARS AGO

A 757 ascending from Newark International screamed low overhead. Among those woken in Ivyland's low-rent district was DH, to whom the jet was obviously a choir of robot angels. Here at the tail end of an epic binge, with uncomfortable morning wood, DH scoured his cartwheeling mind for a fitting song title.

This concern was eclipsed by the realization that he was curled up atop a streetlight. He cast frayed eyes down to Garden Avenue, almost falling right away. The pole was a smooth twenty feet, the spindly arc that connected his perch to it worse than unfriendly. He pulled himself out of a fetal bunch and straddled a domed surface that held sturdy glass in place, marveling less at the height he'd scaled than at how he'd stayed on the thing while sleeping.

Hadn't climbed one of these since high school—someone must've dared him, really gotten under his skin about it, doubting he still could. And before he'd finished rounding out the scenario, DH was convinced of two things: 1) that a psychological prank like this bore Lev's splattered-bug signature, and 2) that Lev had long since tumbled into the sleep of phony insomniacs in a stranger's bathtub, wildly unconcerned with consequences.

DH began to fret over how he might pee. Away from home three days, he calculated to distract himself, the last evening there one of spaghetti, barely thawed peas, and burnt bacon, forced upon him by Hecuba, who said she'd be damned if her son would starve. She'd planted him in the same old kitchen chair. The TV was chattering excitedly about a second space age even while reporting that next year's moon visit would suffer further delays. The news didn't agree with Hecuba; she tossed pots and pans back into their cupboards with a recklessness that bordered on real violence, got the whole kitchen clanging.

"Any tomato sauce maybe?"

Hecuba reached into the fridge and threw a ketchup bottle at him. He mumbled gratitude but set it aside, went to work on the bacon.

"Don't do that," she said.

"Don't do what?"

"Don't eat all of one food and then move onto the next. It's psychotic."

"How?"

"Because," she blurted into the garbage disposal, "the polite thing to do is to try a little of everything, going around the plate. It's polite to the cook."

"Why are you crying? Food's not bad. Look, I like it. Mmm." He choked down a few icy peas. Then he chewed on the tines of the fork, tasting cheap metal, and as much as he wanted to, he couldn't stop, the sound of imitation silver on enamel nicely deafening within his skull. Hecuba shot him a bleary glare.

"S'matter? Menopause or something?" DH asked.

"Wish."

He only now fretted over that reply. The intensity of his grip on the slick roost, his hand making sweatprints on the silver ... silvery thoughtforms and the promise of something new ... each idea followed its parent in such relentless procession, sparked a flash and crumbled into darkling holes, forgotten. He let go of the sequence and stared at the brick wall of the MexiLickin'SurfHog where Hairy Duane from around the block had been shot on his graveyard shift, watching layers of graffiti surface and sink. In front was the dirty unused payphone Leo had used to call in terrorist plots to school, enough to garner a *Bomb Threats* spread in the yearbook: stills of kids pouring out into black-and-white, pre-bust Ivyland, some seizing the chance to sneak off, others growing bored with spurious threats on their lives, maybe starting to crave the real thing.

The stuff, he concluded, hadn't left him yet. New Forest Adderade cocktail was no-shit good. The dripper they bought from—one of Lev's med school colleagues—said the filtration was swimming with recombined premium Endless shit designed to boost all the right neurotransmitters in harmonious waves, showed DH the cheap basement lab while expressing a profound need for smaller E-flasks, then pitched his idea for smart TVs: couples would watch different shows on the same screen, each half of the sound and image confined to a sliver of private angles. "What do you think?," the guy asked, like his survey was what mattered.

This drip made one feel, DH and Lev agreed, in possession of Satan's powers. There was the *edge*, they'd shrieked giddily, like badass snakes swimming off your body. You craved a tribal drumbeat to explain it all and even then you'd just dance till clarity dissolved, till nothing was left but the charge of synapses firing joyously, axons overloading. They'd sat on Lev's porch and watched the night's drunk drivers careening by with sirens in tow, flattened people stumbling home, stopping to lean on their shadows for support, sneakers that swung from sagging power lines in the pre-dawn breeze. One guy went up to a house across the way and knocked, but DH said: "No way this guy's getting in." Lev said, "He will, there's a light. TV's on." DH said, "Trust me." The TV glow quit. Guy stepped back to scan the house for life, waited a beat, and walked away, drawing an awed gasp from Lev.

Except DH cried: if he was right about such things, then the world was broken, had something unnameably awful at its core. "Did you know that would happen," Lev asked, "or did you *make* it happen?" Satan's powers. DH instantly wished a hex on Lenny to protect himself, and especially Mom, in case he had the devil's touch after all.

*

There's a spot along a river in South Jersey's pine barrens, between the shore and garbage dunes, where the water isn't the common tea-brown, not even greenish, but dazzling, icy azure on top, crushing whale-blue below: a well without end for all we know, stashed away in an igloo of rock. Kurt, DH's father, had taken him there, shown him how you could weight a hook and always run out of line before you hit bottom. DH would complain that the grotto offered no fish for the catching.

"But look," Kurt would say. "Something strips the hook."

Something always had.

"Then we're just wasting bait," DH finally countered one day.

"*Some*body's making use of it. What if a water nymph lived down there? Like your Greek myths book."

"Yeah, right. Prolly just gets caught on the rocks."

"You dive deep enough, she'll hold on and suffocate you with a kiss."

"You're making this up."

Kurt grinned like: so what? As if yanked by wires, a honeycomb of bubbles broke the surface. This, DH had to admit, was more difficult to explain away.

They emerged from the limestone cave onto thick Jersey jungle yawning mist in summer, miasma of leafy shadowplay and strange humid rot. DH's eyes imagined movement, suspecting the elsewhere-eye no doubt focused on them, judging the pair and rimmed with wonder. Sudden tang of rancid flesh. Out of stillness came a rising, nauseous buzz. Trying to move forward, Kurt's body stalled, lapsed into private wilderness.

"What?" DH asked.

"You've got to live like no one can see you," he said. "That's the only way to win."

From early on, New Jersey had foiled DH's attempt at invisibility: the Johnstons' God-fearing foster home, its curdled smell and no-shoes-inside rule untranslatable idioms, where he was the kid who didn't get piano lessons. A beer-soaked high school with one or two unbroken teachers, where he'd been held back again and again until one day he was at prom with children. Convenience stores at 3 a.m., cake frosting colors and Mr. Clean's biceps bursting forth to console him. Cold train-station bathrooms, where he'd calmly hallucinated green worms that swarmed over his skin, tunneling in and out of pores. Cars parked up in the Reservation's murder-ready set-pieces with girls who knew he was holding enhanced goods. Prone alongside dusked highways, too weak to fend off mosquitoes, the seep of his vomit filling rumble strips. Newark homeless shelters where he'd been dumped by Good Samaritans. Lev's place of disarray, with décor to stimulate the overstimulated, and a futon that had caved in the shape of DH's body.

The labyrinth ended here: paralysis in a crow's nest. The last direction left had been straight up, and after making minor progress along that axis he was stuck. Didn't trust himself to get down safely, not when he was so out of practice. Just a few Belltruvin would've killed those nerves. Wind was picking up. DH carefully stretched cramped limbs one by one and focused his ears on a pair of competing car alarms in the distance, two pitches of horn grating against each other in staggered blasts, eventually alternating. The increments of empty space shrank again till the horns were aligned in rhythm, only to un-synch once more. DH heard it as the synching and un-synching of an adjusted universe. Midday, the sun backlit a gray canvas, giving it a luminosity he thought gray hadn't earned. It annoyed him how a red-tailed hawk did effortless surveillance in druggy loops above.

A period of actual thumb-twiddling came and went, temperatures dropping, worrisome throat-clearings of thunder a few towns over. People started noticing him, especially the ragged high-schoolers cutting class. He couldn't hear them, just saw them pointing. People pointed at him a lot these days. On the bench directly below, a pinstripe-suited man was shaking a two-liter Atlas Adderade bottle, opening it slowly to relieve the carbonation's pressure, then taking hideous gulps. DH watched as the man repeated the process four times, its loop first irritating, then torturous, accusing. He wished, as a flock of teenage poppers passed underneath, one flashing an unmarked orange bottle to the others, that he was addicted to the right stuff. That he would never again watch Hecuba standing over the sink, distracting herself with dirty dishes while Lenny called him the last of the hippies and the future of junkies.

People had plenty of warning before the storm really started in—by the time a pulverizing rain developed, DH had the town to himself. Lightning split the air like crooked heaven as a pair of headlights came to life a few intersections away, then began to weave unnaturally in the downpour. Of course: it had to be Wednesday by now. And his mom drove Wednesdays. And she drove poorly.

To the west, gobs of smoke bubbling up near the lot where Viking Putt sat. When he was young, and industry booming, Ivyland's outskirts gave off plumes of such unexplained smog at regular intervals, and he was given to asking adults whether it was a fire raging a few miles off. "It's nothing," was the automatic reply, no mystery dispelled. Of course it wasn't *nothing*, you'd have to be living inside-out not to see it was *something*, and this non-answer one day confirmed an ultimate childhood dread: that no one, not even grown-ups, knew what made black wraiths ascend only to break against clouds of concrete.

*

"Dad, what's your job?" DH had asked Kurt as they trekked the muddy trail from fishing spot to parking lot.

"It's not important," Kurt said.

"Leo Clafter says you shovel shit from the smell of it."

"Language. Tell Leo I work in South Woodbane, a town where a lot of chemicals are processed in big important factories, and if he knew anything he'd know that factories smell bad. The more important the factory, the worse the smell. So people who smell bad are the most important ones around."

"Even if they're homeless?"

"Especially if they're homeless," Kurt clarified.

"Am I ever going to be homeless?" DH asked. "Maybe, right?"

"Maybe."

*

DH tried to watch the approaching bus, but the rain began to sting his eyes. This water had an element of grease to it, which he assumed was a Jersey thing. He sat up, put his back to the wind and looked out over the muddy knoll where a house once stood and a checkerboard of parking lots at his back, a small cemetery among them, which was hard not to think of as a parking lot for dead people, and to South Woodbane's grid of electricity hubs and warehouses, the stubby cylinders of chemical plants and sewage treatment centers, a tissue sky with shafts of paradise angling through clouds, and he even saw the smell. The city should've been an open book to DH, transparent. Instead it brimmed with lacks and surprised him: They tore that place down? When had the pawn shop moved to the corner opposite? Had New York always looked that close? Might Dad have paused to lean on this streetlight? As though Ivyland were a Buddhist conundrum that would blink into nothing if he stopped asking.

He turned back again. His mom's headlights veered confidently, came straight for him. Can't be fought or figured. He squinted against water and clung to his slippery silver dome with legs and arms. Halfway up the block, Hecuba lost the last relevant degree of control but wouldn't know it for another half-second. Unbelievable, DH thought: she's actually met the inevitable. Her bad fantasy. A performance of what she'd rehearsed forever. But cause and effect get confused here, he recalled Lev saying some day and a half ago. So it was not without precedent that his streetlight cracked at the base even as Hecuba jumped the curb. Whether the gale or age had done it was moot: her bus sprang up like a massive stapler and sideswiped the pole, which shuddered uncertainly and groaned backward, pitching him into untouchable gray, time spent in midair marked by a doubt he'd fallen in the right direction, whichever one that was.

*

DH awoke in a sterile room, everything in it a neutral gray.

He was in a body cast, but the bed was a silken king-size.

A nurse in a hazmat suit walked in.

She gave him a shot that robbed the world of stakes.

She left.

That's funny, DH thought when he saw them: Most people come in pairs, and here are some fellows who come three abreast. Two in white biohazard numbers fitted with black glass expressions and the letters END branded across chests, a third whose outfit was clear plastic to show off the seersucker suit underneath. At first his face was just more steam, but it dawned on DH that he was, rather incredibly, smoking the stub of a cigar within his protective cocoon, with no way of manipulating it save his mouth. A backpack ventilator seemed to suck away the clouds he made.

You'd appreciate a friendly face, the gray smudge said, though of course it could've been anyone who said it. His ventilator sounded, a symphony of baby buzz-saws, and smoke pulled apart to show bloodshot eyes, a sweaty brow and hair that matched the sterile prison. And at last DH recognized his father.

"Meet your half-brothers," Kurt said above the whine of his ventilator, and this time his teeth showed first. "From the other family. Twins, though you can't tell. Much older than you, my secret baby boy, my little late mistake."

DH's eyes were too numb to make tears.

"Wanted to meet you for ourselves," a twin said.

"We're greedy things," Kurt confessed, cigar tip pulsing. "I stayed with you as long as I could, to make sure you'd grow up in one piece. But I'm greedy for what's new. What's next. Is there desire like that in you?"

DH considered his question as the twin biohazard suits lifted him with care. The back of the non-transparent suit in front of him read LESS.

"Dreams where you drown and it doesn't hurt," DH announced.

They carried him and laid him on a gurney.

"Yes," a voice chimed. "That sort of flash, the ecstatic wisdom. What's the difference between eternal life and taking forever to die?"

"I don't know," DH said as they pulled a blanket up to his chin.

"Nobody does," they replied with small laughter.

"Sometimes I suspect there is no past," Kurt said, his face dawning alongside DH's. "And people sprang into consciousness seconds ago, with artificial memories. That we're a quantum innovation, and some kinks will need to be worked out."

DH fought sleep. He struggled to work his mouth. His eyes fell shut, and he watched blood cross the lids in orange fields.

I think about you every day, DH, a voice or negative print of a voice continued. *I miss you and your miracles. You at a magic show, whispering to me how every trick was done. Nothing escaped you. So you must already know why I left. To carry the banner of sudden immortality's church, a nation of infinity, a molecular force for unshaping all things, stone and bridges and people and moons and someday even quasars and space. Mythology to square with what we've learned, said a lone man in three-part harmony, telling DH in a melted accent: a black hole, you go into a black hole, you never come back.*

*

"Hec."

"Len?"

"Thought you'd never come around. Look, they have *Jeopardy!* Here."

Hecuba shed a tear for the baby she knew was gone. Who else would? DH lay nearby, snoozing in traction.

"There, there, little crying frog."

"Happened to him?"

"His mother."

All she could do was wince, but barely.

"What is Shamanism. O hey, check it out." Lenny brandished an envelope stamped with an insurance company's insignia. "Time to collect. Officially retired."

"Congratulations."

"Have to give some credit to your old folks. What are phonemes."

Hecuba gritted her teeth to make sure they were there. Somebody's dollars went negative on TV. DH stirred, his wires creaking in their pulleys. She wanted more than anything to tuck him in, cut holes in the blanket for his suspended limbs.

"What is the Whig party."

"Ever answer right?" she struggled to say.

"Not really. Always first, though." Lenny sliced the envelope open.

DH's eyes fluttered. "Is this jail?" he groaned. "Mom?" Lenny chuckled quietly, unfolding his letter.

"No, honey," Hecuba said. "I'm so sorry."

"Food was fine," DH muttered. "Stop apologizing."

Lenny shook the envelope, looking for a check that wasn't there and would never come. The letter requested an audience with him—just a few procedural questions.

A Daily Double was posed.

"What is a cryptozoologist," tried Hecuba, to fill the silence.

"Beats me," mumbled DH. "Was having such a good dream." The show had already blipped off, breaking news claiming priority. But talk of a bridge collapse—Europe's first since the American rash—faded to sonic wallpaper in Hecuba's ears, which only now regained a tenuous hold on the wider moment: the grind of skateboards in the parking lot outside, an argument down the hall about kosher status of IV fluids, voices and beepings and idle clatter that would have been unbearable were it not for DH's delirious humming, a tuneless thing you couldn't be sure of.

AIDAN /// IVYLAND, NEW JERSEY

There's a rustle and a moment of phone lag before Phoebe's voice reaches me with an irritating echo attached.

"Aidan?" she says.

"Hey."

"What's up? Can't cover a shift tonight."

"It's about Henri," I say.

I'm standing by the front door, phone pressed hard to an ear that's gone damp. The reception cuts in and out, static mixed with drumming rain and thunder. "I think he's sick."

"Has he seen a doctor?"

"He says so." Outside, a hundred umbrellas have bloomed into a circus tent of observance. The Virgin tree alone goes unprotected.

"Little confused as to why you're calling me, then. Trying to pick a get-well card?"

"I want to help him, but he won't let me."

"Why do you suppose that could be?"

I don't have to suppose. He thinks I'm every bit as helpless. But I have the awful need to hear what I'm helpless against.

"He's building something."

"Doesn't sound too sick. What is it?"

"I haven't looked."

"Because."

"I don't ... I'm pretty sure he doesn't want me to see."

I leave the window and let myself lie face-down on the

floor. This was pointless. Got to make up for it. A curious but unavoidable thought gathers steam.

"I miss you," I say into the carpet.

Forest of hiss on the other end, then the last word of a clipped-off sentence that never made it through, lost between satellites:

"—too."

And I can't ask her to say it again.

"Chin up, Aid. He'll come round again."

The connection drops out, and it's not worth calling back. Outside, some have put down their umbrellas and opened themselves to the elements, praying—how much prayer does a soul require?—while their kids stomp puddles. Budding thunder hasn't moved them to safety. And doubtless the conviction that they act in bulletproof harmony with nature is what scares me most. Nothing to do but march back upstairs. The door of Henri's attic sanctuary is closed, as I left it last.

"I need to know what's happening, here," I tell him.

"Favorite songs have you ache all the right ways."

"What?"

"Remember Halloween? Trading candy from the pillowcases?"

"Yeah. After Cal wouldn't trick-or-treat anymore."

"Just us. And you liked all the candy I didn't like, and vice versa."

"So The Trade."

"The Trade."

"What about it?"

"Like chicken or the egg. I wonder if we started out with the preferences or evolved a liking for what the other threw away."

"I had to grow into *you*, certainly."

"I'm an acquired taste," he laughs, but the laugh without his smile plays badly. Isn't it too soon to be talking like this? It snuck up on me; we each became appendage to the other, fused and easier to ignore. World should have ended a decade ago, but people slog through the coda, bewildered by an accidental era that cannot close. So much untended history settles on our debts to friends, plagues a moment whose weightless calm ought to be enough.

"Having all these people here …" he starts.

"I'm taking care of it; they'll be gone tonight."

"It changed things. I knew it was getting worse. Didn't know … so quickly."

"The story of modern religion is a morbid affair?" I offer. Which seems the wrong tack. I hear soft purposeful movement, items being put away, maybe the bedspread getting tucked in. I can picture him cleaning up, thoughtless, alone.

"You have to tell me what's wrong."

"No way to begin to say."

Then a clatter, a sudden trashing of whatever order's been established, dry fluttering of book pages, the ceramic explosion of what must be the lamp.

"Henri? You can start somewhere," I plead. "Please, this isn't you."

"Every start is false. Me. You."

"That doesn't make sense."

"I know you think that. I always had it with you. Before the others."

"Had what, Henri?"

There is that butterfly-caught-in-throat moment where a question proves unanswerable and words should be put aside. Life's been grabbed at either end and wrenched too tight, the last drops of relief long spent. It makes my forearm tingle where Cal would give me Indian burns, skin twisted in contrary wheels. Henri sighs.

"Back then, I thought *you* were doing it."

The house groans. Banshee winds bend around its frame. Lashing unreal wails. A splintering boom. Otherworldly heat blasts my face, which all but comes apart. It's something, my mind has the terrible peace to reflect, like a nightmare I've had. There's a light so vicious as to blind me, and I trip backward down the stairs in a Cubist blur, down and around the jagged spirals. My back unravels as I fall, shoulder blades grinding under flesh, trying to lacerate their way out. Muscle splitting and bone scrambled.

It stops. I run fingers over my forehead. The same faint ridges. On my back, at the foot of the stairs. Aside from the bruises and cuts, this body is intact. Eyes are quivering in their sockets, sight rimmed with fog-light halos. When they open they can barely align, too hamstrung to dart around.

The broken front window is now fully shattered, constellations of glass strewn in the carpet. Rain coasts lazily through the opening. Outdoors, shouts and cries and repeated words I can't translate. Breathing through my nose inflames things, a scorched sensation. I go shell-shocked through the front door; the screen is ripped from the frame.

The tree is a smoldering pit. Lightning forgets where it's already been. Or runs out of new coordinates. The congregation has been leveled, and those quick to recover shake others still sprawled in the flooded grass. No one dead or badly hurt, just rattled. The rain leaves tiny gray streaks on my clothes—ash of the exploded maple suspended in each drop. A siren yaws through the departed storm.

I look at where the Virgin once stood and wonder why I stayed far from it since Anastasio showed me what it was, avoided it like the epicenter of infection. I wanted it gone. So how can it seem stolen?

People are oblivious to the still-gnashing wind and water, pushing themselves off the ground. And though they ignore me, turning toward the revoked miracle, I know what their faces say.

I know because their faces must mirror Anastasio's, the only one I can see, aimed not at the charred remains but up at the house, at the attic window, agog with sadness, features defying his regal control, melted by rain into childlike wonder. A look that summarizes—*we will be alone again*. Then his eyes find mine, make me remember.

Henri.

My wet clothes weigh a million pounds. Knees will barely bend. But I throw myself into the house and up the staircase, step by unbearable dripping step, half-crawling, shouting his name, expecting him to come casually around the curve any moment and ask me what's going on, whether I'm okay, and if this whole week is not getting curiouser by the minute. Nearing the room, the stairs are tiny waterfalls of ash-water.

I don't know what was wrong with me, he'd go. *I just haven't been myself.*

"Henri," I say so inwardly he couldn't possibly hear. "Henri."

I reach the landing. His door has been blown off its hinges. The frame comes unfixed in space, swooning back and forth. I try to steady myself, to make the scene stop swaying. The broken lamp, the journals stacked neatly except for one sitting open in the center of the room: I notice the trivial things first. Ash everywhere. A pool of grayed water by the window, seeping toward me in bleak rivulets.

And something else curving out of the lake of ash, a great deserted mass that presses the breath out of me till I choke on new air. My legs give out. Lungs collapse, the spine dissolves. I fall to a kneel in the polluted water beside him. Some mournful calculus pushes towards the simplest absence, with weak smoke curling off.

When I touch his head, a red line eases out of his nose.

"It's my fault," comes a sightless voice.

"O," I say when I try to say "no."

"Can go to sleep now."

"You don't have to, Henri."

"But I can go."

He goes.

*

Aimless police patrol the house with blank notepads out. A white truck with men in white biohazard suits is gone. Vacate the house ASAP, they said, we don't want to be back here next week. Phoebe

standing next to me, red-eyed. Anastasio called the monsignor.
They sit on the couch across, hands folded, heads held stiffly. We
listen to the murmur of Vince, the sergeant, on the phone. He
tells his wife he'll be home at the normal time.

"He giveth and he taketh away," the Monsignor thinks.

I *think* he thinks.

When I'm allowed upstairs, only ash is left, a faint outline
where it collected around him. A cartoon: the pursued passes into
solid rock, leaving a hole in the shape of his body.

"Did Henri seem different—depressed or unstable recently?"
Vince asks. Ed and Bert, who I can't believe are still cops, stand
around in the hall awaiting dismissal and don't hide their snickers.
Wouldn't you be? I swear one whispers. He couldn't have said it—
Vince doesn't even flinch.

"He was keeping himself holed up in here."

"Avoiding going out? Trouble engaging others."

"I know why you're asking this," I say. "And where they took
his body." I don't want to imagine those final wild shifts, his brain
bending at deadly angles. "But if you heard—it was still him in
there."

"H12 can leave people highly functional," Vince says. "Right
up till a hemorrhage."

"He had VV."

"You still see infections now and then, especially long-term
incubations."

"It isn't that simple."

"It usually is."

"I," I say. But there's no way to paint the force that diced me
as I lost him. I put two fingers to my upper lip and they come
back red.

"Sir, might want to get checked out yourself."

"That's not all," I stammer, wiping the blood from my nose.

Vince sighs. From the sound of it, the assholes in the hall are
leafing through one of Henri's journals.

"I'll tell you what. We'll leave this one open for now. You

get some rest. Think about what led up to this and tell me your opinion—nobody knew him better than you," he says. "Maybe go over those notebooks."

Casually, his voice betrays a wound.

*

I start with an open journal on top of the stack. I sit on the squeaky bed and let the book lie open across my palms.

Went riding with Grady to the duck pond again. Couldn't stay as long. Always reminding me of the day with Aidan, running from crazy old gun-toting Clafter. Somehow after making the connection I owed Grady something. His past makes it hard.

I skip ahead.

Grady's bad Hallaxor reaction was horrifically delayed. Seemed the VV had been a success. Soon after, a classmate has a birthday party at MexiLickin'SurfHog. Playing in that kiddie ball pit, Grady, fine till now, starts convulsing, puking, bleeding from his nose, and the other kids start clambering helplessly through the churning colors to get away from the freak. Grady's vigilant father sees this from his table, charges into the tube entrance of the ball pit but gets stuck at the waist and is reaching desperately out to his sick kid, saying Grady, Grady, Come To Me, with a dozen kids trying to beat him back through the blocked opening. Grady licking at his nosebleed, wiping fluids on the plastic balls. Soon other crazed mothers and fathers are pulling Grady's dad out of the tube by his kicking legs, but he's is clawing at the mix, yelling to a son who now sits dazedly, half-buried, watching the war of parental adrenaline; he's telling him they can stop for ice cream on the way home, if he'll just crawl out of there.

Did he steal a file from the Harvey House? Make it up? No one would've told him the story. Grady was certainly unable. I pick up another notebook and open it at random.

These radio transmissions between cops, sometimes truckers, sometimes something else in a technical jargon I don't get.

Tin foil hat on a lark. Maybe schizos on to something.

——Didn't work. No sleep.

Doctors told him there was nothing wrong. Brain scans turned up clean. No evidence of H12, though at first he was sure he had it. No symptoms he could describe, only dissolution of cause and boundary. The affliction went unnamed.

That accident in the car with Aidan. Imagined it the day before.

He slid toward two-way paranoia, blaming himself for distant errors and matters of chance. Thought choice and control were illusions except in his particular case.

Coverage of the moon mission I didn't like the sound of, downplaying the secrecy and apparent blackout on mission chatter. Thought better than to tell Aidan. He wouldn't worry, or think it concerned me. Still. The insomnia, trying to will myself to sleep, what I overheard, and now no contact. I can't be capable of that. Please say I can't have done this. I can't make these things happen. I'm an accidental antenna, perhaps the only free agent left. My signals ripple outward impossibly. All blame redirects here.

Nothing is spared.

Aidan homesick for Phoebe. Want badly to say they can be happy but know there is that toxic strain in it.

I pick up the final journal, flip through to the last written page, upon which there is one muted howl, scribbled in haste without punctuation.

not alone as I look the unquiet

"What made the noise?" I say aloud, tears finally standing at their outposts, the journal slipping with a dry snap to the floor as I cave, not knowing what he might have endured. My eyes trace the rim of a burned portal that will not fade. Henri absorbed in folding space.

"Trust me. Please."

I wait for a sign.

*

I have to wait a day, this shell of a day, before I can go to Harvey House. Phoebe gently nudges me, as she had to, and I stumble out the door into blinding sunlight, past the turned dirt that held our maple, and the unruly grass, still flattened here and there from the tents. I walk along the dirty creek and past Floods Hill and the duck pond and come at last to the squat and sinister building, a normal brown two-story except for the swinging sign out front. Here by the grace of science goes whoever.

For the first time, I'm forced to think of the people ruined. The Grady that was supposed to be. What husk or reverse-ghost he became. Then again, he probably enjoyed life more than me. There's a VV ad for you: *No matter what, you'll see things in a better light.*

The woman at the front desk smiles tiredly, maybe guessing I'm a long-lost brother here to connect with an unlucky sibling. I ask for Grady, holding up the letter, and she directs me to the rec room down the hall.

He's sitting next to this foul case playing both sides of a checkers game, swatting when Grady leans in too close. I say Grady's name; they both turn to stare, agape, hunched.

"Henri's friend!" Grady exults, and the knot in my stomach tightens that much. I haven't told anyone except Phoebe, whom I blurted it to, and Anastasio, who seemed to know already. I asked the stately man what he'd seen that evening in Henri's window, but he shook his head as if to say we would never name that agony.

"Henri's friend," I confirm. The checkers guy sniffs and turns back to the board as Grady shakes my hand vigorously. "Aidan."

"Nice handshake, Aidan."

"Henri wanted me to give this to you."

But when I take the envelope out, a tremor of panic interrupts Grady's face. Henri knew I'd have to read it. I tear the letter open and recite a shakily written sentence.

"I have something for you, in my old room."

Grady waits, spellbound, for the end of the message. But that's all there is.

I ask a nurse doing paperwork nearby whether Grady can go for a walk. He can, he's very well-behaved. Home by 5:00 for house dinner, she warns. Grady throws a teenaged eye-roll my way. I actually laugh.

Grady can't contain himself during our stroll, pointing out his favorite benches in the park and rattling off his names for turtles that tread lazily in the stagnant pond, eager to tell anecdotes altogether thrilling but hard to follow. Daily minutiae elevated to epics. He swabs his glasses with his shirt, tells me that I'm about to step on a caterpillar, picks up the furry yellow-speckled thing and deposits it on a low-hanging maple leaf.

Suddenly, near the creek, he bursts into tears, and I'm sure that he's figured it out. He points to a mangled bike upturned in the water. Judging by how he averts his gaze, it's the one Henri gave him.

*

The house is neutral, scrubbed of its history. I'm supposed to leave. We trudge upstairs and come to the room, Grady's nose twitching anxiously. With my hand on the knob, I pause, then step back.

"Hurt?" Grady asks, looking at my hand. No way to begin answering that one.

"I think you're supposed to go first."

Grady is lost in what resembles reflection for ten seconds. His eyes probe the door, suspicious. Finally, a grin gets the better of him and he shoves it open a little harder than he meant to, not hesitating to whoop with ugly, guttural joy when he sees what's inside. Taking up half the room is a blue habitrail Henri must have finished assembling the other day, a maze of plastic tubes with wood shavings and an exercise wheel and strategically placed water dispensers. Rifling through the circuit is a familiar rodent with white rings bristling on a puffy tail.

"Dr. Hal Rockefeller!" Grady bellows, putting his palms to the plastic bend where the ferret has frozen in its tracks, squeaking excitedly. He pulls apart the tube, allowing Dr. Hal to pour out into his hands and shoot up the length of an arm to settle on his shoulder.

"Thought you was lost forever!" Grady exclaims, laughing at the thing's affection. "Henri found Dr. Hal!"

"He did," I say, already distracted: off to one corner is a brand new mountain bike, complete with bell. A note taped to its handlebars. Grady and Dr. Hal watch me remove and unfold the paper.

Dear Grady,
Found good old Dr. Hal living in our miracle tree stump and didn't think it was too safe for him there. Sorry about your old bike, too. I know this isn't the same, but I hope you like it. Wish I could have given you these things in person.

The house for Dr. Hal is all yours, too. Aidan can help you take it apart and set it up again at Harvey House. He knows what to do.
—Henri

The back of the paper is blank. That's it. Not the barest reassurance. Nothing addressed to me. No explanations. I know what to do? Fuck.

This is what you do in a staredown with demise. Make amends with a failed pet project. You thought this had to happen, but what made its momentum? What made you understand that

Grady's bike was warped and rusting in the creek? You meant me to take care of him in your absence, but looking into those shiny damaged eyes as I tell him the bike is his and what you said, I'm not human enough. He wants to thank you, Henri, and I don't know how to say he can't. So listen to his thanks.

When I say *you're welcome*—say it on your behalf—he nods, the light hits his features a certain way and a simmering fear makes me ask his last name. It's Clafter. His dad, he says, lives on a big hill.

But if you want me to think of this coincidence in fuzzy spiritual terms, Henri, I don't know why. The dismantling we try not to imagine, from whole to final useless cog.

We contradict ourselves. But what else? The meaning evaporated with you.

I tell Grady I'll be back. He's not listening, overcome as he is. I hear my cell vibrating as I come downstairs. I come into the room and watch it buzz across the table. It stops. Then it starts afresh. Something's important. I leave.

Moments turn reluctantly, end over end. Wandering in decayed afternoon. Spring day for child's mischief slipping behind the horizon. An orange pearl of sunset. I come to the creek and sit on the weedy bank, Grady's busted bike a few feet away in the filthy water. I throw pebbles in to see the rings.

A soft crunch. Phoebe's car stopping up on the gravelly road. She gets out and steps down through the high grass to join me. Doesn't need to speak. Don't want her to. Don't want to be right about what she says. I throw a rock at a glass bottle lazing on the brown slick, then another, and another, till it shatters and sinks.

"This is the game we should've played. Submarine."

Cal made up the name, I think.

It's getting colder. The moon etched high. Wonder if he's there yet. Maybe I'd surprise him, show up for his big return. Phoebe picks up another of the hundred glass bottles littered about in the weeds, sets it out to drift. My hand grazes hers.

"Trying to spare me," I say.

A faint breeze pulses, the raised wheel of Grady's bike spinning mournfully in place. A sparrow lands on the crossbar and cocks its head at me. Asking. Asking. I can't breathe. Just can't. I clutch at the ground with my free hand, eyes filling.

We both hear a rustle and turn to look up at the lip of the road and Floods Hill rising across the way. No one. A fine sand on the wind.

CAL

I watch my brother from where the grass rolls down to trickling water. Shuffle through the first dead leaves. He and Phoebe turn to face me. Stare straight and blank. Want to sweep through and make them right. But this is what you get: tread time for one dissolving view.

How do we erase obsession? A riptide that punishes our struggle against it? Children are naturally smitten with anything that weds danger and secrecy, hints at discoveries unmade. The boy who worships Bigfoot can't fathom a Bigfoot hunter as laughingstock. The same confidence crumbles with age: pulled certainly, rapidly out to sea, the current works invisible.

People vanish. Always will. Some bend into nothing, lost in the wrinkles. Some burn away for no reason at all. A young woman, asleep, engulfed in 17th century France. Her husband acquitted of murder. The 1960s fading, a meter reader stumbles upon some doctor's ashes. A weary soul spontaneously combusted: black circle on the floor of her beachfront home. She'll have blown away when they come to see.

Each name reduced to dust in the black-and-white sketches and photos, pages of odd, ignored books. Little mounds of self-destructed person. In youth I traced these pictures and, when those grew stale, invented my own.

At night, riding my bike alone—they were always alone when it happened—I would release the handlebars, balancing, and stretch out my arms, trying to conjure the spark inside. I pedaled furiously, so that as I broke apart, the bike's momentum would keep it coasting in the wash of that rare still-working streetlight, ash running off the seat like the tail of a comet till I was gone forever and the spokes still made their inertial orbit. The bike riding itself in a cone of white. Then it would touch the edge of the pool, be enveloped in the flattening dark.

I don't know when the fantasy failed. I couldn't be one of these molten few. They had something I didn't: access, no choice. Saw flaws and gears behind the days. A vision that blossomed for decades but with age became overripe and unendurable. Strangers' thoughts seeping through cracks, inverting life and sleep. Friends' thoughts a torture all their own. Even loneliness must have failed. Sequestered in bare rooms, staring at walls, shadows liquid in barbaric theater, they would summon my loneliness the same way I called for their spark. They fared no better. Walls came tumbling down. Glistening ids and egos slithered in, shuddering in cool air, unhinging jaws and tasting gray matter.

And as we savaged their minds, eclipsed the real, gnawed on a hollowed rind of soul, the body took pity and forged a diamond flame within. Smoke bloomed out in painless Pyrrhic victory. All escape redirected here. A spectrum of blazing anti-time, incendiary space, blue inward electric waves. Exhausted spark became ash. Meager memorials left behind: a singed shoe, stripped bone.

*

I'm standing in the moon lander's airlock, watching distance between the surface and me diminish—first imperceptibly, now by leaps and bounds. But the moon falls up at me. I pull the same.

I want to touch it, feel its powdered dust on my face, in my pores, in the whorls of my fingerprints. See it cling to the glossy white hair on erupting wrists, its grittiness in my rough chin sprouts. To taste true barrenness and sputter, die, drown in the tranquility, my brains lying next to me and one hand full of alien earth. My eyes cracked glass and overawed at the wasteland I've come home to. My corpse will seem alive in a field so calm, a beacon in the gray.

I'm surprised. A dream, the first I can remember, has stitched itself together from a hundred microsleeps, so incandescent and ripe with future dreads that it took days to recognize. It had actually happened. Aidan was there, toddling along, not wise enough to fear me, in that cheerful oblivion adults spend their lives trying to regain. He sidled along, only half my height then—

I've put aside the notion of not knowing him, the two of us passing on the street as strangers. A moment's codes would yield that face no matter how well encrypted, a face that held the vestiges of an innocence I destroyed and pride neither of us could abandon. We might have talked again, I know, but it was the first note of contact that eluded us always, silence more easy than deliberate.

So: he toddled and I strode, each dragging a cheap plastic sled, beneath a bloodless slate thing that loomed above our town, hearing the friction in puffy snowclothes. As did countless children before us, we breathlessly awaited the moment when Floods Hill would reveal itself in blinding glory, shake loose the bordering trees and houses, become its monolithic self. It might be pristine, mythically unspoiled, or already ravaged by Flexible Flyers, jagged swaths of mud and grass shredding the white to lace. It could be overrun or deserted. Snow that had a crunchy skin but lay powdery underneath; snow that was uniformly wet, packable. The infinite designs and variations ran together and realigned as we walked, but no prediction was ever uttered.

One variant that never snaked through my head was the one we found. It was an invented outcome, transforming as the sky. There were no other sledders ... it appeared none had ever existed. It couldn't be understood till we touched it, and even when our ungloved fingers grazed the rough hoarfrost and the smoother surface beneath, it did not abolish our anxiety.

The hill was sheathed in ice. Pure, unmarked ice that warbled in three dimensions, making bulges and miniature alpine ridges, fault lines and tectonic plates, a geology all its own. In it were trapped tiny pockets of air, freeze-framed bubbles gasping for the surface but locked in time. Beneath, yellow grass bent in static breeze.

"It's ours," is how Aidan summarized it all.

We were eager to ride: our plastic discs slid across the mutated hill with no resistance. I climbed at reduced speed, leaving Aidan to manage the tricky slope himself. Stumbling and losing traction constantly, the summit took ten minutes to reach. After a customary survey of the sleepy valley, I sat and launched myself.

Aidan was a blur. The trees melted sideways. Going too fast, I reached out to control the descent, but my gloves skimmed hopelessly over the ice, capturing ripples in fast-forward. The hill terminated in a line of trees, but I slipped through, flung farther, across a street they never bothered to plow, down the start of a second slope that plunged into the polluted creek. I slammed to a stop in iced high grass. In that dazed moment of blessed immobility, I turned back to see the path I'd traveled, and thoughts came trippingly, taking in the dizzy height, the heart-stopping drop I sought.

Aidan was not yet halfway up the hill, not when I first turned round, not when I crossed the blasted street and started toward him. He faltered, lost altitude, gained some, lost his footing, paused. Starting again, he slipped, moved forward five feet, then dropped his sled. From a distance I watched him try to lunge for the disc while remaining upright, the contortions bringing his body down hard on the ice.

I ran, stumbling and bruising myself the whole way, seeing his shock twist itself into furrowed confusion and then a weary escalating cry. Aidan opening his mouth and producing no sound but surely crying. Then his breath caught and the siren flared up, hurt upon hurt, decibels carrying down the valley. Closer, I spotted the source, a candy-red crescent tented over his left eyebrow, brilliant and crisp.

His cry broke into labored gasps when I reached him and realized I knew no way to dampen the pain. I sat with him and held his shoulders and said I was sorry, sorry that I wasn't there, for bringing us, that the whole thing was stupid and come on, we can go. I touched the red with an ungloved hand and picked up its stinging warmth, then put my hand to the ice.

Perhaps the moon will feel that way: cold, vast, somehow mingled with the warmth of life. Cells slow till they stop. But there's death and there is slow enough. There's this glass. Even nightmares move.

Last breath. Door primed. Helmet, gloves, and boots left behind. Incidental memories, none especially worthy. They multiply, canceling one another. Jaw-clenching spasm of terror like a firecracker lit from inside. The organs xylophone up and down ribs, missing none. Craters and rocks stream by now, more fluid than fixed. The blue aura trembles with menace, acknowledgement of the cinching noose. Of returning weight. Uprush of ground recalls first lessons.

What comes up. Look both ways. Stove hot.

Vision slows, shadows seething. It's not to be believed. Atmosphere turns hazy, blue shot with curious mist. Hand outstretched and fingers splayed. Wait.

Emma drifts, immaculate. The ship will be her tomb.

Not mine.

The door   dreams   of
falling   away

    it

   wakens

       and

           does.

Only

                    betweenness and
                    the
                      cold.

I come apart atom
          by
             atom
starting at the toes.

A glimpse of my hand, full of ash.

Aidan and Phoebe, their paled voices.

I woke up to everything else. The cosmos groaned and realigned. New at the end of unspooling wire and melted dawn. Gravity forsakes its hold, the transformation speeding, wild. Close my fist, it breaks away.

Aidan. Me.

I carried both sleds under one arm, holding Aidan's small hand in my bloodied one. We moved in silence, he sniffling from time to time, me squeezing in reply. And in that last point of contact I felt the world slipping into ghastly futures, its grasp failing. Blue weakness slacked the beaten knuckles. The world a hiding place. Aidan, all that fastened me to it. I bounced his fist, cased in mine, wanting never to release. Certain I would. That I already had.

Mercy, please. I'm not ready to be free. I expected. Let the sun come out again: its warmth will colonize my skin. Let me stretch across the surface—release locks up my heart so tight. I reach and nothing will be held. Stolen moondust takes revenge, escapes, flares outward in decaying spirals, catches a swell that lifts me spinning too with coiled fear, over the creek, through the toss of dancing treetops and up to plumes of restless cloud, and I am turning through the years, I am lighter still.